Not Quite Colonel Brandon

A NOVEL

NOT QUITE SERIES

KIM GRIFFIN

To the one who is lost.
May this book point you to the One who pursues you and offers everlasting,
steadfast, and redeeming love.

"What man of you, having a hundred sheep, if he has lost one of them,
does not leave the ninety-nine in the open country, and go after the one
that is lost, until he finds it?" Luke 15:4

Contents

Chapter One

"... *The more I know of the world, the more I am convinced that I shall never see a man whom I can really love." Marianne — Sense and Sensibility*

"Send them away! I'm not answering any questions!" came a man's shout from deep within the coastal cottage.

Megan shifted the basket of food in her arms and glanced at her friend, Kate. The yelling didn't sound like an old man's as she had imagined, and what's worse, he sounded angry.

"Hi." The dark haired, athletic-looking man at the door winced before calling into the house, "It's Kate and her friend with your food! Don't be such a grump!" He turned to them and pasted on a smile before looking back once more. "I can bring them in to say 'hi.'"

"Don't you dare!" came the gruff response.

"Sorry," mouthed the man at the door before saying, "Let me help you ladies." He lifted the large baskets from their arms as if they weighed nothing and disappeared into the house.

"I thought—" Megan stopped when the man reappeared.

He stepped outside then closed the door. "Sorry about that. He's had a rough day. Actually, every day is a rough day." He turned to

Megan and extended a hand. "Hi, I'm Toby Watts, Kieran's physical therapist and friend."

Megan's face heated at the attention. "I'm Megan Taylor, Kate's friend. I also work for her husband." She pointed at Kate.

Toby's eyes sparkled as he grinned back. "Nice to meet you Megan Taylor who also works for Kate's husband. I would invite you in, but..." Frowning, he looked back at the door. "Don't take it personally. He's always like this about visitors." Toby shook his head. "He doesn't want anyone to see him this way."

Kate didn't look surprised. "No worries. The chicken and roasted veggies are warm but can be reheated if he wants to eat later." While Kate explained all that they brought, Megan's gaze followed the path of the ramp down from the cottage to the sidewalk then to the English Channel. The sound of water lapping against the beach held Megan's attention as she pondered what had just happened.

She should have been angry that the man inside was unappreciative of all the work they had put in to cook him a meal, but instead, she worried his anger covered up depression. Kate had said he was a paraplegic. What would it feel like to not have the use of your legs to walk out to that water and feel it lapping at your feet? Did his handicap cause the anger or was he always that way?

"I'd better get back in before Kieran gets worried. I hope to see you again soon." Toby's voice drew her back to the present, and he winked at Megan before saying goodbye and closing the door.

As they retraced their steps to Kate's family's cottage, Megan noticed a dark cloud developing and quickly blowing their way.

"We may want to run before we get caught in a downpour."

Megan swiped at the hair blowing into her eyes and turned to see rain tracing a path towards them. Picking up her pace, she raced up the stairs of the Corbyn family's cottage and glanced once more at the home of the man named Kieran before stepping into the house. Her mind swirled with questions.

"Tell me about Kieran," Megan asked once they were inside. "Somehow I imagined him as an old man—a friend of Margaret's." She recalled Kate's comment that her grandmother-in-law, Margaret, had been in her mid-eighties when she died a couple of years earlier.

"He was not a contemporary of Margaret's, if that's what you mean. Of course, even before the dementia, Margaret never met anyone she didn't consider a friend." Kate bit her lip. "Kieran Davies is his full name. I actually went out with him a couple of times when I first moved in with Margaret. It was just as friends," she rushed to add. Shaking her head, she walked into the kitchen. "He's a bit of a playboy, or at least was at the time, which thankfully, I figured out before his friendliness fooled me into considering more."

"Why does his name sound familiar?"

Kate filled a glass with water and offered it to Megan. "He's pretty famous here in England as an app developer. At the age of twenty-four, he sold an app he created and made millions. He's done that with several more apps since. He also recently dated Natalia Moreno—you know, the model. They broke up after the accident that caused his paralysis, but he was all over the media while they were dating. Maybe you've heard of him because of that."

"Maybe." Megan searched through the recesses of her mind, trying to recall where she'd heard of him, but gave up. She didn't keep up with celebrities and she'd only been in England for three months. "And he's how old?"

"I'm not sure. I'm thirty-three and I think he's a couple of years older than me. It's sad, really. He had everything the world deems as perfect—brains, money, looks, good health, a beautiful girlfriend—then his life imploded when he crashed his motorcycle and became a paraplegic. He's working again from what I understand, but he's become a hermit."

"That's so sad." Megan imagined how the man with the grumpy voice must feel to have lost so much of himself. "He needs encouragement. Doesn't he have friends?"

"I think his close ones abandoned him after the accident. Toby said he's his friend, so there's him at least. Corbyn has always been friendly with Kieran and tried to reach out." Kate waved her hand in the direction of Kieran's home. "But Kieran pushed him away just like he did to us today."

A lump settled in Megan's throat and she tried to swallow down the sadness. She knew what it felt like to lose something, or in her case, someone, so important that it felt like your life would never be the same.

When Kate's brow furrowed, Megan forced a smile.

"Let's talk about something more cheerful. You looked gorgeous in the picture I saw of you at the British Museum's Benefit for the Arts Tuesday night."

Megan grinned. "Thank you. It was fun."

"And what about the guy you were with? Good looking. Didn't you say he works at the British Museum?" Kate raised a brow.

Megan rolled her eyes. "Peter Nelson. He does. He's the one I told you had worked with my mom on her book that I've taken over—one of the museum curators. But there's nothing romantic between us if that's what you're getting at."

"Hmm."

"There's no reason to 'hmm'."

"From the way he was looking at you in the picture, I think he might not feel the same as you."

"I hope you're mistaken. We work together quite a bit, and I don't want to lead him on. He invited me to the benefit as a friend and said it would be a good opportunity for me to meet other historians who might be able to help with the book. I had no idea he was being honored at the event and so much attention would be focused on us. The media assumed we were a couple. It was a little overwhelming, to be honest." Megan tensed, recalling all the cameras taking their picture throughout the night.

"It's okay, I understand. Before Corbyn, my friends were busy trying to set me up with every good-looking, single man who gave me attention." Kate chuckled and pointed to Megan's necklace. "I love that necklace, by the way. It's the same one you wore to the benefit, right?"

"It is." Megan's hand went to the red pendant on her neck. "My mom said my grandmother used to call it her heritage. I assume it was passed down through her family. My grandfather said it's not from his side."

As she lifted it, she noted the markings on the back. She had examined them hundreds of times over the last few months. "I always figured it was just pretty costume jewelry, but when I wore it to the benefit,

Peter said he thought it looked like it was real and an antique. He thinks it's English in origin."

Kate moved closer and examined it as Megan held it out and turned it around. Her eyes grew wide. "If it's real, it must be immensely valuable. The stone in that pendant is huge. If it's a garnet or ruby...wow!"

"Right? Peter suggested taking it to a jeweler called De Clare's. Have you heard of it?"

"I have. It's the jewelry company that made Margaret's engagement ring back in the late fifties." She flashed the ring on her hand. "That's probably a good place to have it evaluated. They've been around a long time and are well known here in England for carrying only the best. How exciting! It's like a mystery. I wonder what you'll find out about it."

Megan forced a smile as she recalled seeing her mom wear it so many times. It would be interesting to find out the history of the pendant, but she would gladly forgo that if it meant she had her mom back.

Chapter Two

"What man of you, having a hundred sheep, if he has lost one of them, does not leave the ninety-nine in the open country, and go after the one that is lost, until he finds it?" Luke 15:4

Megan stared at the sticky note on the bathroom mirror. This had been her driving force since she began to recover from her mom's death. At fifty-three, she seemed too young to die. Megan had so many things to share with her mom that were yet to happen—finally going to China where she felt God had called her to minister, introducing her mom to her future husband, working on a wedding, pregnancy, and watching her mom cradle grandchildren. Megan's hand found the pendant hanging from her neck and held back tears. Every now and then she was hit with sadness over a future without her mom.

God had pulled her out of that sadness and comforted her time and again when she felt too low to go on. He had placed people around her to speak into her life and carry her through. Navigating adulthood without her mom wasn't a choice she would have ever made, but God trusted her with this path, and he had and would continue to equip her for what was to come. Her mind knew that, but her heart sometimes forgot.

God had placed her here for a reason. She recalled Kieran's angry voice and wondered if he was a sheep she was called to minister to. Maybe if she showed him God's love as others had to her, he would see that even being paralyzed he had so much to live for.

Curling up on her bed, Megan pulled out her phone and searched Kieran Davies. Green eyes stared back at her. His face had a chiseled look, and his ginger hair suited him perfectly. She found herself drawn to the handsome man. Articles about his motorcycle crash topped the page, and she hesitated to open them. Curiosity won out. As she read through the account, her heart ached for his loss.

He looked so healthy in the pre-crash pictures. She clicked back through them. He was young and beautiful, posing in locations across Europe with various women who looked like models. The most recent pictures were of him on a ski slope in the Alps just a week before his accident. The article said he was there with his girlfriend, Natalia Moreno. Megan recalled Kate mentioning she was a model. Not that Megan could confirm it. That wasn't the type of thing she paid attention to. Switching to Instagram, she found Natalia, and there was no sign of Kieran in her posts. Kate had said his friends mostly abandoned him after the crash, and her heart sank. Surely that contributed to his anger.

She laid her phone down and those haunting green eyes filled her mind. Why was she even looking at those pictures? It wasn't likely she would ever meet Kieran. Reaching out and trying to help him further would take a lot of maneuvering. They had never met, and it would be extraordinarily awkward if she suddenly tried to insert herself into his life. The fact that he was so devastatingly handsome also intimidated her.

She had never been one to put herself out there with men. That was part of why, at twenty-six, she was still single. With Peter, that wasn't an issue. She felt comfortable with him and he had become a good friend, but she didn't have those kinds of feelings for him.

Megan's phone buzzed and she looked down to see she had received a private message on her Pulse account from P24,601.

After she had begun healing from her mom's death, she'd signed up for the Pulse app. God directed her to it so she could share hope in

Christ with the world. With the Pulse app being the most-used social media app, it was perfect for a young missionary. The app allowed users to share a "beat" of 300 characters or less and even add a picture, video, or meme. She'd been sharing Bible verses and words of encouragement on it for the past six months.

It was well-received, and in that short time, she had over six thousand followers. People responded positively to Megan's Pulse beats, and most beats had numerous comments. Some followers occasionally direct messaged her with thoughts and questions on the app, but P24,601 was the only person to consistently interact with her through the platform.

P24,601: Another bad day, and I can't seem to get out of it. Any good words for me?

Megan pulled up her Bible app and within minutes had the perfect scripture.

Daily Encouragement: Romans 5:3-8 ESV Not only that, but we rejoice in our sufferings, knowing that suffering produces endurance, 4 and endurance produces character, and character produces hope, 5 and hope does not put us to shame, because God's love has been poured into our hearts through the Holy Spirit who has been given to us. 6 For while we were still weak, at the right time Christ died for the ungodly. 7 For one will scarcely die for a righteous person—though perhaps for a good person one would dare even to die— 8 but God shows his love for us in that while we were still sinners, Christ died for us.

Daily Encouragement: Whatever you think you've done, remember Christ died for you.

When user P24,601 direct messaged her the first time, it felt like she'd found her one—the one who needed to hear how much God loved him. He began asking basic faith questions, but their conversations soon became very deep. She didn't even realize he was a guy until he mentioned it after several weeks of messaging had passed and they already felt like old friends.

P24,601 was a strange username. Most people had their own name or a made-up name like hers, Daily Encouragement. Hers wasn't super creative, but it got the point across. When she received that first direct message from P24,601, she looked it up and saw that it was the prisoner number for Jean Valjean in the play Les Miserables. Throughout the play, Jean Valjean tried to redeem himself from what he did in the past. She wondered what P24,601 was trying to escape from. What troubled and haunted this man?

He claimed her encouraging posts of scripture saved his life, but he never shared exactly what he meant by that. Thinking he meant suicide, she urged him to see a Christian counselor, but he insisted that her encouraging words were enough and counselors had not helped. That was a huge burden, but she prayed daily that God would give her scripture and encouraging words to share and meet his needs.

P24,601: I don't think Christ wants me. Tell me something good about your day.

Daily Encouragement: You are his creation, and he wants to be in a relationship with you. A highlight of my day was walking on the coast.

Megan thought of her walk along the coast by the Kingsdown cottage with Kate before they made the food to take to Kieran. The sun was bright, and the breeze was warm.

P24,601: Do you live on the coast?

Daily Encouragement: Just visited for the weekend with a friend.

P24,601: Oh, that kind of weekend!

Daily Encouragement: What? A relaxing overnight with a girlfriend while her husband watched her kids.

P24,601: Sorry. I thought perhaps it was a boyfriend.

Megan blushed. There was no boyfriend. That hadn't been on her list of priorities since she'd been focused on becoming a missionary. She'd not met anyone who shared her calling and didn't want to compromise.

Daily Encouragement: No boyfriend. And even if there were, there would be no overnights and weekend trips.

P24,601: Right. Marriage first. You're a good girl. That's why God wants you and not me.

With a sad heart, Megan silently prayed about what she could say to help him understand.

Daily Encouragement: It's not anything I have done or anything I will do that earns me a way into heaven. It's just what Jesus has done.

P24,601: He died and rose again. I get it.

Daily Encouragement: And that's what God looks at—Jesus' perfection, not my imperfections. I'm a sinner too, but I do want to please God. He is worth it, and I trust that he wants the best for me.

P24,601: You're very wise. It must have taken you years to learn so much.

Daily Encouragement: I've been a Christian since I was 10. I guess in the last 16 years I've learned something. Enough to know I'm still not perfect.

She felt like she could share with him and wanted to be real about her own burdens.

Daily Encouragement: I think another thing that helped me was going through my mom's cancer and death at the end of last year. It was a relapse and took us all by surprise. She was one of my best friends.

Actually, she *was* her best friend. Every day Megan's pain eased a little more. She thanked God for the years she had with her.

P24,601: My condolences. I lost my dad when I was young. It nearly destroyed me.

P24,601: Yet here I am dwelling on all of my problems when you have your own fresh ones. How do you stay so positive?

Daily Encouragement: It took me a few months, some counseling, and mostly God to get to this point. There will always be sadness, but I am joyful too. I have so much to be thankful for.

P24,601: I want that. I just don't know where to start.

This was it. She wanted so much for P24,601 to understand who God is and that God wanted his trust in him as Lord and Savior so God could free him from the lies that held him back.

Daily Encouragement: By telling God that very thing. He is your creator who loves you and wants to be in a relationship with you. You can trust him. Pray and ask him to show you who he is. And read his word, the Bible. The book of John is a good place to start.

P24,601: I'll try.

Daily Encouragement: I'm praying for you too.

P24,601: :)

Megan started to type a discourse on why he could trust God, but she felt God nudging her to stop and give him time. She had shared verses about becoming a Christian before and lots of other passages. He had to decide on his own.

Megan stared at the messages between her and P24,601. God had given her the ability to reach people through the app that she could never reach in person. The app was great, but sometimes she wondered what else she could do to reach people. Maybe that was why the thought of helping Kieran intrigued her. She did have her two friends she had met at the coffee shop and was doing a Bible study with, but she didn't want to miss any other opportunity that God laid before her.

She silently prayed and asked for guidance in this decision on whether to reach out to Kieran.

De Clare's Jewelers had a logo and the date of 1706 at the top of their website. With such a long history, surely it was reputable. Not that she would doubt the word of the man who had just been recognized as a top historian at the British Museum. Megan scanned the page and called the number listed. Once she explained to the man on the phone that Peter Nelson from the British Museum had sent her to them, he was quick to set up a time that afternoon when she could bring her mother's pendant for them to examine.

The store itself was nestled between several other high-end shops just across from a side entrance to Harrods. As she entered, a bell tinkled above the door and she felt like she'd stepped back in time as she took in the beautifully carved wood and glass cases displaying jewelry and fine china. Before she could get a closer look at a particularly stunning arrangement of an antique china place setting, she was approached by a middle-aged man dressed in a three-piece suit.

"Welcome to De Clare's." His stern expression and stiff demeanor as he looked Megan over left her regretting that she hadn't changed out of the jeans and casual top she was wearing. "How may I help you?"

"Um, yes, I...I spoke to someone earlier about bringing in a family heirloom to be looked at." The man looked down his nose at her, but she forged on. "My name is Megan Taylor. I have an appointment."

"Ah, yes. I'm Steven, the one you spoke with. Right this way." He waved her over to a door, and when she entered, she found what looked like a modern lab. He walked over to a sleek, black desk and pulled out a chair for her before seating himself behind it. "You said it was a pendant with a red stone?"

On the desk sat an unusual-looking microscope and a computer monitor. "I did." Megan pulled the jewelry pouch out of her purse and carefully laid the pendant and chain across the desktop.

"May I?" Steven asked as he reached for the necklace.

Megan handed it to him and watched as he turned it around and examined it. His brow rose when he noticed the markings on the back.

"Do you know what that means?" Megan had always wondered about the triple chevron etched into the back of the gold setting for the gem.

Steven shook his head. "First, I'm going to check to see if it fluoresces with a blacklight. I'll need to dim the light." He held up a remote and touched a button, then placed the pendant on the microscope and tapped some buttons until a blacklight came on. The gem glowed. "Hmm."

"What does that mean?"

"It appears to be a ruby. Let's see what the microscope shows." He switched the lights back on and adjusted the settings so that the blacklight turned off and the computer monitor turned on. After turning the monitor so they could both see, he began to alter the magnification and looked back and forth between the microscope and monitor. He adjusted it every few seconds.

His brow furrowed and his eyes went wide as he analyzed the gem. "It is genuine. I only see this one inclusion, and it is a tiny silk inclusion. I had to use a very high magnification to find it." He pointed to a crystal-like shape on the screen. "This is what we call a VVS grade because of the minor inclusion. It is also triple A which means it has the best color and clarity." He shook his head and rubbed his chin. "We call this color Pigeon's blood red. Based on the way it fluoresces, its deep red hue, and the clarity this is a Burmese ruby. They are extremely rare and some of the most valuable rubies. If you'll give me another few moments, I can estimate its weight. It will only be an estimate because of the setting."

Nodding slowly, Megan wondered how her grandmother ended up with such a rare gem.

Steven pulled out a ruler and laid the pendant down alongside it, turning the pendant in all directions and noting the size. "I'm estimating it at somewhere around ten-and-a-half carats. This is truly impressive." His eyes narrowed as he looked up at her. "You said this has been in your family?"

"It was my grandmother's, but I don't know how or when she received it. She died before I was born, but my mom always said they were a very middle-class family."

"I see." Steven looked perplexed. "Are you interested in selling? De Clare's would love to have a piece of this quality. I am sure we could find an interested buyer in no time."

"Oh, no. I couldn't sell it." This was one of her most valued possessions. It had meant so much to her mom, and now she treasured it as a link to her dearly missed mother. "How much do you think it is worth?" Although she would never sell, she was curious.

"I would estimate it at over ten and a half million."

"What?"

"Over ten and a half million pounds. Has this been insured?"

"Ten and a half million?" Megan reached for the pendant and rubbed her thumb across it as she had done so many times. "How is that possible?" It didn't make sense. Again she wondered how on earth had her grandmother come into possession of such a thing? "Insurance?"

"I can refer you to the company that we use."

Megan's mind spun. "Yes, that would be good." She turned the pendant over in her fingers. "So you don't know what the symbol on the back means?" Now she was especially curious.

"I'm afraid not, but if you have the time, I can ask the manager. He has experience with the more historical jewelry that we carry."

"Yes, that would be nice. I would love to have some clue about where it came from."

As Steven excused himself and left the room, Megan searched her mind for anything her mom might have told her about her grandmother. Unfortunately, her grandfather had passed away several years ago, so she couldn't ask him either. He and her grandmother had been friends since they were children, so even if it wasn't from him, surely he would have known. This was such a strange surprise.

"Hello, I'm Bernard Blake, the manager." Another middle-aged suited man appeared, followed closely by Steven. "I hear you are in the possession of quite a valuable piece of antiquity."

"It would seem so."

"Well, you've come to the right place." He sat down in the seat Steven formerly occupied and reached over the desk to shake her hand. "It's a pleasure to meet you, Megan. I do have some experience with historical pieces of jewelry and would be happy to look it over and tell you what I know."

After handing Mr. Blake the pendant, Megan watched as he evaluated the shape and design before flipping it over. His brow rose and he nodded towards Steven. "Thank you, Steven. You are free to attend to our other customers. I think I've got this."

"Certainly, sir." Steven turned to Megan. "It was a pleasure meeting you. Be sure that Mr. Blake gives you our recommendation for insurance before you leave."

Once the door closed, Mr. Blake spoke up, "He is correct about needing insurance. We can give you an official appraisal. I would normally charge five hundred pounds for an item of this magnitude, but I can tell you were not expecting this to be such a valuable piece and will discount it to one hundred fifty pounds."

Megan took it all in. "Thank you, I'd really appreciate that. Also, can you tell where it came from? Do the markings on the back mean anything?"

Mr. Blake's brow furrowed, and he examined the pendant again. "I cannot tell you what the symbol means, but by the ornate design and size of the setting and the stone's cut, it looks as if it was made in the late Middle Ages." He looked closely at the chain that looped through the pendant. "It appears that this is not the original chain. It likely was attached to a more ornate necklace that also held a number of gemstones. These were often sold in order to obtain money to maintain large estates, while the family kept back the most valuable part of their heirloom." He laid the pendant back down.

"At any rate, what is left is certainly of great value, even without knowing the precise provenance of it." He hesitated and tapped his fingers on the desk while eyeing the pendant. "I can also offer you a space in our vault as an option. You would rent the space and it would be covered by our insurance. For an item of this value, you might find this to be more affordable. I will have to work out a price for you after speaking with our insurance company."

"So I could come take it out any time I wanted?"

Mr. Blake shook his head. "No. It would need to remain in the vault to be fully covered."

Staring at the pendant, Megan tried to make sense of all the new information. "I think I need to talk with my father. This is a lot to take in and I'm not sure what I want to do." She hated the idea of not being able to see or wear the reminder of her mom.

"I understand. There is also the option of selling it. There's quite a market for antique jewelry. We could help you with that. Here." He reached into his pocket and pulled out two business cards. "This is my card and one for the insurance company. I'd also like to get your number in case I think of anything regarding the provenance of the pendant. Do you mind if I take a picture?"

"That's fine." She pushed the pendant towards him, then reached into her purse for one of her own business cards. "I could never sell it. It's too special to me."

Minutes later Megan found herself walking back to the tube entrance while clutching her neck. This time the necklace was hidden under her shirt rather than in her purse. She glanced around, wondering what people would think if they knew she was wearing something so valuable.

Chapter Three

"How's my favorite missionary?"

Megan smiled at the nickname her father had given her. England wasn't China like she'd imagined going to since she was thirteen, but it was the place where God had opened doors...for now.

When she pressed him about where the necklace came from, he insisted he had no idea. Though her father was at home in Chapel Hill, North Carolina, he offered to come to London and help her figure things out. Megan insisted he didn't need to come all that way. This was a chance to prove to herself and him that she could take care of herself, and she refused to cave at the first setback. He did help her find and order a safe to keep the pendant temporarily, but it wouldn't be in for two more days. He also urged her to talk to the insurance company and ask them for options so they could compare it to keeping the necklace in the jeweler's vault.

The insurance company wanted an exorbitant fee to insure the piece, but they also offered her a reduced rate to cover the necklace if it was in the De Clare vault and she only removed it a few times during the year to wear. That sounded much better than never seeing it, and she wondered what the charge to store it would be. She left a message for Mr. Blake to get back to her about the cost of keeping it at De Clare's.

It was so much to process, and she still hadn't wrapped her mind around the fact that she had inherited such a costly piece of jewelry. Despite all of this, the thought that kept her mind working overtime was wondering where it came from. Grabbing her phone, Megan sent a text to Peter.

Megan: The jeweler was able to tell me a time period for the pendant, but didn't recognize the markings. He said it was from the Middle Ages. Do you know anyone who is experienced in that time period? I'm extremely curious about where it came from.

However curious she was about the pendant, it was the ancient antiquities of Egypt that Megan needed to focus on, so she sat at her desk and opened the laptop. *A Practical Guide to Egyptian Antiquities* was what she came to England to work on in her mother's stead.

The book was nearly finished, but she needed to keep up her pace and focus on finishing it by the deadline. Corbyn Publishing Company had graciously extended the deadline when they discovered her mom's cancer. Megan left her job to spend time with her mom and assist her with the project. The publishing company once again pushed back the deadline when her mom died and she couldn't think clearly for weeks after. She would not ask for another extension. Instead, she set a timer, flipped open her notes, and began typing like a woman on a mission.

Peter: I have a mate at Oxford. He'll be in town Friday if that suits.

That was four days away, and after what Megan found out, she was anxious to keep the necklace safe. But more than anything, she wanted to know where it came from. Her family had managed to have it for years with no extra insurance or special precautions. Surely a few days wouldn't make a difference.

By Friday, Megan couldn't wait to leave the mews house. She'd managed to stay on the property all week—only crossing the yard to go to Kate's in-laws' home which was the estate that encompassed the house. While she waited for her taxi to the British Museum to meet with Peter and his friend, every person on the street seemed to be watching her. Who was that man at the corner of the mews road? She'd never seen him before, and he was standing there looking at his phone. What about the woman across the street with a child? Did they look familiar? With the road being a dead end alleyway, she didn't expect to have strangers pass often and definitely didn't expect them to linger.

When the taxi pulled up, she checked the app to make sure it was the correct driver. The ride left her tense, as she anticipated finding out more about her necklace. She breathed a sigh of relief when the taxi approached the museum and she saw Peter waiting at the entrance.

Peter smiled and greeted her before guiding her in and past security. When Megan glanced back at him, she wondered if he had any idea of the value of the necklace she had hidden under her blouse. When she felt his hand touch her lower back, Kate's comment about his interest in her also surfaced, and she was determined not to lead him on.

They wound through several hallways and stopped at Peter's office. "Reece arrived earlier and is eager to meet you."

"Thanks so much for setting this up, Peter. I—" The words died on her tongue when Peter opened the door and she took in the man on the other side. He was devastatingly handsome and she had to do a double take. He looked almost identical to the actor who played Superman.

"Megan." He stood and held out a hand. "Reece Fairfax, professor of Medieval history at Oxford."

She stared at him speechlessly for far too long before gathering her senses and reaching out to shake his extended hand. "Oh, uh. Hi." At a loss for more words, Megan pasted on a smile.

His firm grip and warm hand didn't help her situation, and the moment he released her hand, she reached out to steady herself on a chair at the round table next to them. "I'll just…" She looked at Peter as she struggled to pull the chair back.

Before she made a complete fool of herself, Reece moved the chair out so she could sit. Her jelly legs appreciated the relief. Peter pulled up a chair beside her.

"So, let's see this work of art Peter raves about." Reece sat across from Megan and slid from his jacket pocket a small, black metal instrument containing two magnification lenses. When he noticed her watching, he held it out to her. "This is a jeweler's loupe to help me see inside the gemstone."

"Oh, yes, I've heard of those. At the jewelry shop, the man used a special microscope." She reached up behind her neck to unclasp the pendant.

"They have those here as well, but for our purposes, this will do. Peter said you were interested in finding out where it came from."

Megan nodded and laid the necklace down.

"May I?" Reece questioned and at her approval he reached for it, his fingers brushing against hers. He glanced her way and the corner of his mouth lifted.

Was he flirting with her?

Reece ran a finger over the ruby and then the gold setting surrounding it. "Exquisite. The design appears to be Gothic which is late Middle Ages. I would date it as late thirteenth century." He turned the pendant over. "Yes, there is no leopard's head which is the mark Edward I decreed in 1300, so it was made sometime before that…Three chevrons…Now we're getting somewhere…Maker's marks were not required until 1363, but often families had their marks placed on jewelry so there could be no question who it belonged to." Reece glanced up. "This is from a family coat of arms. It might take me a couple of days to sort it out, but I should be able to narrow it down to a few families this might represent. With that, you could look at family trees to see if they intersect with yours."

"That sounds easy enough."

Reece looked up at Megan intensely and nearly made her forget what they were talking about. After holding her gaze he turned his head and continued using the loupe to analyze the ruby.

"It does look genuine, but you already knew that from the jeweler. This chain is not the original. It would have had an ornamental tiered necklace attached. Likely with more but smaller rubies and scrollwork to match this." He pointed to the gold scrolls surrounding the ruby and she nodded, recalling Mr. Blake's comments.

"Have you considered placing this in a museum collection? Perhaps here." He looked over at Peter. "Though the Victoria and Albert Museum might be the most logical location."

"A museum." She frowned and slid the pendant towards herself. "But this means so much to me. I want to be able to wear it. It was my mother's and grandmother's before that." She added in a whisper, "My heritage."

"Then I suppose you wouldn't want to sell? You would be set for life if you sold it. But if you chose the museum route, perhaps they could work out a loan. Of course, the interest of a museum depends on how this fits into history. Considering the quality of the piece and the size of the ruby, I would think some museum would want it."

He leaned back and crossed his arms over his chest, smiling at her like she was the priceless work of art. "This will have great value to someone. It's your pendant and it's up to you to decide." Glancing at his watch, Reece leaned in more closely and placed his hand on hers as she clasped the pendant on the table. The intensity in his eyes made her breath catch. "I'll be in touch with you soon with more information on the heraldry. Here's my card. I'll get your number from Peter."

"Here." Still rattled from the touch on her hand, she shakily handed him her own card.

He smiled then reached for her hand and brought it to his mouth. "It was a pleasure to meet you, Megan." Her name rolled so smoothly off his lips. "I wish I had time to get better acquainted, but I will plan better next time. I must get to my meeting."

Her eyes trailed after him as he left and once he was gone she realized he'd said "next time." He *was* flirting with her, and she liked it.

When she turned to Peter, she noticed the sad look in his eyes and gave him a weak smile. "So, I figured I would spend some time looking at artifacts for the book while I'm here. Anything new?"

"No, but I have a few more minutes if you need assistance." The tilt of his head and the sincerity on his face made him look so hopeful.

"I think I've got it, thanks." She lifted the pendant and unclasped it while standing.

"Let me help you." Peter stood and reached out.

"Thank you." Megan couldn't deny him that and regretted how awkward she felt. Usually, they spoke and laughed freely.

"If you consider placing the necklace in a museum, you'll want to hire a solicitor to help you draft out an agreement that protects you. I can suggest one if you choose that route."

"Thanks." Megan grabbed her purse.

"I can store your necklace in my office safe until you are finished here." He laid a hand on her shoulder while waiting for a response.

Megan forced a chuckle. "Surely with all of the security in this place, I'll be okay for a few minutes." She glanced at her watch. "I only have an hour before Kate picks me up for lunch. She'll have her girls. Have you met them?" She turned to him now that the necklace was in place.

"I've not." His hand rubbed the back of his neck while he smiled tightly.

"They're adorable." She looked down at her feet, then up again. "Thank you so much for setting this up. I'll let you know what I decide. Now I have even more to think about."

"You do. If you choose to try a museum, you know I'll put a good word in here and elsewhere if needed." He smiled tightly before turning back to his desk. "See you around, Megan."

She stared at Peter's back before turning to leave. The Egyptian early dynastic period held little interest when her mind swirled with thoughts of the pendant, and she found herself wandering to the Medieval section of the museum. There was nothing like her pendant, so she began searching for the triple chevron symbol. That search was fruitless as well.

Her phone buzzed to remind her of her meeting with Kate and the girls. Four-year-old Madeline and one-and-a-half-year-old Margaret were too precious for words, and Megan looked forward to spending a couple of hours with them. She also hoped Kate had some advice about her jewelry situation.

Chapter Four

"Did you two enjoy your macaroni and cheese?" Megan questioned Kate's girls while they all rode home after lunch.

Madeline gave a loud "Yes!" Margaret nodded emphatically at her older sister. When Megan's phone buzzed, she turned to check it.

"Is that Jean?" Kate glanced over at Megan, then focused back on the road.

Megan chuckled at the name Kate had given P24,601. It was certainly easier to say.

"It is. He was just asking how my day is going."

"Have you told him of your strange discovery?"

"No." Megan thought about why she hadn't. "I guess I don't want him to think of me differently. I worry that when people know I have this valuable thing, it will become the focus. Money and stuff can be such a distraction for people."

"Maybe there's a way to talk about it without revealing that it's so valuable. It is a big part of your life right now, and you said you were trying to be real with him."

"True, but it might distract from the chance to talk to him about God."

"Or it could give you more opportunities."

"Maybe. I'll think about it." Megan's phone vibrated again before she had responded to the first text.

"He's persistent today."

"Oh, it's not him," Megan said when she checked the screen.

"Who is it? The insurance company?"

"Actually...it's Reece. The Oxford professor who looked at my necklace."

"You're not fooling me, acting like he's some old guy. I saw the way you got all dreamy-eyed when you spoke about him over lunch."

"You're right. He wasn't old, and he was *very* good-looking. I think he looks like that actor who plays Superman."

"Okay, then. I like the sound of that. Maybe you need to meet with him again."

Megan's face heated as she looked down at the message. "Oh, wow. I...I'm not sure what this means."

"What is it?"

"He says..." She wondered how to phrase it. "I'll just read it. It says, 'Sorry I had to leave so quickly earlier. I'd love to take you to dinner tonight to talk more while I'm in town.' What does that mean? Is it a business 'talk more' or a personal get-to-know-you 'talk more'?"

"He wants to meet with you? Did he give you a reason to think it might be more than business earlier?"

"It did feel like he was flirting with me." The girls were giggling in the back, and Megan gave them a wink. Surely Madeline didn't understand what they were talking about.

"So you're going to say yes?"

"I guess." Tension formed in Megan's shoulders.

"Do you need help getting ready? I can get Corbyn's mom to watch the girls for a few minutes while I help you."

"I—" Megan glanced back at the girls who were chatting away. "Sure. Thanks. But I don't want you to fuss over me too much. I'm not going into this with any expectations. I'm just going to imagine it's business, which it may very well be. He may already have answers for me."

"Got it. That's probably the best approach." Kate turned the car onto Belgrave Mews Road. "By the way, I'm taking the girls to the Kingsdown cottage tomorrow. Corbyn's got a work thing. You should come with us. It will get your mind off all of this pendant stuff, and you can tell me all about your 'business' dinner."

"Deal." They both locked eyes and chuckled. The girls joined in, too young to understand why they were laughing.

"So the little one was putting macaroni in her ear?" Reece questioned with a chuckle as they waited for the waiter to deliver their meals. "How old did you say she is?"

Megan calculated the months until Margaret's birthday. "She's twenty months, and definitely a handful."

"I'll say. Do you want kids someday?"

Megan's eyes went wide, and she froze as he watched her with those enchanting eyes. "Y-yes, if I find the right person to marry." She felt her face heat for the umpteenth time since he picked her up at the mews house.

Reece gave her his suave grin.

"Right now I'm happy to enjoy Kate's children. In fact, tomorrow we're taking them to their family beach cottage in Kingsdown."

"Sounds like you've got a nice day planned."

"Yes." She stopped when the waiter laid their food on the table. "There's something about the sea breeze that relaxes me. I'm looking forward to it."

Kieran flashed in her mind. She'd told Kate she wanted to take him another meal. It seemed God had worked everything out so she would have another chance to reach out to Kieran, and she had to take it. She paused before asking, "Do you mind if I pray over our meal?"

Reece's brow furrowed and he glanced around the restaurant. "Um, go ahead." He frowned, then closed his eyes while she prayed.

Megan felt tension radiating off Reece during the prayer but chose not to comment on it. She looked across at him. "Tell me what it's like being a professor at Oxford." She'd never visited the campus but had often imagined what it was like.

"I love what I do. I love studying history. But let me tell you, it's getting harder and harder to get and hold the attention of young people. They're all into their mobiles."

Megan's phone vibrated and she winced.

Reece continued, "Just like that. Buzzing all the time and they can't stop themselves from checking them. Go on, I'm used to it." He winked and gestured towards her purse.

"No. I'm fine. If it were important, they would call." It was tempting to check it, but she refused to prove him right. She had a feeling it was P24,601. He had a habit of messaging about this time of night. It seemed the time when he felt loneliest. "Anyway, you can't be that much older than me."

Reece bit his lip and smiled. "I'm the same age as Peter. Thirty-eight. He and I were mates at uni."

"I didn't realize that." Neither man looked that old, and she wondered if the twelve-year age difference was too much. She'd not given it much thought with Peter because she only viewed him as a friend.

He reached out and touched her hand. "Does that bother you? My age?"

"Not at all." Maybe she should have paused before answering because she wasn't so sure about his age or whether she wanted this to go further between them. He was making it clear this wasn't just a business "talk more."

"Did you, uh, did you have a chance to look into anything regarding my pendant?"

"I did not." He tilted his head at her change of subject. "I was in back-to-back meetings, and now I'm here." He gave her a smoldering look. "Once I return home, I'll give it my full attention."

"Thank you. It really means a lot to me." She took a bite of Guinness pie and hoped he didn't notice the heat rising to her cheeks.

"Always glad to help a friend."

She smiled. "Peter's a great guy."

"He is, but I meant you."

"Oh."

Megan made it through the meal without embarrassing herself. She worried she might say something that sounded naive and tripped over her words several times, but Reece didn't seem put off by her insecurities. When he returned her home, he opened her door and kissed her hand before promising to call her the following evening to let her know how things were going with the search for the chevron.

As Megan relaxed on her sofa and recalled the evening, she decided that regardless of where Reece was trying to take their "friendship," that was all he needed to be. He was nice and one of the most handsome men she had seen in ages, but something didn't feel right—especially his reaction to her praying.

Her hand went to her pendant, and she decided to look up information on lending works of art to museums. When she looked at the screen, she saw P24,601's message and remembered she'd never opened it.

P24,601: How is your night going? I'm eating out on my balcony and watching gulls try to catch fish in the sea.

Daily Encouragement: That sounds wonderful. Tomorrow I'll be at the sea with a friend and her children.

P24,601: The same friend as last weekend? You'll have a chance for another relaxing walk on the coast.

Daily Encouragement: It is and I definitely will.

It warmed her heart to think he remembered what she'd said about her time the weekend before.

P24,601: I've been praying and reading the Bible like you suggested.

She'd been praying for that very thing. *God, make yourself known to him.*

Daily Encouragement: That's wonderful. What are your thoughts?

P24,601: I have many. After I read the book of John as you suggested, I decided to start from the beginning in Genesis. Once I got to Leviticus it seemed that maybe I should read from the Old and New Testaments simultaneously to balance things out. To be honest, Leviticus was quite tedious and weighty, so reading the New Testament helped keep me going. Numbers was tedious too with so many numbers ;).

Daily Encouragement: You've already reached Numbers? When did you start?

P24,601: I'm in Deuteronomy and about to start Acts in the New Testament. Last Sunday when you told me to pray and read the Bible.

She was floored at how dedicated he'd been.

Daily Encouragement: That was only five days ago! You've been busy. You make it sound like I demanded you do those things. I didn't mean to come across that way.

P24,601: You could never come across that way. I know you meant it for my good. I trust you. That's why I've been reading the Bible so much. I also like to analyze things thoroughly before making a decision.

Daily Encouragement: Let me know if you have questions. I may not know the answers, but I can find someone who does. A lot of the Bible can be confusing at first. Do you have a Bible with cross-references in the margins? That can help.

P24,601: Thanks. I already discovered that. My Bible also has notes at the bottom, but I feel like that's cheating. If God is worth knowing, he is worth me putting in the work.

Megan shook her head. How did he grasp something that so many long-time Christians didn't? For some reason, the nonfiction works of C.S. Lewis came to mind.

Daily Encouragement: Have you heard of C.S. Lewis?

P24,601: I attended Oxford. It would be hard not to. I also read *The Chronicles of Narnia* as a boy.

Daily Encouragement: I love those books. Have you read *Mere Christianity*?

P24,601: I have not. Do you recommend it?

Daily Encouragement: Yes, since you are analytical, you would appreciate the logic he uses to describe why God is who the Bible says he is.

P24,601: If you recommend it, then I have to read it. Like I said, I trust you.

Daily Encouragement: That's a lot of pressure.

P24,601: Is it my turn to encourage you now?

Daily Encouragement: Maybe.

P24,601: I've had a good example, so hopefully I can follow in her footsteps.

She felt herself blushing before his comment about C.S. Lewis came to mind.

Daily Encouragement: You went to Oxford. Does that mean you live in England?

Out of all of the countries in the world, wouldn't it be ironic if she had been messaging someone in England?

P24,601: I do.

Daily Encouragement: I'm an American, but I live in London. Maybe we could meet in person sometime?

Immediately, she wondered if that was a poor choice. With all of the crazy people out there, should she be offering to meet a stranger? But he didn't seem like a stranger anymore. She could meet him at a neutral location and have Kate there in case things got weird.

P24,601: I'm not a social person. Sorry.

It seemed she was worried for nothing. Part of her looked forward to meeting him in person and having a face to put with...his number. Megan laughed out loud. She didn't even know his name, and here she was feeling hurt that he didn't want to meet her.

P24,601: I hope you don't take that personally. I do enjoy our talks.

She *was* taking it personally. Now she was thankful she had not poured more of her heart out to him. She needed to remember that this was a ministry...*God, how do I respond? You led me to this. I trust that you have a plan. Help me not take this so personally.* She did trust God and P24,601 trusted her. She laughed at the realization.

P24,601: Are you there?

Daily Encouragement: Yes.

She couldn't say "It's fine." She didn't feel fine.

Daily Encouragement: I'll be fine.

Eventually. She knew she was making too much of it, but her feelings were hurt. In time it would fade.

Daily Encouragement: Goodnight. I've got some things to do before bed.

ᵗPraying and reading the Bible. She needed some redirection.

P24,601: Goodnight.

As she laid her phone down, Megan looked for a distraction from her conversation with P24,601 and began picking out clothes for the trip to the cottage with Kate and the girls. They planned to take another meal to Kieran. Maybe God was opening one door and closing another.

Chapter Five

"Look, Madeline! Over there is a seal," Megan called.

Madeline squealed and ran closer to where the seal bobbed its head up and down in the water before it disappeared.

"How fun!" Kate joined Megan and Madeline with Margaret in tow. "We almost never see them out here. You got to see something special, Madeline. We'll have to look up information on seals tomorrow when we have some free time. But right now it's nap time for both of you."

"Aw, Mummy. Do we have to?"

"Mummy, have to?" Margaret copied her sister.

"Yes, you do." Kate reached down and lifted Margaret into her arms and chased after Madeline who had begun running in circles and giggling.

"Let's get sister, shall we?"

Madeline dropped to the pebbly shore in a fit of giggles.

"I've got her." Megan joined in the mayhem and picked up Madeline, then swung her around before leading her towards the cottage.

As they came to the gate, Megan's eyes drifted to Kieran's cottage, and she wondered if they would have an opportunity to speak to him when they delivered his food. Before she turned her head, she noticed a figure in the downstairs window. It was him, she was sure. His physical therapist had been much broader. A ruffle of the curtain and he was gone.

"I hope Kieran doesn't yell at us like he did last time," Kate commented as she tossed a salad to take to him. "I'd rather the girls not be upset that way."

"It *was* disturbing. I'm happy to take the food myself. I can carry two baskets filled with all of the food."

"Oh, no. That's not what I was getting at. I'll just explain that he's a grumpy old man."

"I thought you said he wasn't old."

Kate chuckled. "To us he's not, but to a little person, mid-thirties is old."

"Oh, dear, their grandparents must seem absolutely ancient."

"Something like that." Kate's mouth lifted to one side and she nodded towards the oven. "Do the veggies look done?"

"They look like they could use a couple more minutes. I'll get the chicken out of the pressure cooker while they finish off."

Fifteen minutes later, Megan found herself knocking on Kieran's door while holding two baskets in her arms.

"Toby," she said when Kieran's physical therapist opened the door. "Do you remember me from last week? I'm—"

"Megan," he cut her off. "How could I forget a lovely lady like you?" He looked down at the baskets.

"I can help you carry them in."

Toby glanced back into the house. "Sure. Just don't go past the kitchen, please. It's the first door to the right, off the hall." He grabbed a basket from her before turning back into the cottage.

Megan quietly followed Toby in, carefully taking in her surroundings. Though the home looked like a well-kept old beach cottage from the outside, the inside was nothing like Kate's antique filled family cottage. Instead, she spotted contemporary furniture as she followed Toby's direction to the modernized kitchen of sleek granite countertops, dark cabinets with clean lines, and stainless steel commercial grade appliances.

"Do you think I could maybe speak with Kieran?" Megan softly asked as she placed the basket on the counter.

"Sorry. He's still not up for visitors. Yet." Though Toby tried to lower his voice, it carried through the house.

"Ahem." Someone cleared their throat in the next room, and Megan looked up at Toby who just shook his head and grinned.

"We hear you," Toby called. "This nice lady, Megan, who brought you food again, is not going to bother you."

"Well stop flirting with her. And tell her thank you."

Megan bit her lip at Kieran's retort.

"She can hear you. You could come tell her yourself."

Now there was silence in the other room.

"I left this note for him." Megan spoke loud enough for Kieran to hear and pointed to a piece of paper in one of the baskets.

"I'll make sure he gets it." After emptying the baskets, Toby returned them to Megan and guided her back to the door.

"Bye," she said to Toby, then just before stepping out she turned back and spoke more loudly, "Goodbye, Mr. Davies."

"Mr. Davies. Hmph," Kieran mumbled.

Toby gave her his signature wink before saying goodbye.

Megan wondered what Kieran would think of her note of encouragement. She'd included two Bible verses. *God, I pray that you take those words and pierce his heart in a way that helps him feel alive again and helps him see you.*

"I did it! Well, sort of," she called out to Kate as she entered the Corbyn family cottage. "I didn't get to see him, but Toby let me go into the kitchen. Kieran spoke to us from another room. Then when I left, I loudly called out goodbye. Oh, and also I mentioned that I had a note for him and said that loudly so he could hear."

"Well if anyone can get through to him, it's probably you. I've been looking at your Pulse Daily Encouragement beats and the responses. You are making a difference. Keep it up."

Megan fiddled with her thumbs then looked up and smiled. She wasn't looking for accolades, but the words still encouraged her.

Dinner with the girls was an adventure as always, and before she knew it, they were returning to London. Almost instantly the girls fell asleep in the back seat after the busy day.

"Too bad we didn't get to see your friend Hayley. I was hoping to finally meet her and see her baby."

"You'll just have to come back with me and we'll try again."

"That would be nice. I do love it out there." Maybe next time she would get to meet Kieran in person.

"So what's next with the necklace?" Kate questioned.

Megan watched the coast fade into the distance as they turned away from Kingsdown. "I'm still waiting to hear back from the man at De Clare's. The price the insurance company gave me was outrageous, and I'm looking for other less expensive options. Mr. Blake made it sound like it would be cheaper to store it there because they have discounted insurance since their items are heavily protected."

"That would be helpful."

"I don't think I'm going to take the museum route. It seems like I wouldn't have access to it if I wanted to wear it." She pulled out her phone and shrugged when she saw there were no messages. "I was supposed to hear back from Reece today. The professor at Oxford. I guess he didn't find anything yet regarding the chevron design."

"That's right, the handsome professor who took you to dinner."

"Mhmm. Don't read into it too much. I don't feel like he's someone I'm supposed to date, if that's what you're thinking."

"I won't do that to you. Like I've said before, I know how it feels to have everyone around you pushing you towards dating someone when you aren't ready."

Megan grinned. "Well, it does seem to have worked out well for you."

"Corbyn is the one man that no one was trying to push me towards. Well, there was one person. Hayley was pro-Corbyn from the beginning.

She only quieted about him when I made her feel guilty because I thought he had recently broken an engagement. But I do remember the added stress of so many people trying to play matchmaker, so I won't pester you. On a different topic, I am wondering what's going on with Jean, spiritually I mean. You said you thought he was close to becoming a Christian."

"I did, but now even more so. Yesterday I found out that after I recommended he read the book of John, he decided to read the whole Bible from start to finish, and when he got bored with Leviticus he began simultaneously reading the New Testament. In five days he had already read to Deuteronomy and was about to start Acts. There's no telling how far he's read by now.

"He messaged earlier today while you were putting the girls down for a nap." She recalled him talking about how the Pharisees of Jesus' time were like the hypocrites of today which made him not want to be a Christian. She had been flattered when he said she was changing his mind because she wasn't like that. Their conversation flowed normally, but she'd work hard to squelch the sting from the fact that he didn't want to meet her.

Kate glanced over. "What's that face?"

"I...I found out that he lives in England and suggested we meet, but he's not interested. It kind of hurts."

"Oh, Megan, I'm sorry, but don't you think that's a good thing? You shouldn't go off meeting strangers, even ones who seem nice and who you're witnessing to on Pulse."

"I know, but it still hurts my feelings. I was excited when I realized he was so close. It seemed like a God thing. I would have taken precautions like having you or someone I know nearby."

"I'm terribly sorry your feelings are hurt. But I still think it's safer this way. You have enough to worry about without having to be paranoid about meeting a stranger who started messaging you on social media."

"You make him sound like a stalker. He seems like a normal guy who is working through things."

Kate placed a hand on Megan's shoulder. "You're right. I don't mean to downplay what's been happening with him. It does sound like he's sincere. I've been praying for him and for your interactions with him."

"Thanks. I'll get over it. His relationship with God is the most important thing."

Megan's thoughts drifted to her next steps with the necklace, and she looked at her phone, once more checking to see if Reece had texted.

As they turned onto the mews street, Megan smiled. It was a pretty little street in the center of Belgravia with quaint homes attached to one another. The street boasted potted topiaries on the ground level, second-floor flower boxes, and a cobbled street. She couldn't have dreamed up a more perfect London abode.

It had been a blessing for her to have such an upscale place to live while working in London, and it was a huge factor in her father not giving her a hard time about moving so far away from her North Carolina home.

She grabbed her backpack and hugged the girls, who had awakened in time to go to their grandparents' estate on the other side of Megan's backyard. "See you later, girls. Thanks for letting me hang out with you and your mom."

"You've become a dear friend, Megan. I'm so glad to have you as part of our lives. When you've completed this book for Corbyn Publishing, I'll make sure Corbyn offers you a permanent job that you can't refuse."

"You know, I think I might like that." She smiled back at Kate.

Corbyn was the CEO of Corbyn Publishing, and it flattered Megan when they let her complete her mother's book. She'd always imagined her time in England would be a short-lived experience, but the thought of staying a while longer sounded intriguing. She was coming to love London and the other towns she explored on her day trips. God was even opening doors for her to share her faith, and she wondered if he wanted her to hold off going to China or maybe even change directions altogether.

"All right then." Kate slipped Margaret out of her car seat and set her on the ground. "Girls, wave goodbye to Miss Megan, then we'll go visit with Nan and Pop."

While climbing the steps to her second-floor bedroom, Megan

pondered the thought of living in London for several more years and quite liked the idea. She shifted her backpack off her shoulder and moved towards the bench at the end of her bed when it hit her that clothes were strewn around the floor and on the furniture. Clothes she hadn't placed there.

Her heart raced as she glanced around and silently retraced her steps down the stairs while muffling a scream. As soon as she exited through the back door into the yard she began screaming, unaware of what words came from her mouth.

"God, you are my fortress and my shield! God, you are my fortress and my shield!"

As she approached the back door of the estate, Tracey, Kate's mother-in-law, opened it. "Megan, come in! You're shaking and look like you've seen a ghost. What's happened?"

"I-I think I've been robbed! I don't know if they're still there."

"I called nine-nine-nine. They're sending Bobbies over straight-away," said Tracey's husband, Richard as he joined the ladies.

The next thirty minutes were a blur as they awaited the police and a detective questioned Megan. Several policemen checked the mews home and the surrounding property for signs of the intruder. Once she was given the go-ahead, Megan returned to the home. Her heart raced as she turned the doorknob and wondered what she'd find missing.

Chapter Six

A thorough search revealed the only thing missing was the large safe Megan recently purchased for her necklace. Her hand went to her neck and she silently thanked God she was wearing her treasured heirloom. Before leaving that morning, she had almost placed the pendant in the safe. Instead, the burglars would be disappointed upon realizing they stole an empty safe.

At almost one hundred and fifty pounds, three feet tall, and two feet square, the safe should have been difficult for someone to maneuver. It had taken Kate's two nephews, who were eighteen and twenty, to set it in place. Who were these people who invaded her home?

As Megan walked around her bedroom looking at the disaster, she noticed her grandmother's antique wooden jewelry box open on the floor. Wood splintering out from the side made her heart sink. Bending down to look more closely only brought more pain, and she moved away, not wanting to dwell on the broken piece of her history.

"Do you have any idea what the thief may have been looking for, miss?" the detective asked after she informed him that nothing but the safe appeared to be stolen.

"I do." Her hand touched her shirt where it hid the necklace, and she hesitated. A sudden wave of paranoia filled her. Could she tell anyone else of its value? She had only spoken to a few about it. But then, there were also the pictures the media put out showing her and Peter at the arts benefit. The pictures placed her pendant on full display. Would someone have recognized its value from a picture online?

Her eyes darted around. Kate was the only other person in the room. The others had gravitated to the reception room. She would tell him as little as possible. "I recently found out my necklace," she lifted it from beneath her shirt, "is quite valuable. It was my mother's, and she passed away last year." The detective typed into his electronic device.

Megan wondered how much he needed to know. "A friend of mine pointed out that it was probably valuable and I should have it looked at, so I went to a jeweler and also had a historian from Oxford look at it. I've spoken with an insurance company as well." She stood up and stared down at the jewelry box, longing to examine the damage more closely. "Oh, and I wore it at the Benefit for the Arts held at the British Museum. It was almost two weeks ago. Pictures of me wearing it were all over social media the next day." She blushed, realizing how that sounded. "It was because my date had been honored."

The detective nodded. "Have you noticed anything these past couple of weeks that's seemed strange?" he continued.

Megan started to shake her head. "I remember having a strange feeling that I was being watched the day I discovered its value." She thought back to the day and then shook her head again. "But now that I think about it, it was probably just me feeling paranoid because of what I'd discovered. No one looked suspicious." She frowned at the floor and then looked over to the detective again. "Forgive me, I'm just rambling."

"It's fine, miss. Everything can mean something. Don't hesitate to tell me any little detail. If you can please give me the names of the people who know your necklace is valuable?"

Thinking back through her encounters, Megan didn't want to believe anyone was responsible for violating her personal things and trying to rob her of something that meant so much to her.

At her hesitancy, the detective tried again. "Who was the friend who recommended you have it looked at?"

Peter's face flashed before Megan's mind. Surely not. "Peter Nelson. He's a curator at the British Museum."

"Okay. I'll need the names of the jeweler, Oxford professor, and anyone you've spoken with at the insurance company."

With a racing mind, Megan pulled out her wallet and found the cards for the jeweler, insurance company, and Reece. After handing them over she noted, "I met with two different men at the jewelers. The second one is on the back." Again she tried to imagine how any of the men could be behind the break-in. They all seemed so nice. Her buzzing phone drew her thoughts back to the present. The flash of Reece's name seemed ironic, and she sent his call to voicemail.

"Do you need to answer?" The detective nodded towards her phone.

"No, I'll speak with him later."

"Is it one of the people you've given me the name of?"

Megan furrowed her brow, torn between worry that she might get the wrong person in trouble and worry that she might fail to provide vital information about the one who actually did it. "It's Reece."

"Hmm." He typed something into his device. "Who on this list knows where you live?"

"You know that anyone can find that information out nowadays with a quick internet search. My name was in the paper." When the detective raised his brow and continued to wait silently, she sighed. "Peter and Reece."

After a grunt of acknowledgement, he asked, "Have either of them been inside your home?"

"Only Peter," Megan answered softly, not liking the idea that he thought her friend was a suspect. Should she be suspicious?

More typing, then he began snapping pictures. "I'll be looking at everything. By the way..." He led Megan and Kate downstairs to the entrance hall and pointed to the console on the wall. "This alarm system is dated and works on radio waves that can be mimicked. Anyone with the proper gadgets can shut it off. Whoever did this is experienced. For now, I'd suggest you put your necklace somewhere that is actually safe." He pointed towards the entrance door on the ground floor which had a broken lock and busted frame. "You also need to find somewhere else to stay tonight."

"Don't worry. We'll take care of her," Kate broke in.

Once the officers left, Tracey confirmed that they had a hidden built-in safe in their home that could house her necklace. "I'm so sorry this happened. I had no idea the security system needed updating. It's concerning that they were able to disarm it. We'll have the entrance door replaced and the security system upgraded. We insist you stay in our home as long as you need to feel comfortable. We have a state-of-the-art security system in the main house."

Richard nodded in agreement. "I feel like I'm in place of your dad here, and I know I would worry for my daughter's safety after something like this. I would also suggest you have someone accompany you to places for a few days until the police figure out who might be targeting you. Since they didn't accomplish their goal, I'm guessing that they're not finished." He glanced at Tracey. "We might even speak with our head of security for the office and see if his company has anyone that can follow you for a few days."

Megan rubbed her temple when Richard mentioned her dad. She dreaded calling him and explaining what happened. Ever since she'd discovered the material value of her pendant, it had begun to feel more like a millstone around her neck.

"How about we gather these clothes strewn around and take them to the cleaners," Kate offered.

"Okay." Megan appreciated Kate taking the decision-making away. She was overwhelmed with choices and worry.

"You can go upstairs and pack a bag to take to Tracey and Richard's while we gather the clothes."

"Thanks." Megan found herself wandering around her room with a lack of focus when her eyes landed on the broken jewelry box, and tears began to flow. Crouching down, she examined it more closely. There on the floor surrounding it lay the few necklaces and two bracelets of little value that had filled it. A packet of letters peeked out.

She lifted the box to reveal the packet which was wrapped in a pale blue ribbon. She'd never seen the letters and looked again at the busted jewelry box. The faded burgundy lining had separated from the top and exposed them. She gingerly pulled out an envelope. The yellowed paper was brittle as she unfolded it.

Dear Nancy,

Since the first time I saw you in the café reading Emma, I've not been able to get you out of my mind.

Megan skimmed to the bottom of the letter.

Yours, Robert

Nancy was her grandmother, but her grandfather's name was Walter Douglas Moore. She double-checked the date, and it was from April 1970. Barely more than a year before her mom was born. Interesting. It seemed her grandmother had an admirer.

"Are you okay?" Kate joined Megan on the floor.

Megan looked over at her friend and realized she had momentarily forgotten about the robbery. "Yes. Look." She pointed to the letters. "These were in my grandmother's jewelry box hidden behind the lining." She carefully tucked them in her messenger bag to examine later.

The guest room bed lured Megan in and she dropped onto it. How did such a beautiful day turn into a nightmare? She reached for her grandmother's letter that had been calling to her since she'd first opened it, but her phone sat next to it and she knew what she had to do.

An unanswered message from P24,601 stared at her from the phone. In the chaos, she'd not had a chance to reply. He was the one person she wanted to talk to about the robbery. Her hand hovered over the keyboard and she squeezed her eyes shut. The thing she needed to do worried her almost as much as the thought of someone coming after her for the necklace. She switched to the phone screen.

"Hey, Dad."

"My little missionary sounds tired. What's up?"

How could she explain without making him panic? Best to get it over with. "Dad, I've been robbed."

"Megan? You're okay? Were you mugged? Where are you?" She heard shuffling papers. "I'm looking up flights right now."

"No, Dad. It's not like that. It was the mews house while I was gone."

"Thank you, God! My precious girl, you're okay. I don't know what I'd do without you. It's too soon after losing your mother. If you had— Wait! Where are you? Are you at the mews?"

"No. I'm fine and safe, I promise. I'm at Tracey and Richard's home. The mews was inspected by the police, and Richard hired a security team to patrol the home tonight."

"Okay. Okay. But what about your grandmother's necklace? It was so special to you and your mother."

"It's fine. I was wearing it at the time. The safe we bought was stolen though, but that's all."

"They stole that huge safe? I'm sure they had quite a disappointment. But that's not good, Megan. You said that's all they took. It sounds like they came for the necklace."

Megan's mind wandered to the scene in her room and her hand found the spot where the necklace usually hung.

"Megan? Did you hear me?"

"Yes, Dad. It does."

"Then I'm definitely coming there. I'd prefer you come home to me, but you're as stubborn as your mother."

Megan swallowed hard and clung to the memories that bounced through her mind. As a teenager, she'd had many arguments with her mom resulting from their similar trait. They'd always managed to forgive one another, and as she matured their arguments grew further apart.

"It looks like I can leave in the morning. Unfortunately by the time I get to you, it will be two days for you with the time difference. Will you be okay? Where is the necklace right now?"

"It's in a built-in, very secure safe here in Tracey's home. Don't worry."

"Can they keep the guards with you until I get there? I'll pay them back."

"That seems extreme." Or maybe not. She had no idea what was best in a situation like this. Was her life at risk? *Please, God, show me what to do.*

"No, Megan. I'm not risking your life. Please do this for me."

The brokenness in his voice shook her. "Dad, I love you. I'll let the guards protect me. I promise."

Chapter Seven

"Corbyn spoke with Kieran about your situation."

Megan's eyes widened at Kate's comment, and she scanned the church parking lot. After the break-in the day before, she was vulnerable and hyper-aware of her surroundings.

"Don't worry, he didn't tell him specifics of who or what."

"Thanks. At this point, I'm feeling paranoid about everyone. I'm trying to trust God. I've never been in a situation like this. I'm sorry if I'm overreacting."

"It's fine, Megan. I can't imagine how I would respond. Corbyn is always good about praying over me when I am stressed. Can I pray for you?"

"Yes, please."

"God, please give Megan wisdom in this. Calm her heart and help her know what to do each step of the way. I pray for protection over her and over the pendant. Not because of its monetary value, but because it is special to her. Bring her father safely here as he travels. In Jesus' name, amen."

"Thank you. What were you saying about Kieran?"

"Oh. Right. Kieran has some experience with the dark web and—"

"Dark web?"

"Yeah. According to Corbyn, it's as shady as it sounds. People buy and sell things on it anonymously. You never know who you are dealing with. People pay with bitcoin and other hard-to-trace currencies. You can just imagine what kinds of things that leads to. People can hire hackers, buy guns, drugs, stolen art, stolen jewelry."

"Stolen jewelry?"

"You can understand why Corbyn thought Kieran might be helpful."

"The dark web. It sounds so ominous."

"From everything Corbyn has told me, it is. So will you let Kieran help with this?"

Megan sent up a silent prayer for wisdom. "I think so, but can I let you know in the morning?"

"Of course. Why don't you join Corbyn and me for lunch? We haven't decided where to eat yet, so you can help us choose. You can also ask Corbyn more about the dark web. I can tell you have a million questions."

Megan couldn't stop yawning during their meal. When Kate looked her way, she tried to stifle another one.

"I imagine it was hard to sleep last night after all you had been through."

"It was hard to get settled down, but I ended up messaging back and forth with Jean until well after midnight. I told him my home had been broken into but didn't say why. I admitted I was worried about my safety, but felt bad that I wasn't trusting God. Then he tried to distract me by asking loads of questions about God and the Bible. It was a good distraction."

Megan yawned again. "Sorry, I should get home before I fall asleep here at the table. You two probably want this time to yourselves anyway since Tracey is keeping the children for the afternoon." Megan nodded towards Corbyn.

"We're fine. She gives us lots of time alone. She dotes on the girls endlessly."

"It's true," Corbyn spoke up. "Mum loves the girls and they love her. Just let me know what you decide about Kieran's help. He may be grumpy and going through things right now, but he has a good heart and it might also be helpful for him to have to interact with someone besides his physical therapist friend or his computer."

"At this point, I think I'll run it by my dad when he gets in tomorrow morning. I hate that my dad has to use his personal leave days to come all the way over here."

"That sounds like a good plan. I know you feel like you're inconveniencing him, but trust me, dads feel very protective of their girls." Corbyn gave a pointed look at Kate.

"Yes, dear, you are very protective of our girls. I feel bad for the men who want to date them someday. No one will be good enough in your eyes."

Corbyn chuckled. "You may be right about that."

Megan smiled as she watched Kate and Corbyn's banter. She'd never been in a serious relationship. There was always something else drawing her focus and driving her heart. Being a missionary was her passion. Now that she had followed God's lead to England, she began to wonder if God might have romance for her after all.

She thought back to her interaction with Reece. Even though he didn't seem like her type, the attention had been nice. He drew her out from the awkwardness she usually had around men she didn't know well. Then she remembered...

"Reece never contacted me back."

"What do you mean?"

"He promised to call yesterday to update me on his discoveries. He never did. I briefly thought about it, but have had so much on my mind I forgot."

"Megan, what are you thinking? You have that look you get when your mind is whirling," Kate said, causing Corbyn to laugh.

"It seems odd. The timing. He knows where I live, and he's seen my pendant. What if…"

"You think he might be the one who broke in?"

"This is where Kieran's skills could be helpful. If this Oxford professor stole something like that, or anyone for that matter, they wouldn't be able to sell it to anyone legitimately and they wouldn't be able to use it for any notoriety if it has historical significance. Their only option would be the black market." Corbyn paused and frowned. "I'm not trying to pressure you to speak with Kieran. I just think he might be able to give you some direction."

"It's fine. I'm leaning that way, but I'll wait to hear my dad's thoughts."

Reece Fairfax
    Bernard Blake
    Steven ?

She'd not gotten Steven's last name. Megan looked at her list, then reluctantly added another name.

Peter Nelson

She stretched across the bed. All these people knew of her pendant's value. There were likely a number of others at the Benefit for the Arts who could have guessed its value, but she would have to get a list of names and it was a large crowd. There was that one man at the benefit who commented on the necklace. She'd met so many people that night and couldn't remember his name.

Megan's eyes began to close and the page became blurry.

A buzz woke her from a sweet dream where she was with her mom and dad, running in a field. There was that buzz again. She felt around the comforter until she touched her phone. "Hello," she answered groggily. Another buzz and she partially opened her eyes to see it wasn't a call but a message from P24,601.

P24,601: How are you doing today? I haven't heard from you.

Daily Encouragement: I was napping because someone kept me up last night.

P24,601: Someone probably wouldn't have slept either way. I was helping.

Daily Encouragement: That is true. Thank you.

P24,601: Feeling better today?

Daily Encouragement: Other than being tired ;) Yes. I am actually. The thought that my dad will be here in the morning to help me figure things out takes away some stress.

P24,601: You must be close to your dad.

Daily Encouragement: Very. Especially now since my mom died.

It was getting easier to say.

P24,601: Same for me since my dad died.

Daily Encouragement: I'm so sorry. When did he die?

P24,601: Years ago when I was a kid. I'm okay, but we were close. I love my mum and make sure she's taken care of. Glad your dad is coming to take care of you. I finished reading Hebrews. Interesting book. Especially with the way it ties into the Old Testament.

Megan walked to the window and took in the view of Belgrave Square Garden. The garden reminded her of the dream she had just awakened from, and that longing for her mom returned. She tucked those thoughts deep down and began typing on her phone.

Daily Encouragement: What are some of the things you found interesting?

P24,601: Melchizedek. Didn't think much about him when I read through Genesis, but I want to know more now. Order of Melchizedek? Without father or mother or genealogy? I think I get that Levi was still in the loins of his ancestor. His name means king of righteousness. That is interesting since he is tied to Jesus. This is a lot to process. I feel like it's something big, but this is all new to me.

Daily Encouragement: Turning to Hebrews now.

It would be so much easier to call Jean, but she didn't want another rejection after his response about meeting in person.

Flipping between Genesis 14, Psalm 110, and Hebrews, Megan recalled the things she had studied in the past. She turned on the talk-to-text so she could get all of her thoughts out more quickly.

Daily Encouragement: You have to keep in mind that the writer of Hebrews was writing to Jewish Christians. They were raised around the Levitical priests, daily sacrifices at the Temple, and all of the Old Testament laws. Along with that, the Jewish leaders of the time had been telling them the Messiah would be a leader who would come and free them from the rule of the Romans. They were expecting someone to come in commanding political power and monetary wealth while setting up an earthly kingdom.

Instead, Jesus came in humility and to serve as he pointed the people to God and helped them understand that their sins needed to be forgiven permanently to be in a relationship with God. Only Jesus, fully God and fully man, could provide the way for that permanent forgiveness.

The sacrificial system with the priests was never intended to save the people. It was instead to help them see that they could never be good enough to get to heaven on their own. People can never be good enough. The Old Testament laws and sacrificial system made up the Old Covenant and were to prepare the way for the New Covenant. With the New Covenant, Jesus is not only the priest, who intercedes for the people, but he is the sacrifice for sins. If he had been of the lineage of Levi, the people would have tried to tie the two covenants together.

That's where Melchizedek comes in. God intentionally had the writer leave out any references to his lineage so he could be seen as a literary type of Christ. A representation that in some ways pointed to the real Messiah to come. Melchizedek laid the foundation for a priest who was not part of the Levitical line and was not tied into the Old Covenant and its sacrificial system. Jesus was not in the order of Levi but in the order of Melchizedek. His authority didn't come because of his lineage, but because of God's design.

Her heart raced as she looked back over what she had just texted and then sent it. Talking about Jesus was what she was made for. She stopped and flipped through the concordance.

P24,601: It's still a bit fuzzy, but I'll keep studying it with these things in mind.

Daily Encouragement: Matthew 5:17 says Jesus "didn't come to abolish the Law or the Prophets, but to fulfill them." He is the permanent and only solution to mankind's sin. His one sacrifice is effective for people who lived before he was on the earth and everyone else until the day he returns. Be sure to look at Genesis 14:18.

She wondered if she should say more or leave it there. It was a lot for him to work through. If they were in person, she would be able to read him better to know if she should go on. Her eyes roved the street outside that met with the garden. Movement in a white car on the street caught her eye. Was that man taking her picture?

She began to shift away from the window but decided against it. Two can play that game. She shifted her phone ever so slightly so she could take his picture. The driver would be blurry, but she was mainly trying to get the license plate, then she forwarded it to the group text of the guards patrolling the house for Tracey and Richard.

Her gaze drifted several cars down where one of the guards sat in a gray van. It blended in with the vans for the embassies housed on the street. She watched as another vehicle drove up and parked next to the white car. When the driver exited she recognized he was another one of her guards. He got out and strolled towards the park, then stopped and leaned on a post before messing with his phone.

Megan wanted to go down there, too, except she would be tempted to knock on the door of the car and demand to know who he was and why he broke into her home. Likely not the best idea, but she was tired of being fearful and it was turning into anger. Were there phases for feelings after being robbed like there were for grief? Her phone pinged.

P24,601: Still there? Thanks for sharing your thoughts. It was helpful.

Daily Encouragement: Yes, still here. I got distracted. I'm being watched.

She was glad she'd explained the basics of what had been happening to Jean so he wouldn't think she was crazy for thinking she was being watched.

P24,601: Watched? Are you safe?

She started to answer with an immediate yes but realized that the man could have a gun and aim it at her before she had time to move. Okay, maybe sitting in the window wasn't the best idea. She no longer felt brave as she moved away with one last glance at the guard who was looking between the white car and her. *God, show me what to do. Help me not make stupid choices.*

Daily Encouragement: Now I am. I moved out of the window. A man was taking my picture from a car across the street.

P24,601: I'm worried about you. Your dad won't be there until tomorrow.

Daily Encouragement: I'm with friends.

She hesitated but then added:

Daily Encouragement: And there are guards watching the house.

P24,601: Okay. That's better.

Megan found herself pacing back and forth but couldn't take it any longer and moved closer to the window. Just close enough to see out. The white car was gone. Her phone buzzed and she saw a call coming in from one of the guards.

"Hello."

"He left. Thanks for moving away from the window. I was about to text you. I hate to limit you so much, but until we get a better idea of how serious it is, sitting in the window is not a good idea. When you leave the house, someone will go with you."

"O-Okay."

"We ran the tags and they were stolen, so no leads there. We contacted the police and they were on the way to confront him. There's still a chance they may find him. We sent them a picture of the car."

"Thank you. I don't plan to go anywhere until we pick up my dad at the airport."

"Just let us know. I'll update you if anything new comes up."

"Thanks, I'll do that. Bye."

Daily Encouragement: The person taking the picture left and was using stolen car tags. The police have the information though.

P24,601: Do you have any plans to leave the house before your dad gets in?

Daily Encouragement: No.

P24,601: Wise decision. Keep me updated. Is there someone who can help you get to the bottom of this? Do you have any leads on who it is? I wish I could help.

Daily Encouragement: Not really. You can pray.

P24,601: I can and I will.

A thrill went through Megan. Jean was definitely close to becoming a Christian.

Thank you, God, for letting me be part of Jean's transformation. Help him to understand all that he needs to in order to lay down his life and accept Jesus as Lord and Savior. And help me to not get so caught up in this situation with my pendant that I miss more important things, like opportunities to talk with people who need you.

That evening, Megan wore her pendant as she ate dinner and spent time with Tracey and Richard. It would be a while before she wore it again.

Her father had been in discussions with Mr. Blake at the jewelry shop and thought that their best course of action was to make a show of having an armored car come to take the necklace to De Clare's. There it would be tightly guarded around the clock in their vault along with the jewels of other customers. They planned to take the necklace after her father arrived and was settled at the house.

She'd never thought of herself as materialistic, and the financial value of the necklace had no bearing on her feelings. But the thought of parting with it gave her anxiety. It had become a link to her mother whom she loved and her grandmother whom she had only heard stories about. It felt like a test. She closed her eyes and touched the pendant. *God, nothing is more valuable than you. It is yours to do with as you please.* She meant it but was still sad.

When she settled down for the evening, she was determined to read some of her grandmother's letters. Maybe they would provide information about the necklace. This time when she pulled them out, she noticed it was written to her grandmother at a London address. Megan never knew that her grandmother had lived in London. She flipped through the others and they had the same address. Curiouser and curiouser.

As she flipped through the letters, she found them in order by date. The one she had started was dated April 9, 1970, and was the first. She opened it and read. This Robert guy was clearly enamored with her grandmother. He elaborated on her grandmother's beauty and urged her to meet him for lunch the following week at the same location. Hmm.

In the next letter, Robert thanked Nancy for meeting him, and it was clear that they had some deep conversations from the things he said about faith, family, and their jobs. Her grandmother worked at the U.S. Embassy?! That was a revelation. There was talk of Vietnam attacking Cambodia. Robert also mentioned his thoughts on the Apollo 13 launch over the weekend and he referenced the discovery that an oxygen tank in the service module failed.

Megan stopped and looked up the information on her phone. On

April 11, 1970, Apollo 13 was launched. If nothing else, her knowledge of history would be enriched. It was fascinating to think of her grandmother being alive during events that seemed so distant.

A yawn escaped, and she had to fight to keep her eyes open. Although Megan wanted to read more, she decided a good night's sleep was in order before she met up with her father in the morning. They had a busy day ahead.

Chapter Eight

"Dad!" Megan threw her arms around her father and melted into him. Scott Taylor felt like safety and home as he hugged her back. She didn't realize how much she needed him. The past week had frayed her nerves.

"My precious pearl." He pulled back and looked Megan over then lifted a hand to her brow. "You hold your stress in your eyebrows just like your mother." His wistful smile reminded her that he had lost his best friend and the love of his life.

"I'm okay, Dad, especially now that you're here." She grabbed his hand and pulled him towards the car one of her guards was driving. The trip back to Belgravia went quickly as Scott caught Megan up on all of the goings on in her hometown of Chapel Hill. He'd been allowed a family leave even though the classes he taught at UNC had only begun the week before. While in England, he had video lectures to do online which meant he would be busy in the afternoons.

"I've set up a phone meeting with Kieran for this afternoon. After what he told Corbyn about the dark web, and especially after being photographed, I think we need to look at every angle."

"Photographed?! What happened?"

Megan watched the buildings rush past as she framed her thoughts. She forgot he didn't know about that. "While I was sitting in the window yesterday, I noticed a man in a car on the street taking my picture."

"This is worse than I imagined." He lowered his voice. "Maybe you should consider coming home. I'm sure you can work something out with the publishing company to finish the book there."

Tension filled Megan. "No. We can figure this out. If someone wants my necklace that badly, they may even follow me back to the U.S. Anyway, once we send it to the jeweler, they'll probably stop altogether." She hoped.

"Megan, my pearl..." Her father's brow furrowed, and he held her gaze. Megan's name meant pearl, and he always used that nickname when he was serious. "I...I know you feel like God placed you here for a purpose, and I would never want to keep you from his will. Right now my emotions are clouded, and I've had a long trip. Why don't we both pray about this over the next few days?"

He squeezed her hand, and the pain in his eyes was almost too much to bear. Megan's throat tightened. "Okay. I love you, Daddy."

As much as the events happening because of the necklace worried her, she couldn't imagine leaving. It didn't feel right. She knew that God had led her here for a reason. Trusting him meant that she couldn't cave every time bad things happened. Trusting God also meant if he wanted to direct her differently, she would follow. She would pray and try to stay open-minded.

It was strange watching the armed guard carry out her necklace in a metal case secured to his wrist. If anyone was watching, they were in for quite a show. The guards took their time entering and discussing things inside so that the armored vehicle could sit in front of the house long enough to cause a stir. Megan prayed that the dramatic display accomplished its purpose and was thankful for De Clare's help.

At lunch, peace fell over the home for the first time since the robbery. Wanting to be clear-headed during their discussion with Kieran, her father followed lunch with a nap. Tracey and Richard had errands to run that they had put off for days in order to stay close to Megan. The house was quiet and tension eased from her body. Maybe she should take a nap too.

Before she could settle, she messaged Jean, excited to share the events of the day with him. When her phone vibrated, she checked to see his response.

Corbyn: Kieran wants to do a video chat instead of a phone call. Kate and I can be there if you would like.

Megan blinked and read the text again. Kieran wanted to video chat? The same Kieran that didn't want to see her when she took him food? Her shock quickly turned into a case of nerves as she recalled his pictures on the internet. He was one of the most handsome men she had ever seen.

Moving to the mirror on the wall, Megan wondered if she should fix her hair or change clothes. *Don't be so vain*, she chastised herself. When she dropped to the bed, her phone bounced, reminding her she'd not answered Corbyn.

Megan: Dad and I will be fine. There is no reason for you to continue to be the intermediary.

Corbyn: Okay, but know that we are still here to help in any way we can.

Megan: Thanks. Does he have my email to send me the link?

Corbyn: I just sent it.

Megan sent him a thumbs up and then lay back on the bed. She was too wound up to rest and reached for the book she'd been reading—*Sense and Sensibility*. It was her favorite book, and she'd read it more times than she could count. Where was she?

Ah yes, something about Colonel Brandon's appearance not being unpleasant despite being on the wrong side of thirty-five. Though Edward was generally considered the favorite hero of the book, she'd always preferred Colonel Brandon. Often underappreciated, he was the most constant and helpful male character. His age had benefited him and he'd learned from his previous poor choices and inaction how important it was to exert himself on behalf of others. In the back of her mind, she held up Colonel Brandon as her ideal.

Megan prepped her father as they arranged things for a video chat.

"Kieran might seem...cold, but he has had a hard time since his motorcycle accident. He's now a paraplegic, and according to Corbyn, it's made him become a recluse and changed him from the happy-go-lucky guy he was before."

"If he's going to be difficult to work with, maybe we should look elsewhere for help."

"Corbyn assured me he wants to help and is very good at what he does, though it is surprising that he wants to do a video chat. We should at least hear what he has to say. Maybe our performance earlier with the armored vehicle has already deterred whoever it is, but it would be rude to cancel at the last minute."

Despite her anxiety, she still hoped to establish enough of a relationship with Kieran to allow her an opportunity to tell him there is hope in Jesus. Every time someone mentioned his name, she felt the Holy Spirit's nudge in that direction.

It was funny how, though she was shy, God had given her the desire to speak to people who intimidated her. The Holy Spirit won out time and time again when her natural self said she could never say what was necessary. The amazing thing was that God had shown her each time that he was bigger than her inadequacies. She had spoken to all sorts of people of influence in her hometown and often been able to be part of their salvation story.

The same God that gave her strength on U.S. soil would provide abundantly for all that he called her to in England. *And my God will supply every need of yours according to his riches in glory in Christ Jesus.* She internally recited Philippians 4:19 which she had memorized to help her when she was nervous before speaking to someone.

"Okay. I'm not willing to take chances where you're concerned. Assuming it's over could be risky. If Corbyn believes this man can help us, then we'll start with Kieran." Her father glanced at his watch. "Are you ready? It's time isn't it?"

"It is." Megan clicked around on the computer that she had raised with several books on the dining room table, then sat back, unsure of what to expect from Kieran today. "Dad, will you pray before the meeting?"

"Of course." They bowed their heads. "Father, I don't know what is happening here, but you do. Go before us and make the path clear. Help us to know what questions to ask, and help Kieran to see the things he needs to see to help us. And be with Kieran as he navigates his new situation. Help him to find hope in you, and let us be a light in his life. In Jesus name, amen." He looked up at Megan. "You want to tell him about Jesus, don't you?"

Megan bit her lip to hide a smile.

When Kieran first appeared on the computer screen, she anticipated a disheveled, withered version of him, or maybe a scar. But other than his hair being a little longer than the pictures, he still looked devastatingly handsome. He was frowning, and Megan's heart sank.

"Mr. Taylor, Miss Taylor." Kieran spoke firmly and looked at both of them.

"Please call me Scott, Kieran."

"Certainly, Mr...Scott."

"That's better. So—"

"And you can call me Megan." She smiled, though tension filled her body.

Scott glanced at Megan, then back to the screen. "What are your thoughts on our situation? Megan said you have some experience with something called the dark web and that it may come into play with such valuable jewelry."

Kieran's brow furrowed and he shifted his gaze to Megan, leaving her paralyzed. Those green eyes had flashed through her mind so many times since she'd looked him up, and now those eyes were looking into hers. She expected to see frustration there or anger at what his life had become. It's what she'd visualized when she heard his voice snapping each time she took him food. Instead, she saw worry. That was better and might allow her a chance to speak more freely with him. *God, direct me in this conversation.*

"Megan's correct." Kieran continued to watch her. "When Corbyn told me about the situation, I began searching the dark web for anything related to expensive jewelry. I found a site that deals in priceless jewelry and says it has a unique historical piece coming soon. I'm keeping an eye on that. I also noticed a request for surveillance in London. The day that you were being watched, I went back and checked and that request was removed. It concerns me." He looked at Scott. "I'll keep watching it. How long are you here, Scott?"

"I can take as long as a week."

Kieran nodded. "That's good. She needs someone with her until we see if anything more comes of it now that the necklace is at the jeweler's. How did that go?"

Megan spoke up. "They made a dramatic show, and I received an email with confirmation and a photo showing it in the vault a little while ago. Hopefully, the danger has passed now. I just wish I didn't have to leave my necklace there to feel safe."

"I'm sorry. I understand it has personal meaning to you."

"It does. It was my mother's and my grandmother's before that." Her heart picked up speed. Was he actually concerned? It was not what she had expected.

Kieran shook his head. "It shouldn't be this way. People shouldn't have to worry about things like this. What is wrong with people?"

Megan saw her chance. "Sin."

Kieran's lip quirked up. "Ah, yes. Sin. It is the pride of man and drives him to what he doesn't need, regardless of the peril or pain it leaves in the lives of others."

"How insightful. Do you read the Bible?"

Her father shifted in his seat as he watched the exchange.

"I do. I would not quite say I am a Christian, but I am considering the claims of Christ."

This was good. Kieran was open to the things Megan wanted to share, and she hoped there would be ample opportunity to discuss those things with him.

"But to get back to the subject at hand, I have also sent an inquiry to the person who posted about the antique jewelry. I'd like to see what their response is now that the piece is locked up or if it turns out to be an entirely different piece of jewelry."

"Thank you for going to so much trouble. Surely it will be better now that we made a show of sending it to the vault."

Scott spoke up. "Thank you, Kieran. Though Megan wants to believe it's over, and I certainly do too, I don't want to leave any stone unturned in finding out who is behind this. If there is a chance it may protect her in the future, then I agree that I would like for you to continue monitoring that. Like she said, that necklace means a great deal to her, and she may want to wear it to an event at some point. If this person is left on the loose, she won't ever be safe to do that."

Megan tensed. She hadn't thought of that. Her phone began ringing, and she reached out to silence it but stopped when she saw the name. "It's Reece," she said to her father.

"The history professor from Oxford who was supposed to tell you more about where the necklace might have come from?"

Megan nodded and reached again to silence it.

"Answer it. I'd like to hear what he has to say," came Kieran's voice from the computer. "It could be helpful for me."

Megan quickly reached for the phone and answered it on speaker. "Hello?" It seemed strange that he had failed to call two days earlier, then immediately after the necklace was taken away, he called.

"Megan, hi. Look, I have to apologize for not getting back to you Saturday like I promised. Saturday morning my sister called saying my mum had been taken to hospital. She had a heart attack and they had to do emergency surgery. It's been very touch and go. She's stable now, so I came back home."

"Reece, that's terrible." Guilt twisted within her for thinking the worst. "I'm glad she's stable. I'll be praying for her to recover well. What's her name?

"Thanks. It's Valerie."

"Heavenly Father, I lift up Valerie and pray for complete healing from her heart attack. God, I pray that you would strengthen her heart and help her to lean on you in this. Help Reece to be comforted as he worries, and to have wisdom about how he can help. In Jesus name, amen."

"That was...beautiful. Thank you, Megan. I hope you won't take it personally that I didn't get back to you. The timing just wasn't good. Believe me, though, I was thinking about you. How could I not?"

Megan's face heated and she glanced up to see her father's brow raised.

"Anyway, I do have information for you. It will require you to do some more digging, though, to see if there is any way the family tree lines up with yours. There are several families that used the three chevrons through the years, but only one with the wealth and prestige to have had a piece of jewelry like this. All my research seems to point to the de Clare family."

"De Clare?"

"Yes. Peter told me that was the name of the jeweler you used."

"It is."

"You can ask them if they think there's a connection. The last of the de Clare line died in 1360 with a woman named Elizabeth. By then the line had split quite a bit, but it seems likely that something of this value may have come from her or one of her full siblings. Her father, the wealthy and prominent Gilbert de Clare married Joan of Acre, daughter of Edward I. It is possible that in order to win approval from Edward I, a gift of great value may have been promised to show he would suitably take care of the princess. Joan of Acre and Gilbert de Clare had six children, but only three of them had children. From there the family tree splits in a myriad of different directions. Regardless of whether it is from that branch of the line or another, the de Clare family was very wealthy."

"That's a lot of information." Megan was frantically taking notes in the notebook she used to keep track of everything surrounding her necklace. "Can you send it to me in writing? I'm afraid I may have missed something."

"Absolutely. I'll also send you a picture of the family tree. I wanted to speak to you about it first, and of course, I needed to apologize for taking so long to get back to you."

Megan glanced at the computer and caught Kieran rolling his eyes.

"Yes, I...uh, thank you. This is so helpful." It seemed like more than a coincidence that her necklace was at De Clare's Jewelers.

"Glad to be of use. Are you sure everything is okay? You seem a bit distracted."

"No. Thanks. I'm fine."

"Okay then. Please call if you have any questions. I'll be in town next week. I'd like to take you out again."

"Sure, sounds good. I'll speak with you later then. Bye K—Reece."

"Goodbye, Megan."

She looked up from the phone and found her father with a raised eyebrow. "What?"

He mouthed, "You'll go out with him?"

"What?" She tried to recall the last part of their conversation. "Oh!" Megan threw a hand over her mouth. "I didn't mean to say that. My mind wandered. Surely I can rectify that later. Right now I can't stop thinking about De Clare's. I'd like to go there and see if they know anything about where the necklace came from. Maybe someone else there can tell me. I should look up who the current owner is." She turned back to the computer and there was Kieran. "Oh, I..."

"I already pulled up their website," Kieran said. "Just a moment." The De Clare website popped up on Megan's screen and she recognized it from when she looked them up before having them evaluate the pendant. "It doesn't have the coat of arms anywhere on the site that I've found."

The page changed to the history of the company and Megan quickly skimmed through it.

De Clare's Jewelers was first opened in 1706 by Henry Stafford, a master silversmith; his grandson became a crown jeweler. The original founder of De Clare's had a fascination with exquisite gemstones and jewelry through his own family's collection, some of which date back to the medieval period and the house of de Clare.

Megan's heart raced. Could this be what she was looking for? She skimmed farther down.

The Stafford family branches off from the house of de Clare which was one of the wealthiest families in the thirteenth century. The de Clare family dates back to Richard the First, Duke of Normandy.

De Clare's Jewelers has been passed from son to son and is currently owned by Henry Stafford VII, a former British Crown jeweler.

Megan watched as Kieran scrolled through some of the crown jewels they designed. It was astounding to think they had created jewelry for royalty, but her mind was hung up on the store's owner. "I was hoping the current owner was named Robert." She looked at her dad and recalled how perplexed he'd been when she'd told him about her grandmother's letters.

"Robert?" came Kieran's voice through the computer.

"Yes, I just discovered that my grandmother, who gave the necklace to my mother, spent time in England before she married my grandfather. I found some love letters addressed to her during that time and they were signed by a man named Robert. Since the necklace is of English origin, it's possible the man who wrote her gave her the necklace. Maybe Robert is Henry's dad."

The computer page switched to show black-and-white pictures of the Stafford family and another with two men. Underneath it, the caption stated it was the current owner and his father, William.

"Never mind then. I guess I will be doing some digging later to find out who Robert is," Megan said. Scott reached over and squeezed her hand.

"That would be nice to know, but let's not forget that right now the most urgent issue is to find who is after that necklace." Kieran switched the screen so they could see one another.

"I thought it might all be tied together." She felt deflated and blew out a breath.

"To set your mind at ease, you can speak with the owner and have him confirm if it is from his family. However, it doesn't seem likely that if your necklace came from his family, they would try to steal it from you. They *are* in the fine jewelry business and part of their business is documentation. If your grandmother, sorry to say this, got it in a less than legitimate way, they should have documentation that would prove it belongs to them. No need for them to steal it. If it was a gift from the family, it doesn't make sense that they'd steal it back either. Also, they have too much to lose with their reputation. It's got to be someone else."

Megan nodded. "I was thinking the same thing."

"What's the story with that Reece character?" Kieran's voice took on a harsh tone.

Once again heat rose to her face when recalling her earlier mistake at the end of the conversation. She glanced at her father. Not that he could undo her blunder. "Peter, my friend from the British Museum, put me in touch with him. He's a history professor at Oxford. His specialty is Medieval history."

Scott spoke up. "Kieran, you may be right that he is someone we should look into. Megan, didn't you say he picked you up for dinner Friday night? So he knows where you live. Then he didn't contact you Saturday like he said." Megan opened her mouth to speak, but he continued. "I know, he claims his mother was in the hospital, but it seems strange that he calls now of all times."

"He asked if you were okay, almost like he was fishing for more information from you," Kieran offered.

Megan shrugged and bit her lip. She didn't like thinking the worst of anyone, but she had already been considering him as a possibility when he didn't call as he'd said. How hard would it have been to call and say, "My mum's in the hospital. Let me get back to you."

"Reece is on my list," Megan admitted.

"List?"

She nodded at Kieran and turned to the list in her notebook. "Reece Fairfax is the first name on the list, but I also included Bernard Blake who is the manager at De Clare's I've been communicating with, Steven who also works there, and Peter Nelson. I hate to name Peter. He's been such a good friend and support to me, and he helped my mom when she came here to work on her book. But I did put him down because he knows the pendant is valuable and he does know where I live."

"Corbyn did mention your mum. My condolences for your loss. She was here working on a book before she died?" Kieran asked.

"Yes. Thank you for your concern. It's getting easier for us to bear." Megan glanced at her father whose face had tightened. "She was here off and on, and I helped her work on the book from Chapel Hill when the cancer returned and she could no longer travel. So that's how I know Peter. I had met him before when I came on one of my mom's trips and we hit it off. He's always seemed like a great guy."

"Hmm, so Peter's asked you out?" Kieran questioned.

Megan glanced from the screen to her dad. He knew she had gone to the Benefit for the Arts with him. Her eyes found Kieran's again. "We went to a Benefit for the Arts together. He asked me. I didn't think anything of it, but Kate thinks he is interested in more than friendship. Do you think that affects things where the pendant is concerned?"

"Perhaps. It's hard to say. His last name is Nelson?"

"It is."

"Got it. I'll check him out along with the others."

"Thanks." It made her uneasy to have people checking into the life of someone who was supposed to be her friend, but she wasn't sure if it was more because she believed he was innocent or because she was worried about what Kieran might find. If her friend was involved some-how, she would find it hard to trust her own judgment in the future.

Megan had been on the fence about Reece from the very beginning, and looking into his life didn't bother her. After initially being in awe of his good looks, she found herself less enamored when he seemed caught off guard by her wanting to pray before their meal.

He might be a great guy for someone else, but she always envisioned herself marrying another missionary or a pastor. She wasn't just looking for someone who wouldn't hold her back from following God's call and speaking Jesus into others any chance she could. She wanted someone who would actively partner with her and come alongside her to spur her on in her relationship with God and their mission as Christians to be Jesus' witnesses in "Jerusalem and in all Judea and Samaria, and to the end of the earth," just like Jesus said in Acts 1.

"Is there anything we should be looking into?" Scott questioned.

"Right now, focus on trying to get in touch with De Clare's owner so he can say if the necklace came from his family. I'll look into the people on your list in case Scotland Yard misses anything, and I'll keep an eye on the dark web."

"Thanks." Scott patted Megan's shoulder. "We can go together to De Clare's."

"Okay. It sounds like we have a plan," Megan said.

Kieran cleared his throat. "If two people at De Clare's are on your list, how did you end up having them store your necklace? Is that the best idea?"

"I wanted it away from my daughter. Scotland Yard told Megan that they checked out the facility there and did a background check on all of the employees, and they think it will be safe. They had some behind the scenes things going on there that they weren't at liberty to mention, but they have eyes on it."

"Hmm." Kieran rubbed his chin. "Okay then."

"Dad, will you pray for us before we end the call?"

"I will."

Once they were off the call, Megan was anxious to get started and looked at her watch. "I know you're tired, Dad, but De Clare's doesn't close for an hour and a half, and I would like to run over to see what we can find out. You don't have to go if you're not up to it."

"I think I have a little more in me. Let's go see what we can find out."

Chapter Nine

"Is everything okay?" Mr. Blake hurried around the jewelry counter to greet Megan. "Ahh. And you must be Mr. Taylor!"

"I am. Scott." He shook Mr. Blake's extended hand.

"Then I insist you call me Bernard." He looked between Scott and Megan, then lowered his voice. "Your delivery arrived earlier just as planned. Would you like to join me in the security room where you can see it on the camera? Or I can bring it out to you if you need to see it in person."

"No, thank you. It would be good to speak somewhere private, though," Scott asked.

"Certainly. Right this way."

Scott led them to a small room similar to the one where they had inspected Megan's pendant and offered them both seats.

"How may I help you? Did the guards do something wrong today?"

"No, they did everything they should," Scott assured him. "We have some questions about the de Clare family line."

"Good, good. I'm glad everything was to your satisfaction. Your pendant is in good hands. Now what is it you would like to know about the de Clares? How are they connected to our store, perhaps?"

"Something like that," Scott answered.

Before he could continue, Bernard spoke. "The last de Clare passed away in the thirteen hundreds if I remember correctly. The current owners are distant relations to the family that started De Clare's. That information can be found on our website if you want to know more."

"We've seen that, thank you," Megan jumped in. "We found out that the three-chevron symbol on the back of the pendant is from the de Clare crest. I realize it's a long shot, with the family tree spreading out in so many different directions, but I was wondering if there was any way that I could find out if my necklace at one time belonged to the family that owns De Clare's. It would be nice to figure out how it came to be in our family. Maybe I could speak with the owner, Henry Stafford."

"I can imagine that information would leave you quite curious. The truth is that Mr. Stafford has pulled back quite a bit from the store as he is getting up in age. I am married into his family, and I have never heard of such a necklace. The family has always kept extensive records on their jewelry holdings, though, and I will be happy to check into that for you."

"Would you? Thank you, that would be wonderful."

"Certainly, it will be no bother. I'll also check with Mr. Stafford. I must say that may take a few days. Mr. Stafford sometimes... Well, sometimes he struggles to remember things, so I'll have to get him at just the right moment."

"Thank you, Bernard." Scott reached out to shake his hand. "We appreciate all of your help with this matter. I am not exactly sure how long I will be here. Likely just until the end of the week if things go well. But you can always contact Megan."

"Perfect. Let me show you your necklace in its new home." He pulled out a laptop and logged into the security feed. "And there it is. Safe and sound. I do hope this puts your mind at ease."

"It does. I'm glad that you had a reasonable solution for us. The appraisal came as such a shock, and the necklace is very sentimental, so it's something that we plan to keep."

"I understand and am honored that we can serve you in such a way. Is there anything else I can help you with at the moment?"

"I think that is all for today. I look forward to hearing back from you regarding the de Clare family and the necklace." Scott stood and shook hands with Bernard, followed by Megan.

Bernard escorted them to the front of the store.

"Thank you, Scott. It was a pleasure meeting you. Have a wonderful visit. Hopefully, all will calm down now and you will no longer have to worry about Megan's safety."

As they traveled back to the house, Megan thought through all she had to do—research the de Clare line, do some research for her book, read more of *Mere Christianity* so it would be fresh in her mind as Jean asked questions, and at least skim through some of the chapters in the books he was reading from the Bible.

In addition to her regular quiet time, she was spending extra time in God's word studying for discussions with Jean, and she loved it. She also knew she had a job with deadlines, so she had to figure out how to balance it all.

"We should let Kieran know we didn't find out anything at De Clare's and are waiting to hear back." Scott tapped Megan on the arm and drew her from her thoughts. "There's a chance that may affect what he's working on. You had me worried about Kieran's attitude and that it might make him difficult to work with, but I thought he seemed appropriately concerned. He has an understanding about things I could never help you with, so I really appreciate that."

"You should tell him that. Maybe you should be the one to speak to him."

"We can put him on speakerphone. That way neither of us misses something important."

Megan nodded and thought about their video chat earlier. Somehow she'd expected him to look frazzled and maybe even a bit unkempt compared to the pictures she'd seen online. She'd imagined that he'd become so frustrated with life that he had let himself go. He had not. He was even more handsome in a live video chat than in the online pictures. If she ever saw him in person, she would find it very hard to focus.

Not only were his good looks distracting, but her dad was right about him having a good attitude. Not one time did he seem to resent helping them. Maybe he enjoyed feeling useful.

After arriving at the house, they found that Tracey had dinner ready early so Scott could get a long night's sleep after traveling. It was hard to focus on the conversations at the dinner table with thoughts of the day rolling around her mind. She was also anticipating their call afterward to Kieran.

"Kieran, this is Scott. You're on speakerphone, by the way. Megan is also here. First of all, thank you for helping us. I really appreciate it. It's nice to know there are people here who will help Megan and make sure she's safe, especially with me heading back home at the end of the week."

"It's no trouble, sir. It's the least I could do after receiving such delicious meals." Megan thought it sounded like he was smiling and wished it were a video call.

"She did mention that. Megan is an excellent cook, as was her mother. I miss having my girls around for many reasons, but their cooking is definitely one of them."

Megan saw tears beginning to form in his eyes.

"Enough of that, though. I wanted to touch base with you about our meeting at De Clare's. Henry Stafford wasn't available, so we met with Mr. Blake. He did not have any recollection of the necklace from the family records but said he would check into it. Mr. Blake married into the Stafford family and seems very familiar with their family dealings. He also said he would speak with Henry Stafford, though he made it sound like he has dementia. He said it may take a few days to get anything out of him."

"Thanks for the update, Scott. Megan, I'm sorry you weren't able to find anything more out. I can tell it's important to you."

"Thanks. I haven't had a chance to look at the information Reece sent, and once I do, I will contact my mom's brother and see if any of the names sound familiar. When I checked with him before, he didn't know anything about the necklace, but maybe one of the names would mean something to him."

"Megan, Kieran, I think I've hit a wall. I'm going to head to bed."

"Oh, okay. I guess this is goodnight then, Kieran." Megan looked at her dad and smiled.

"No, no. You two go on. I can find my way to my room. Goodnight, my pearl. I love you, dear." Scott leaned over and kissed Megan on the forehead then left the room.

"Your dad really cares about you."

"He does." It was strange remembering it was just her and her dad now. Their little family of three had been so tight-knit. "So, where do we go from here?"

"It's just a waiting game. I'll keep digging around on the dark web to see if anything pops up. You look into your family history. Also please let me know if Bernard Blake comes back with any information. By the way, I didn't find anything of concern about Bernard or the others on your list. Not that it means they are innocent."

"Okay. I'll keep that in mind." She didn't want the conversation to end before she spoke to him about spiritual things. *God, give me wisdom.* "You said—"

"You and your dad are—Pardon, go ahead," Kieran offered when they both spoke at once.

"You said you were considering the claims of Christ. What did you mean by that?"

"Funny you ask that. I was just going to ask if you are a Christian. You and your dad pray a lot."

Megan grinned to herself. *Thank you, God.* "Yes, we are both serious about our relationship with God. Jesus has given us so much. Do you have things you're confused about when it comes to Christianity, or is there something holding you back from becoming a Christian?"

"You are very optimistic despite your loss. And you ask tough questions."

"I have so much to be optimistic about. I'll see my mom again. I'm not saying it's easy. I miss her dreadfully, and Dad misses her more. But I take joy in God and am at peace knowing things are in his hands. As for the questions...You did say you read the Bible, and you said you are not quite a Christian. That makes me think something is holding you back."

"You're right. I take the decision seriously, and honestly, I'm struggling to let go of the anger I've had towards God for my accident and long before that for taking my father so early. I felt like I had to be the man of the house at age eleven, caring for both my mum and sister. That's part of why I am amazed at your optimism so soon after her death. In twenty-four years, I've not been able to let go."

Megan pondered his statement. "Maybe that's part of the problem.

The anger has become so much a part of you that it seems wrong to let it go. Maybe it's your tie to your father. Was he a Christian?"

"He was. I know what you're about to say, and it makes sense. I should want to be a follower of the God that my dad followed. My mom has told me that so often."

"Satan does twist things in our minds. It makes me think of C. S. Lewis's book, *The Screwtape Letters*. Are you familiar?" It was funny how C.S. Lewis's books kept popping into her mind lately.

"I remember seeing the name of it, but I haven't read it. Should I?"

"I think you should. It's something to ponder as it's a made-up story of what might be happening in the spiritual world when the demons try to lure us away from God. We don't know exactly how those things happen. The Bible doesn't give a lot of information, though it makes it clear the demons are fallen angels. It also talks about angels in battle. Occasionally God even revealed the angels to people. The Bible speaks of specific demonic attacks and also mentions in James One that temptations aren't from God."

"I recall reading the James verses and I think I read an Old Testament story where God said he was fighting for his people, and he opened the eyes of one of his followers so that person could see that the enemy was surrounded by angels. I'll add *The Screwtape Letters* to my reading list. Any other of his books that you'd recommend I read?"

"I started rereading *Mere Christianity* recently after recommending it to another friend. It's really good for people who are considering the claims of Christ. You should read it."

"You recommended it to another friend?"

"Yes, a guy who wants to know more about Christianity." It hit her that Jean never had said what brought him to his crisis of faith. Though she felt close to him and considered him a friend, there was so much she didn't know. He still held things back. Yet she had even told him about her necklace, though not how valuable it was.

"Oh, a guy?" She heard mirth in Kieran's tone. "He must be a good friend for you to be reading along with him."

"I'm not actually reading along. I'm skimming through it since I read it so long ago."

"Is this *friend* on your list?"

"List?"

"Your suspect list for your necklace."

"No, of course not." She blushed thinking about the truth. "I've never met him in person. He doesn't know where I live. Or even my name."

"He doesn't know your name?"

"We started talking on the Pulse app. I began using it as a tool to encourage others and point them to Jesus after my mom died. It hit me that others were going through hard times too, and I could help them that way."

Crickets.

"Kieran? Is that weird to you?"

"No. It's not. Can I call you back tomorrow? I've got something I need to take care of."

"Yes, of course. Goodnight, Kieran."

"Goodnight, Megan."

Megan hung up and stared at the phone. His voice sounded off at the end of their conversation. Did the fact that she called someone a friend whom she didn't know in person weird him out? Did he think she was too pushy with her faith?

She started to pick her phone back up and message Jean about it but didn't feel right. Instead, she decided to work on her book. She could message Jean later.

Chapter Ten

Daily Encouragement: Sorry for not messaging last night. The day got away from me. The necklace is safe and my dad is here.

Two hours passed after Megan sent her message to Jean and she worried something was wrong. He was usually quick to respond.

Her father had been up since five and was ready to go sightseeing. He texted Kieran to confirm that he had found nothing new on the dark web. Even though Kieran had not seen anything suspicious, Scott insisted they have a guard follow them. Megan gathered necessities into her purse and met her father on the ground level when her phone buzzed.

P24,601: I'd like to meet in person.

"Your online friend?" Scott raised a brow after reading the screen.

"It is."

"I know this is a different day and age, but I would like to be there.

See if you can work it out to happen while I am here. Today or tomorrow would be great. I'd like to save the end of the week for tying up loose ends with this necklace situation."

Daily Encouragement: Do you have time today or tomorrow?

P24,601: I'll see and let you know.

The rest of the week flew by uneventfully. Kieran received no response to his dark web antique jewelry inquiry, and he'd not seen anything pop up that appeared to have ties to Megan or the necklace. The guard who followed them throughout the week saw nothing concerning either. With the positive news from all sides, Megan felt more at ease.

Things with Jean had been quiet as well. He said he was unavailable this week to meet and didn't message or respond as often as usual. Scott was not happy that their meeting didn't happen while he was in England to accompany her and requested that if she met with him, she have a man with her. Both Peter and Corbyn volunteered. She was concerned her father's presence kept Jean away, and that didn't sit right with her. With the way things had been going, she wasn't sure who she could trust anymore.

When Scotland Yard confirmed nothing concerning was happening with Megan's case, Scott decided Megan was out of imminent danger and returned to North Carolina at the end of the week as he'd originally planned.

The surprise of the week came from Kieran.

Megan called Kate as soon as she finished texting Kieran. "You'll never believe what happened."

"They caught the person after your necklace?"

"No. That would be great though. Kieran is coming to London and asked me to meet him at his London flat tomorrow."

"You're kidding. I don't think he's been back to London since he got out of the hospital. Did something happen with your necklace?"

"I don't know. That seems likely. It caught me off guard so I didn't think to ask. I agreed to meet with him."

"It's a huge step for him. I don't think he's wanted to be out in public since he's been in a wheelchair."

"I have to admit I feel intimidated about meeting with him in person. He is so smart." And she wanted to add *really handsome*. "Our conversation went well when my dad was here, and he seems to have moved past snapping at everyone, so that doesn't worry me anymore. Also he is interested in Jesus, so I'm hoping we have a chance to talk about that. I could use some prayers for our meeting."

"Consider it done. Let's pray right now."

"Thanks."

"Father, I lift up Megan and pray that you would give her peace about this meeting. Give her words to say to point Kieren to you and help him understand what it means to be a Christian. Help him to accept his new normal and move forward in his life. In Jesus name, amen."

"Thank you. How has your day been?"

"Very productive. Corbyn took the girls to his parents' house after church, and I've had the afternoon to clean and even time to relax and read."

"Nice. It's great that you have his parents nearby."

"It is. I'm sad that my parents miss out on that, but video chat does help. And this fall we'll go there and stay in Memphis for a month. Corbyn will work in the Memphis satellite location and fly up to check on the New York offices. We're all looking forward to the visit."

"That was so sweet of him to open that location so you guys can go back regularly and spend time with family."

"He's a pretty amazing husband," Kate said with a dreamy sigh.

"You've been through so much. You deserve a godly man like him." Megan recalled the things Kate told her that she'd discovered after her first husband was killed. He'd been cheating on her since before they were married and he was psychologically abusive. Megan couldn't imagine how Kate felt. The way Kate not only recovered from such trauma but poured into the lives of others was a testimony to God's work in her life.

"Thank you. I never imagined I would get another chance like this after my first husband. Corbyn was a wonderful surprise."

When Megan hung up, the image of little Madeline, Margaret, and their family came to her, and she smiled, wondering if God would ever surprise her with a family of her own. Lately, a longing had begun developing in her heart to have her own family—just a seedling of an idea.

As Megan's taxi approached Kieran's building, it looked like she had gone to another city rather than just cross the Thames. The street was lined with what looked like modern towering office buildings, though she knew some of them had been transformed into apartment buildings. Here and there a little historical building was tucked in, reminding her that she was still in London.

A case of nerves hit once again as she entered the elevator with several people. *I can do all things through him who strengthens me.* She silently recited Philippians 4:13 while the elevator rose to the top and periodically stopped for the others to get off. When it was her turn she found that Kieran's flat was one of only two on the penthouse floor. From the hallway, she caught a glimpse of the Thames and Westminster Cathedral in the distance.

Turning towards Kieran's door, she discovered it was already opened. Kieran bit his lip as he sat fidgeting with his shirtsleeve while watching her from his wheelchair. He looked...nervous? Once again she was hit by his good looks and those green eyes that were even brighter in person. Something was different about him.

"The doorman rang me." Kieran smiled at her. The first real smile she had seen him make. That was the difference, and it made his whole countenance light up.

"Kieran, it's so good to meet you in person. I can't thank you enough for your willingness to help."

"I haven't done much of anything yet. Come in." Kieran waved her forward, and she noticed Toby holding the door open.

"Toby, how have you been?"

"Good, thank you. No basket of food today?" His eyes twinkled.

"Not today." Megan glanced at Kieran who just shook his head.

"I apologized for that and don't appreciate you reminding her about my poor behavior."

"As long as you realize it was poor behavior," Toby chastised him and closed the door before disappearing farther into the apartment.

Kieran led the way to a living room with a huge wall of windows overlooking the Thames and numerous windows on two other walls. There was a dining room enclosed by glass that also overlooked the Thames. It had a wall on the opposite side with windows looking out into the city.

"This view...It's stunning."

"That's what drew me to this place. I like the modern look too."

Megan scanned the room and noticed it was filled with mostly sleek contemporary furniture. There were a few antique tables, but they meshed well with the rest of the room. Rather than appearing jarring, they added character and warmth.

"Why don't you have a seat?" He pointed to the seating area in the middle of the room. "Can I get you anything to drink?"

"No, thanks." Megan found a spot on one of the sofas just as her phone buzzed. She ignored it. "So what did you want to talk about?"

Kieran rolled his chair close to hers and reached for a Bible from a nearby table. "I was hoping you would talk to me about becoming a Christian."

Megan's heart raced. This is what she'd been praying about, but for some reason, she didn't expect this response from him so soon. "Of course. You said you've been reading the Bible?" *God, help me to clearly speak your words to him.*

"I have been reading the Bible, but I'm still confused about exactly what I need to do to become a Christian."

Megan's phone buzzed again.

"You should check that."

"Surely it can wait." She didn't want such an important moment in Kieran's life to be interrupted. *God, please intercede here.*

"They've messaged twice. You should check it."

"Okay." She quickly looked down and saw it was Jean. Before she shut it off again, the beginning of the message caught her eye. "I have been reading the Bible..." She opened it fully and found that was the beginning of the second text. The first said, "I was hoping you would talk to me about becoming a Christian." When she scrolled to the second, she found the full message said, "I have been reading the Bible, but I'm still confused about exactly what I need to do to become a Christian."

A chill ran down her spine. "How?" Megan looked up at Kieran, then glanced around, expecting someone to jump out from a nearby room. Heat rose to her face and she fought not to say something hateful. "Is this a joke?" She shifted to the edge of her seat preparing to leave.

"Wait. Of course not. It's...I'm prisoner 24,601. I wasn't sure how best to tell you. Please don't leave." Kieran's brow furrowed, and he frowned.

"Jean?" Megan whispered and tried to wrap her mind around what Kieran had just said.

Kieran's face brightened. "You call me Jean?"

"It's easier than saying P24,601 every time I talk about you. Kate started it."

"Kate knows about me? Or about Jean?"

Megan relaxed, then nodded. "She's my best friend here. I was excited about helping him...helping you get to know Jesus Christ." She froze midway into sliding back into her chair. "Was all that real?"

"Yes. So real that I was scared to share it with anyone in person. I wasn't ready to admit I had those questions to anyone who knew me and might get upset if I didn't like what I learned about God."

"Do you?"

"Do I what?"

"Like what you learned?"

"I didn't at first, but the more I read, the more I know that it is true. Once I began to accept that, I realized how perfect he is and how perfect the salvation he offers is. But I'm not clear about what needs to be done. I was baptized as an infant and lived like the devil for years, so it's clear that isn't what makes a Christian."

"That's true. Baptism is a symbol of a decision you have made. Just like wearing a wedding band doesn't make you married, but it shows others you are. You've read Romans, right?" He nodded.

It didn't seem possible that he was the same man she'd been messaging for months. It made her feel simultaneously more comfortable and more anxious. *God, give me words and strength to say what needs to be said. Calm my heart and mind.* She could think about her feelings later. "If you turn to Romans 10 and read verses nine and ten, you will see how simple it is to become a Christian."

"'Because, if you confess with your mouth that Jesus is Lord and believe in your heart that God raised him from the dead, you will be saved. For with the heart one believes and is justified, and with the mouth one confesses and is saved'." Kieran paused after reading. "So if I believe, I just have to say it out loud?"

"Yes, but bearing in mind that God knows if your belief is real or something you are just saying. It can't be only intellectual assent that God is in existence. James 2:20 says, 'You believe that God is one; you do well. Even the demons believe—and shudder!' Belief, as referred to in the Romans verse, means you believe that you are a sinner and that Jesus is the only one who can pay the price for your sin so that God can forgive you. It involves repentance—confessing and turning from your sin."

"I do believe all of those things. I battled with trusting him, but I've been praying what that father in Mark nine said to Jesus, 'I believe, help my unbelief,' and I have repented and asked him to forgive me for my sins. I fully believe that Jesus is Lord and has saved me from my sins. I can't do it myself, and I don't want to live without him anymore."

"Then you are a Christian. You believe everything necessary for salvation and you have spoken it. You can pray those things back to him right now."

He tilted his head and knit his brow. "That's all I need to do? It seems too simple."

Megan nodded. "Jesus did the hard part, and you believe. The prayer is just you talking to God and confirming what you already believe. Then you'll want to be baptized and tell people the good news. You can continue to do what you've been doing—praying and reading your Bible to grow your relationship with God." *Thank you, God, for helping Kieran find you.*

Kieran grinned and his face relaxed. "Okay then." His prayer was short as he repeated what he had already told her.

When his voice choked up halfway through the prayer, her heart went out to him. She'd never imagined Kieran, the harsh, angry man she'd taken food to two and a half weeks earlier, had such a sensitive, gentle side.

After he was done, she lifted her eyes and looked into his. Who was this man? Kieran? Jean? Was he still her friend? Her gaze drifted to the wall of windows and the buildings on the other side. She wanted to say something but didn't know where to start.

"Would you like to see what I've been searching on the Dark Web?"

Still unable to voice the feelings bubbling up inside, Megan turned back and nodded. "I have been curious."

Kieran rolled his wheelchair forward to grab his laptop from the coffee table and then turned in the opposite direction. "Come join me at the dining room table."

One space at the table had no chair and Kieran rolled to it. Though the angle of the wheelchair made it awkward, he pulled out the chair next to him effortlessly. "For you."

Before Megan was fully seated, Kieran began pounding away at the keyboard. As she watched him, she thought through all that happened since she entered the apartment. "Did Toby text me the messages earlier from Jean?"

The corner of Kieran's mouth curled up but his typing continued. "No." He finally looked at her, then turned the computer so she could see better. "It's a program I created to do timed messages. I triggered it when you got here."

To Megan, the program code looked like a foreign language. "That's impressive."

He shrugged. "Thanks. It wasn't that difficult. If you'd like, I can show you how to do it yourself sometime."

"Maybe. But I don't see myself needing that capability."

They both chuckled, and some of the tension Megan felt melted away.

Kieran's words broke into their laughter. "I apologize for catching you off guard. When I first thought Daily Encouragement was you, I wasn't sure how I felt about it. I had worked so hard to keep that part of my life separate, so I could decide what to do about God without feeling pressure. When I saw you that day..."

"When you saw me? What are you talking about?"

"The second time you brought food...I saw you earlier that day. You were outside with Kate and her daughters."

Something welled up inside Megan. "I remember. I saw you at the window. At least I thought it was you. You weren't as grumpy when I left the food that day as you had been the first time. But you were still quite curt."

"I'm trying to change. I just now became a Christian. Give me some time." He drew the computer back and started typing again.

Megan thought she saw a smile reflected on the screen. "I can give you time." But what she really wanted was an explanation. "How did you figure out I am Daily Encouragement?"

"I first suspected it that day when I saw you through the window. On Pulse, you had said you were going to the beach, and I knew Daily Encouragement had been to a coast in England the week before. The eastern coast is easy to access from London, though it could have been Brighton. Then you left that note that had the encouraging verse with my meal. When I saw it, I felt it had to be you. When I found out about the robbery from both Daily Encouragement and Corbyn, I knew it was you. I wanted to say something sooner, but I didn't want to talk until it was just the two of us."

"My dad will be relieved. He was worried Jean was waiting until he was gone for some nefarious reason."

"I analyzed my options from so many angles, but I'm not good at factoring in human nature. I should apologize to him."

"That's a good idea. It might be better if you explain it to him."

Kieran nodded and frowned. "I also was embarrassed."

"What do you mean?"

"I've not wanted anyone to see me in a wheelchair. It took a while to have the courage to face you." He looked at her with shame. "I know it's vain. This past week, it hit me that I can't keep running away from life. But you've shown me who God is and how to know him better. It's changed everything for me. Thank you." Megan felt a tear fall to her cheek, and his brow furrowed. "What's wrong?" He reached over and wiped the tear away.

"God continually amazes me. The way he brought us together virtually and in real life...“

Kieran held her gaze. "I agree. I still can't wrap my head around it."

The significance of how God orchestrated it all hit her full force. What else was God going to do through their connection? As she looked back into Kieran's eyes, she wondered if he felt it too.

"I...What were you going to show me?" Megan basked in contentment and joy.

Kieran swallowed and his Adam's apple bobbed. "The dark web." His hands moved across the keyboard before he drew his eyes away.

Words like VPN, Tor browser, and Torch search engine were tossed about as Kieran worked his way through dark web searches that looked remarkably similar to standard internet searches.

"Here it is—the website where I saw the advertisement for the soon-to-come historic jewelry. There hasn't been any update of it since your necklace was put in storage." Kieran pointed to the screen. "I'm going to check something." He typed some more. "I'm looking to see if there are any advertisements for surveillance in London in the chat room where I found it before."

The site had discussions on so many unsavory topics Megan had to look away.

"Bingo. The same person is looking for surveillance on someone in London. See. Here are my screenshots from before. Hopefully, this isn't related to you and the timing before was a coincidence. But I don't think you should take any chances. I would suggest getting the security guys back. If that's not doable, at least have people with you and make sure someone is aware of your whereabouts at all times. Also, have someone you trust with access to your location tracking through your mobile. I can help you come up with other ideas too."

All the joy from earlier disappeared. Megan pushed back her chair and walked to the window. "I need a minute."

She rubbed her temple as she watched the cars speed past below. *God, show me what to do.*

Chapter Eleven

A minute turned into several as Megan contemplated this new development.

"It may be nothing. Why don't you come sit down, and I'll see if I can find out more," Kieren offered.

"Okay." Megan turned back with a sigh and hoped he was right. But she needed to know if he wasn't. "What are you going to do?" she asked as she sat back down next to him.

"Apply for a job doing surveillance."

"What do you mean? You…You can't do that." An image of Kieran following her in his wheelchair popped into her mind, and she realized it wasn't the wheelchair that made her think he couldn't apply for such a job, but she didn't want to impose on his life.

"We'll see." He grinned a sideways grin that made her lose focus.

Megan watched as he typed a message asking for more details about the job. "What will you do if they hire you?"

"If it really is you they want followed, I'll hire someone to do the job for me. If it's not, I'll make up an excuse and bow out."

"You'd hire someone to follow me? What if I don't want to be followed?"

"If someone is going to follow you, would you rather it be someone who wants to harm you or someone who is looking out for your best interest?"

"If you put it that way, I suppose I don't have a choice." It was logical. "How much will that cost? You'll need to talk to my dad about how much he will spend. Surely that would get expensive."

"I imagine so, but the person who hires me will be paying me."

"True." Why didn't she think of that? When his eyes caught hers, she realized why she'd not been thinking clearly. Those emerald green eyes could weaken the resolve of Pharaoh when Moses said "Let my people go." She broke the trance when a change on the screen caught her attention. "What are they saying?"

Kieran angled the screen. "Seven a.m. until eight p.m. most days and until ten or eleven p.m. weekends. A three-mile radius centered around the Belgravia area with occasional trips out of town to places like Dover. I'm not liking the sound of this." He typed: Guy or girl? Length of time? Any physical or verbal interactions? Terms?

Another window popped up on Kieran's screen and he quickly typed in code that made no sense to Megan. That window began producing its own code.

The answers to Kieran's questions popped up on the first window: Woman. Minimum two weeks, possibly more. No physical or verbal. Will carry mobile with GPS and take pictures. £10,000 per week. Mobile provided. Extra for trips outside of London and daily travel to follow in tube, taxi or other forms of transportation.

After rubbing a hand down his face and checking the second window, Kieran typed: I'm in.

Seconds turned into minutes before an answer came: Job is filled. Check back in two days. I may need an extra.

Megan stared at the words as Kieran's fist hit the table. She jumped.

"I thought I was in or that I could track him at least, but he cut out too fast for my program to lock onto his location. We're getting a guard for you." Kieran grabbed his phone and started texting.

"What? Wait…Why am I getting a guard?"

"Someone was hired to follow you, and we don't know why. I want to know who they are reporting to and what their plans are."

"I need to check with my dad."

"He would want this. I'm texting the company that was following you before."

"But my dad needs to approve the funds. Maybe it's not for me."

"Not taking chances. I'll message your dad. We'll make it happen. You will be safe."

"I don't know. This is all so much. I can't believe this is happening again. I thought for sure it was over after we had the armored car come."

"Unfortunately it's not over, and I want to know why." He dialed a number on his phone. "Toby, we need you to order dinner. Thanks."

"'We need him to order dinner? I can eat at home."

"Megan, you can't leave until I have someone with eyes on you. I'm sorry." He dialed another number. "Scott. It's Kieran." He switched the phone to the speaker.

"Is everything okay?" "Unfortunately it's not, sir. I have Megan here and you're on speaker."

"Megan? You're okay?"

"So far." She didn't know where to start.

"She's here with me searching the dark web, and we found a request for surveillance from the same user I was watching before her break-in. I told the user I was interested in the job and asked some questions. They all point to her." Kieran listed all they found out and told Scott about his plan to hire guards. "This time I want the guards to be invisible so they can find out who is trailing her. I'm hoping if we find them we can get a lead back to the person who is after her."

"That all sounds like a good plan. Thank you, Kieran. I want to—" Kieran switched the phone off speaker and rolled his chair into the living room. Megan heard him talking, but it was obvious he didn't want to be heard.

Once again she felt helpless. *God, give me strength and wisdom in this. I don't know what is going on, but you do.*

Periodically, Kieran looked over at Megan through the glass and the serious look on his face left her both worried and flattered that he was so concerned. Toby entered the living room, and Kieran waved him towards Megan.

"I've got local menus if you want to see what you're in the mood for." Toby laid a pile of printed menus on the dining table.

"Are there any sushi menus in there?" At the moment, food was the last thing on her mind, but eventually, she would be hungry.

"This one's Kieran's favorite for sushi." He pulled one of the menus out.

"It's not your favorite?"

"I don't eat sushi. But Kieran says theirs is good. He's starred his favorites," Toby said as he flipped open the menu and pointed to some marked ones.

"Thanks. How long have you worked for Kieran? What's he like to work for?"

Toby chuckled. "I've only been his physical therapist since the accident, but we've been best friends since we were kids." The smile left Toby's face. "This accident has changed him, and it's been hard to watch. He's always been outgoing and happy.

Being a grumpy recluse is so far from who he was. Did he tell you his dad died when he was eleven?"

Megan nodded.

"After that, he had a hard time and was depressed for a few weeks, but then he seemed to snap back because he knew his mom and sister needed him. He'd become the man of the family. I sometimes wonder if he bottled his dad's death up too quickly and now, years later, this pushed him over the edge."

"I understand how hard it is to lose a close parent. My mom died last year." She could only imagine how hard it would be at such a young age and feeling like he had to take care of the women in his life. As she thought about Kieran's loss, she remembered how she felt when she learned Jean had lost a parent. It was almost too much trying to merge what she knew about Jean with Kieran. "Did he mention our other connection?"

"That he's Jean Valjean and you're the Bible girl?" Toby chuckled. "When he told me he was reading the Bible, it took me weeks to get out of him that he was messaging some woman who was teaching him about the Bible. When you left him the Bible verse after delivering food last time, he told me he thought it was you."

"Maybe you should be Kieran's counseling therapist instead of his physical therapist."

"Sometimes it feels that way." Toby smirked and looked up as Kieran was approaching.

"You two look chummy?" Kieran's voice had an edge to it as he looked between Toby and Megan. "Did you decide what you wanted?"

"I'm looking at the sushi menu." Megan scanned down it, looking for anything that jumped out at her. "The ones you've starred look great. Why don't you tell me your two favorites and I'll get them."

"Or we could share several, and that way you can try more."

"That works for me. Toby, what will you get, since you don't like sushi?"

"No worries. I'll eat their hibachi steak. It's just sushi I don't like."

Megan noticed Kieran gesturing for Toby to leave just before he said, "You can go order that."

"Thank you, Toby," Megan called out then tapped Kieran on the shoulder and mouthed *thank you*.

"Thank you, Toby," Kieran said. The smile trying to break through on his face gave Megan hope that things were changing for him. Or better yet, God was changing him. "You and I need to talk. The security company is sending over two guys who will take shifts guarding you and watching for the person following you. Once we figure that out, they'll be monitoring that person and we'll try to figure out who he is."

The reality of what he said clicked. "So now three people are going to be following me?"

"Technically only two at a time. Well, maybe three if I watch from a distance."

"You might watch too!" Megan's brows shot up and she imagined a man in a wheelchair and two others following her around. How did her life become so complicated? "Maybe I should just stay home."

"That would be the safest."

"I'm joking. I couldn't live like that."

"It's worked for me." Kieran's mouth quirked, then he shook his head. "Actually, no, it hasn't. I want to start living my life again and accept the life I have now." He glanced in the direction Toby had gone. "Toby will be happy to hear that. I think he's starting to lose his mind living in my seaside cottage. I think I heard him talking to his socks the other day." He chuckled to himself.

"I'm glad you're willing to take a chance and engage in life again. I'll be praying about that for you. That's the kind of thing you should talk to God about too."

"Oh, I have been. I've been telling God I can't do it, and he's been making me feel bad by pointing me to verses like the one that says, 'I can do all things through him who strengthens me.' It's in Philippians somewhere."

"Philippians 4:13." Megan grinned back at him, thrilled he was learning to apply scripture to his life.

"Right, I remember now. Usually, numbers stick with me. I've read so much so fast that it's getting jumbled up." He shook his head. "Enough about me. We need to focus on your situation."

Kieran pulled a notebook out of the side pocket of his chair, and Megan thought of her own obsession with writing things down on physical paper. For a computer programmer, his low-tech notebook surprised her.

"What about your list of suspects?" Opening his notebook, he flipped to a list that matched hers. His list had each name numbered with corresponding paragraphs and notes below. "Anything new with the men on your list? Has Reece been back in town to take you out on that date?"

"It's not a date." From her perspective.

"Really? From what I heard, he wanted a date. When are you going out?"

"Friday night." Something in Kieran's look made her worry. Should she have said no to Reece? "I just agreed to get him off the phone. But I'm also hoping it will help me figure out if he's had anything to do with the break-in and person watching me."

"At least there will be a guard watching you. We may even need to have you wired so the guard and I can listen, in case things go wrong."

"Is that necessary? Maybe I can come up with a signal so the guard will know there's a problem."

"Too risky. This is for your safety, Megan. Your dad told me to do whatever is necessary. Please don't make it more difficult for us to protect you."

Megan bit the inside of her cheek. This was all so far beyond her comfort zone. *God, guide me.* Her eyes once again drifted to the windows and she looked down the thirty floors to the cars zipping past on the road. Her life felt like it was moving past just as fast, leaving her out of control. Yet something inside told her to trust Kieran and she knew it was God nudging her. "Okay, let's do that." Once she agreed, peace filled her.

"So now that we've got a plan with Reece, what about Peter?"

"My dad and I went to the museum, and I introduced them. When I fished for information, he didn't respond in a way that led my dad or me to believe he had anything to do with the burglary. He also checked on me by text the other day, but that's it."

"Is that normal? Just a text?"

"We used to talk more, but I think at the Benefit for the Arts he realized I'm only interested in him as a friend. Since then, he hasn't contacted me as much as before."

Kieran nodded and tapped the paper with his pen before writing something down. "And the two employees at De Clare's?"

"Dad went into the store before he left and spoke with both men, and Mr. Blake opened the vault so he could view the pendant in person. Dad said he didn't notice anything unusual about the way either man acted. Though, I'm not sure he would know if they were lying. Truthfully, nor would I. Neither of us knows them well enough to tell the difference."

"I agree. The police have your suspect list, and if things progress, we can suggest they do lie detection tests, but those aren't always accurate. I've also done some research into each of the men and have not found anything suspicious. None of them has a criminal record. They all look like upstanding men on paper."

He again tapped on the notebook before laying the pen down. "For now we'll stick with the plan to have you protected when you're out and see if that gives us any leads. If something doesn't rise to the surface, we can also work on getting the list of attendees at the Benefit for the Arts. Everything started soon after that. Whoever wants that necklace knows its value and may have been there."

"Thank you. I apologize for pulling you into this. What if this person on the dark web is after someone else entirely? We may be going through all this for nothing."

"That could be, but it's not a chance your father or I am willing to take. I've been watching it for days, and since your break-in, this is the first request specifically for London. If after a week there is no sign of someone following you, we can reevaluate things. Will that work for you?" His phone buzzed but he maintained eye contact with her.

It seemed pointless to argue knowing that her father wouldn't agree to anything less, so she nodded.

Kieran held up his phone. "Looks like our food is here. Let's eat before your guards come. A few minutes to clear our heads will do us some good."

"I couldn't agree more."

"You never mentioned what your uncle said about the necklace."

"He had no idea where it came from. He was like me and always assumed it was costume jewelry. He also didn't know that my grandmother had lived in London. When I mentioned the de Clares and some of the various last names tied to that family, he said he didn't know of any ties, family or otherwise to any of those names. That's a dead end for me. I've spent hours searching the internet with the de Clare family tree, and it branches out in so many directions. I've only searched through a small fraction and already come up with thirty-six last names. It's confusing too, because many of the titled families intermarried with one another so their family trees cross back and forth. They also use the same first names over and over. In the case of dukes, they don't even have a last name. That keeps throwing me off because there are quite a few of them in the different branches."

Keiran laid a hand over hers, and tingles shot off where they touched. "I'm sorry that you have to go through so much. Do you think your grandmother's love letters might have information?"

"Maybe, but I haven't read past the first two because I was so caught up in tracing the family tree. Also, I was trying to keep up Bible reading with a *certain* other person." She smiled and looked at Kieran pointedly.

He raised his brow and grinned just as Toby entered with their food.

"Am I interrupting something?" He looked between them, then down at their hands.

Megan pulled her hand back and her heart raced. "No, come join us." It came out shaky and uncertain.

Toby chuckled and side-eyed Kieran as he spread the food out on the table. "Care to update me on the necklace situation?"

Megan looked to Kieran, and he nodded. "Toby's a good guy. I've told him some of what's going on. If it's okay with you, I'd like to keep him abreast of things. Especially since he may need to help me."

Toby did seem like a good guy, and it was obvious that Kieran would need someone to help him on occasion.

"Okay. Sure."

The next thirty minutes were spent explaining things to Toby and answering questions, then preparing a plan for the guards before they arrived. Megan hoped by the end of the week she could get rid of them. It was going to be a long week.

Chapter Twelve

P **24,601:** Psalm 118:5-6 "Out of my distress I called on the LORD; the LORD answered me and set me free. The LORD is on my side; I will not fear. What can man do to me?" I know you are anxious today about going out. God has got you.

Megan's heart soared when she saw the message the following morning. She thought after Kieran revealed he was Jean he would stop messaging her through the Pulse app.

Daily Encouragement: Thank you. I'm surprised you are still using the app.

P24,601: It's my turn to send you biblical encouragement.

Daily Encouragement: A Christian for only one day and you are already ministering to others in Jesus' name.

He continued to message on the app, updating her on what he read in the Bible that morning and his thoughts on it. She'd never known someone to jump into studying the Bible so enthusiastically that they read nearly the whole thing in only a couple of months. Not only was he reading it, he was understanding it. She imagined he must have something close to a photographic memory and she wouldn't be surprised if he scored in the genius range on IQ tests.

Her phone rang and she smiled when she saw it was Kieran. "Good morning. Did you get tired of texting?"

He chuckled in the background. "I didn't want to talk business through the app for various reasons. The security company your guards are from is setting up an office in the home next to yours. I contacted the estate agent and leased it from the owners. This way they can keep an eye on things in case someone comes after you at home.

"If you see any of them coming and going, you can have short, friendly conversations with them. I know you southerners from the U.S. like to do that, so do what comes naturally. But don't talk to them about anything related to your case or their line of work while outside. You'll still need to call them to talk about those things. Your actual guards won't be going there so they can avoid being associated with you by whoever might be watching. Any questions?"

"You don't think that's overkill?"

"That's what we're trying to avoid."

"What?"

"Sorry. Bad joke, but your necklace is very valuable, and I don't think someone would go to the trouble of the break-in and having you followed if they weren't capable of much worse than jewelry theft."

Megan's insides dropped—the reality of her situation worsened by the day.

"Megan. I doubt God brought us together to let you get hurt. Regardless, I know that you belong to him and this world is not your home. Don't let the forces of this world cause you to lose hope or trust in God. Nothing will happen outside of what he allows, and I know you enough to understand that you don't want to be outside of his will."

She tried to control her breathing. "You're right. It's just taking my heart a minute to catch up with my mind." How was he speaking to her like someone who had been studying the scriptures for years?

"God, help Megan lay this burden at your feet. Help her...help us see and understand all that we need to so we can keep her safe. In Jesus name, amen. Did I do that right?"

"As if you've been doing it for years." Joy and peace welled up inside Megan, and she knew they were gifted to her by God. They weren't joy and peace that come from things turning to good or a guaranteed positive outcome. They were from trusting that her future was secure regardless of the present. "Thank you for standing in the gap for me when I was blinded by my circumstances."

"God is giving me the words to encourage you, and I will continue until we get through this. You stood in the gap for me as both Jean and Kieran when you didn't know me and what you saw of Kieran wasn't worthy of your effort. Because of *you*, I have a hope and a future. Thank you. Now, despite having full faith in God, I believe he has given us abilities and resources to protect you. You have me and the security company on speed dial?"

"I do." Her "shopping" trip was designed to draw out the person following her, and she wanted it to be successful.

"Hmm. And do you have the voice recording app pulled up and ready in case you need it?"

"Yes."

"Good. Don't go anywhere without Kate. Not to the loo or a separate part of a store. Even though you have a guard, there are some places he won't be. He'll likely stay outside at some of the smaller shops."

"I promise I'll be careful." Little girl giggles filled the entrance of the home. "Kate's here. I should go."

"I'll be praying and watching your progress."

"Thank you. I'll talk with you later, Kieran."

"There you are," Kate called out as she joined Megan in the living room. "I left the girls in the kitchen with Corbyn's mom. Are you ready?"

Megan nodded. "I think so. I'm certainly ready to get this over with. Do you know where we're going? It's been a while since I've been to Marylebone, so I don't remember many of the shops there."

"I have a plan for the day. I talked it over with Kieran, and we came up with a map of sorts. It lists the shops and a place for lunch." She pulled up a picture of a map on her phone and shared it with Megan.

Kate and Megan ducked into a home fragrance store with a dark-haired man close behind. He had been trailing behind them as they window shopped, and Megan suspected he was following them. She and Kate greeted the shop clerk and moved to a display that allowed them to watch the entrance.

Several minutes later, the man entered while talking on his phone. He glanced at Kate and Megan, hung up, then headed to the clerk and pointed to something displayed on a shelf. He didn't look like someone who had evil intentions. He looked like he was in his thirties, clean-cut, and dressed like he came from an office. In most circumstances, he would blend right in. If he was following her, that was the intention.

The man glanced their way again, and Megan picked up an item from the display. She analyzed it as if it were part of a test.

Kate joined in and nodded. "Yes, I quite like that. Maybe it would work at the beach house."

Megan put it down and reached for another item when she noticed the man turning to leave with a bag in his hand. Once the door closed behind him, she breathed a sigh of relief and the tension in her shoulders eased. She looked at Kate who raised an eyebrow. After taking their time browsing, they purchased a scented soy candle, left the store, and set off for the restaurant.

The few yards from the store to the restaurant felt like miles as Megan tried to nonchalantly keep an eye out for the man they'd seen earlier. She didn't see him and wasn't sure if she was glad or bothered by it.

The restaurant had quirky yet elegant decor, and something savory wafting through the air reminded Megan that it was past her normal lunch time. Once seated, she scanned the menu and was pleased with the selection of seafood dishes. The miso glazed black cod caught her eye right away. It wasn't until Kate cleared her throat twice that she looked up, worried about her friend. "Are you okay?" She glanced around looking for a waiter to bring water.

Kate patted her chest. "Yes. I'm okay, thanks." She slid over a few inches on her bench and raised a brow, then mouthed something.

Megan tried to decipher Kate's words, but she had never been good at reading lips. Maybe she wasn't a Nancy Drew in the making. She furrowed her brow, and Kate mouthed something again. Still not understanding, she guessed maybe it had to do with the man they'd seen following them. "He's here?" Megan mouthed as she glanced side to side without moving her head.

Kate mouthed, "Yes."

At least Megan recognized that word. Kate reached for her rolled up silverware and slid it to Megan while using her pointer finger to point to Megan.

"Me?" Megan mouthed.

Kate's finger twitched again on the top of the silverware roll. It pointed straight at Megan.

"Behind me?"

Kate smiled and nodded. "We should share some of the small plates." She pulled her hand back and gestured to the selection of small plates. "Their pan-seared scallops and crispy calamari are delicious, and the grilled goat cheese is almost a salad with all the greens. But you really can't go wrong with anything on the menu here. What do you think?"

"That sounds good. I'm up for sharing." She was glad it did sound good because with the way her mind was racing, she didn't have the brain power to decide on food.

"Great. I also think you'll like their sticky toffee pudding for dessert."

"Count me in."

As they ordered and then waited for their food, Megan tried to listen for sounds coming from the booth behind her. She wondered if he was facing them or not. Either way, it made her nervous. How did he know they would be there? Or was he taking a break and someone else was watching them too?

Megan had previously texted her security team with the man's description and saw her guard eating across the room. That eased her worries.

A woman with long, blonde hair entered the restaurant and waved in their direction. Megan laid a hand on her chest in question, but the woman walked past, and she heard the man behind them greet her as she sat. Both Megan and Kate raised their brow.

"Jack. Thanks for waiting on me," the woman said. "Did you get our order placed?"

"Yes," came Jack's quick reply.

Megan shot a text to the security group with the man's first name. She listened as Jack and the woman discussed mundane plans for the week followed by frustrations with their coworkers. Once Jack and the woman's food was served, they had little to say. Megan tried chewing as quietly as she could so she didn't miss anything important. She and Kate kept their conversations low.

Despite listening intently, nothing in the conversation behind them seemed to be helpful. When the waiter brought Jack the check, she was disappointed that other than his first name, they hadn't learned anything.

As he and the woman walked by to leave, Kate stood up. "Jack? Is that you? I haven't seen you in ages. How have you been?"

Megan studied his face while Kate questioned him. He was very plain looking up close—a guy who could easily blend into crowds with his dark hair and eyes and average build.

Jack's brow furrowed. "Forgive me, what's your name again?"

Megan looked over and saw her guard leaning forward to stand up. She subtly shook her head.

"Kate...Kate Fitzgerald. I'm sorry, but I've forgotten your last name."

"It's...um...Talbot." He glanced at the blonde woman who pursed her lips and raised a brow at him.

"I'll be sure and tell Corbyn I saw you. It was great seeing you." She smiled at the couple who nodded awkwardly and left.

"Kate, you had me and the guard both on the edge of our seats. It was quick thinking though. Great job at getting his last name—if it is his last name."

"I couldn't just sit here and let the opportunity pass. Sorry if I worried you. I figured in this crowd and with the guard nearby we would be okay."

Megan sent a message to the security group text with the last name and an explanation of what Kate had done. The guard gave them a look and texted that he would prefer for them not to interact with people they suspect are following them.

As they finished their shopping excursion, they didn't see Jack again. Megan remained on edge until the moment they were safely back in the car and returning home.

"Today seemed like such a long day. Tomorrow I'll be doing it all over again when I go to meet my Bible study girls for coffee and then Corbyn and Lucy for lunch. Do you think we scared Jack off when you spoke to him, Kate?"

"If he was hired to do a job like this, surely not. I hope the security team gets the information they need from Jack quickly for your sake."

"Me too. I just wonder how hard it will be to get that information." Megan's thoughts went back to Kieran and all he had done for her. He was changing and she liked what she saw in him. "I'm glad Corbyn was able to get in touch with Kieran's mom and sister to have them come to his baptism tonight."

Kate smiled. "You may not be in China, but you're having an impact right here in London."

"You're safe." Kieran rolled his wheelchair Megan's way with worry etched into his brow. "We've convinced Scotland Yard to take this seriously, and they are having this Jack Talbot's accounts watched."

"I'm amazed they're doing that for me." Megan didn't expect them to help out an American citizen.

"Not only is your necklace a historical artifact, but when I showed them the information I found on the dark web and the other jewelry listed, they were able to connect it to a larger jewelry trafficking scheme that Interpol recently requested member countries to look out for."

"Interpol?"

"The International Police Organization. The United States is connected with them too."

"You're really knowledgeable about all of this. Are you secretly an undercover agent for Scotland Yard? Or maybe you're a vigilante like Batman."

Kieran chuckled and tapped his wheelchair. "Yes, this is all a ruse. When no one is around, I can walk just fine which is helpful for chasing the bad guys."

Megan frowned. She rarely even thought about him being in a wheelchair and hoped he didn't think she was making fun of him.

"Don't feel bad about the comment. It was probably this sleek wheelchair that made you think of Batman and all his cool gadgets."

She'd not paid much attention to it before, but it was a futuristic looking black wheelchair. "I honestly forget about your wheelchair." He tilted his head and furrowed his brow, and she hurried to explain. "There is so much more to you than this wheelchair. You know that don't you?"

His smile returned, and he winked. "I'm starting to get that idea. At least around certain people."

Heat rose into Megan's face. "When are your mother and sister arriving? I'm looking forward to meeting them."

"They're excited to meet you too. They'll be here any minute. Be prepared for them to gush. You're the woman who got me out of my slump and helped me become a Christian. To them, that's a big deal."

"Megan, you are heaven-sent to my Kieran. I have been praying for something to change him back to himself." Susan, Kieran's mom, turned from Megan and looked at Kieran who was making an 'I told you so' face at Megan. "It's true. Well, maybe not exactly the same as he was. I always hoped you would turn to God, but was starting to doubt. God had his perfect timing and way. Right, Paige?"

"Yes, Mum. We *have* been praying for him." Kieran's sister leaned down and hugged her brother. "I'm glad he finally came round. Megan, thanks for taking on the headache I like to call my little brother." She grinned and fake-punched him in the cheek.

"He even looks healthier than he did last time we saw him," Kieran's mom proclaimed.

"Okay, Mum. Megan gets the idea. Why don't you two come meet Declan's family and the pastor."

Kieran's name for Corbyn caught Megan off guard and it took her a minute to remember that he went by Declan with his non-work-related friends. Corbyn was his middle name. Kate had told Megan how hard it was for her to change to calling him Corbyn when they were first engaged.

Megan smiled while watching Kieran interact with his mom and sister. They were spunky women who clearly loved him and brought out a different side of him. He had his mom's green eyes and he and his sister shared the same dark ginger hair. His mom's was dark brown with whisps of gray highlighting it. They were a stunning family.

"Have I got stories to tell you?" Paige grabbed Megan's elbow as they followed Kieran.

Chapter Thirteen

When Megan woke the next morning, she thought of all the stories she heard about Kieran from his mom and sister. She could write a small book. She learned he had been very active as a child and into adulthood up until the motorcycle accident.

It was also clear that he was a very determined man who pushed past obstacles to achieve great things. He had been determined to protect and provide for his mother and sister after his father's death, so he studied hard and worked odd jobs after school when other young men were playing around.

As a young man, he realized he had a gift with computers and math, which he inherited from his mom who taught A-level maths. He then directed his studies to be the best programmer. According to *Computer Tech Magazine*, he was.

His mom said it wasn't until the accident that he lost that drive. But in the past week, Megan had seen him transform into a force to be reckoned with. He had poured all of his expertise and energy into helping her, and though they had yet to find answers, she felt safer and more at peace.

Kieran Davies was like no man she had ever met. At every turn, he surpassed what she expected. When she spoke to him about baptism, she thought with his handicap he might want to hold off to figure out the logistics and hoped it wouldn't discourage him. Instead, he was determined to be baptized the next day.

Megan never imagined she would attend a hot tub baptism, but it was the most memorable one she'd ever seen. Though Kieran wanted to go out in public and share his newfound faith, he didn't want his baptism to become a media spectacle. The private venue of Tracey and Richard's home with Kieran's family and Corbyn's fit his preference perfectly. The little room that held the hot tub was packed. In addition to Corbyn's parents and his own little family, his sister, Chloe, came with her husband and one of her two boys.

Kieran's testimony would forever be etched in her mind.

"Six months ago I thought I'd lost everything that mattered. I wished I was dead yet feared death at the same time. When I finally came to the hospital, there were these scripture verses posted by a stranger on Pulse that drew me in and made me want to know more about such a great God. The verses told of his love, his sacrifice, and his holiness.

"I was getting so close to becoming a Christian, then God threw the very person who had pointed me to him on Pulse into my real life. It broke that last prideful part of me. I knew that there was so much more to our great God than I could ever imagine. Up until that day, salvation through Christ seemed logical, but in that moment, he touched my heart. He showed me that he cared about me so personally that he had orchestrated an amazing and unique way for me to find him.

He had looked at Megan and held her gaze before continuing. *"The Holy Spirit stirred something deep within, and for the first time in my life, I felt alive. I still have a lot to work through, but I know that I belong to Him, and I will keep working on that relationship my whole life— however long or short it may be. Philippians 1:21—'For to me to live is Christ, and to die is gain.' I no longer fear death, but look forward to the day I can see my Savior and Lord face to face."*

Megan wondered if her feelings were something like what people felt when they fell in love—not that she was falling in love with him. But the passionate way he spoke about God reflected the passion of her own heart towards God. His joy and excitement about his salvation stirred her love for God.

Megan's phone vibrated and drew her out of her reverie, and she glanced at her phone. It was Kieran on the Pulse app, and her heart leapt.

P24,601: 1 John 4:4 You are from God and have overcome them, for he who is in you is greater than he who is in the world.

Daily Encouragement: Just what I needed to start the day!

Once again, Kieran shared from his Bible study that morning and gave Megan a chance to share from hers through the app. After they finished, Kieran called. It was starting to seem like a routine. He prayed for her at the end of their conversation. Though he worried he still wasn't doing it right, his prayers were heartfelt and to the point. She loved hearing him pray.

Today, she planned to leave the house alone and appreciated the prayers of Kieran and all her friends and family. Once again, Kieran had worked with the security company to help them plan her coverage every step of the way.

They gave her very specific instructions for travel from the house to the bus stop—text the security team before leaving, then wait thirty seconds before stepping out of the house.

Outside, she noticed one of the security company's men picking up a bag from the ground. When he stood up, she smiled and walked on, knowing he was taking the same path as far as the bus stop. On the bus, one of her guards, who had gotten on two stops before, waited. She recognized him right away but made sure not to make eye contact. When she got off the bus, another guard was walking down the street in the same direction as the coffee shop. Just before entering the coffee shop, she recognized another guard across the street.

Kieran told her all the guards had tiny video cameras hidden on their clothing and the footage was being analyzed at the security office. With so much effort centered on her case, surely they would find what they were looking for. She'd been checking her surroundings but didn't see Jack, the man from the day before.

The two young ladies she was meeting, Yasmin and Chelsea, were unaware of her guards and the situation with the necklace. As much as she wanted to tell them, there was too much at stake to share that information with anyone else.

After their Bible study, she had lunch scheduled with Corbyn and the Academic Publishing Director, Lucy, from his office. It was only one block away. She left the coffee shop and noted that the outside guard had moved to her side of the road. Inside the restaurant, Corbyn was tasked with wearing a video camera so no guard would be necessary there. Megan entered and smiled at the way he had situated them so they had a corner table and he was facing the restaurant with a clear view.

"Megan, you remember Lucy?" Corbyn greeted Megan and let them get reacquainted.

"Corbyn mentioned you came from a Bible study. How did that go?"

"Good, thanks." Megan sat in the chair Corbyn had pulled out and looked at Corbyn, wondering how much she should say.

Corbyn nodded towards Lucy. "Lucy has been leading women's Bible studies in her church for years, so I'm sure she would enjoy hearing the details."

Megan sat back and elaborated. "I met Yasmin and Chelsea at a coffee shop a week after moving here. We hit it off and soon they were asking me about Jesus because I kept talking about him. About a month ago, they decided we should do a Bible study. My friends had no real knowledge of the God of the Bible. Now they're excited about what they're learning from it. Today they said they'd like to come to church on Sunday. It's going to be an exciting day with them there and Kieran too. I think they are close to becoming Christians."

"That's wonderful!"

"Great news!" Both Corbyn and Lucy enthused simultaneously.

Over lunch, Lucy talked about future projects that Megan might want to help with until she was experienced enough to write her own books. She enjoyed editing the book that her mom had done so much work on, and the research and writing she had done to fill in the gaps after her death had been a good experience as well.

Though she wanted to be fully engrossed in the conversation over lunch, she couldn't help but scan the room looking for Jack or some other familiar face from the past two days. Not one person in the restaurant looked familiar and she wondered if they were outside waiting for her to leave. Worry crept in, and she hoped that there wasn't anyone watching her at all and her dad and Kieran would call off all of the cloak-and-dagger efforts they had in place.

Before Corbyn and Lucy dropped Megan off at home, he informed her he was bringing Kieran over later to "go over some things." They had been careful not to let Lucy know about her situation. She knew it was necessary, but hiding parts of her life felt foreign to her.

"We've got lots to discuss tonight," Kieran said as he exited the elevator in Tracy's home. He pulled out his computer and rolled into the living room. "Jack is not the man following you."

Megan thought back to the day before and recalled feeling sure he was. "I don't understand." She settled into a chair next to Kieran's wheelchair.

"The security company had him followed and found no unusual activity and no attempts to follow you. The woman he had lunch with is his wife. I verified that on his Facebook." Kieran opened a window with Jack's Facebook page, and there he was with the blonde woman and a young boy that looked like Jack's mini-me except for his eyes which matched the woman's. "Besides the fact that there is no unusual activity with his bank accounts and he's been at work all day, I don't imagine a man who treasures his family like he seems to would post pictures of his family on social media and leave it set to public if he was involved with underground activities."

"Oh. That would be bad. So does that mean no one is following me and we can cancel all of the security?" She knew it was a long shot, but one could hope.

Worry was etched on his face. "No. Though nothing points to Jack Talbot, we've got our eyes on two other men we know have been following you." He opened two new screens with images of two men. One looked vaguely familiar but not the other.

"I think I recognize him." Megan pointed to the familiar face. "I think he came into the coffee shop where I met my friends today."

Kieran nodded and pulled up another window. "Both of these chaps have been arrested and convicted multiple times. The man you don't recognize is working with the one you do, and they have been trailing you since yesterday."

Megan's stomach lurched, and she slumped against the arm of the chair, closing her eyes. Up until this moment, she held out hope that taking the necklace to the jeweler's had ended the worry of being targeted. Why was this happening?

"Megan, it's going to be okay." Kieran placed a hand on hers, and his words along with the contact drew her out of her thoughts.

"You don't know that." She looked at him and wished he could say he did.

He stared right back. "No, but I know someone who does and so do you."

She closed her eyes again and squeezed them tight. "You're right. I know this, and after being a Christian for so long it should be second nature to trust God. Sometimes I can't stop my mind from going to dark places first." Again, she opened her eyes and looked at him. "Thank you for the reminder."

"I haven't been a Christian for long, but I am guessing that there will always be a battle between your will and what you know is God's will—until heaven at least. I think I remember Paul saying something about doing the thing that he hates because of sin that is within him. That was Romans, I believe."

Shaking her head, Megan chuckled.

"What?"

"You, barely a Christian, sharing just the right scripture with me. I needed that reminder. Also, your memory continues to astound me."

"I'm glad it's good for something." He squeezed her hand.

"Still, I am scared." She couldn't shake the feeling as she imagined the men pictured watching her. "I've always felt like I was strong and invincible because God is with me. I don't know why I'm having such a hard time trusting." Her heart began to race and she tried to regulate her breathing.

Kieran tugged Megan's hand as he leaned over the side of the wheelchair and pulled her into a hug. "God, I don't know what's going on. Please help Megan. Give her peace. Help her trust you. Please. In Jesus' name, amen."

She relaxed into his arms and silently agreed with all he had prayed. *God, help me.* There was a battle going on for her mind, and she wasn't going to let herself give in. "Thank you," she whispered.

Kieran gave her a quick pat on the back then leaned away. "It wasn't very eloquent, but I imagine God knows what I meant." He tilted his head and looked closely at her. "I hate to bring us back to the subject, but there is another thing I wanted to discuss with you regarding all of this."

"Okay." She nodded slowly.

"I've developed software that will essentially hack into someone's mobile. It's called bluebugging. It will give us access to their contacts, messages, web pages visited—everything, including listening in on conversations."

"Is that legal?"

"Both Interpol and Scotland Yard approved it. Tomorrow when you go visit Peter at the British Museum, at some point, you will need to go to a fairly crowded space and spend some time there. The hope is that whichever man is following you will be there and our guy can wander around like he is analyzing art while using his mobile to hack into the other man's mobile. It would be best if you could pick a location in the museum tonight so the security team can map it out to get their guy in place quickly tomorrow. You'll need to text them right before going to that location tomorrow."

"I can do that. Thank you. This sounds promising."

"It is. We're going to do all we can to end this quickly and keep you safe."

"I appreciate it, Kieran. I have to admit I'm overwhelmed by all that you've done for me."

He looked at her before shaking his head. "It's not exactly a chore. I'll do whatever it takes."

"All this computer stuff is in your wheelhouse, that's for sure."

"Even if it wasn't, I would figure something out. You are worth it."

Now Megan's heart raced from happiness and not fear. It was a common occurrence around Kieran. "I know I keep saying it, but thank you. I've never had to depend on people other than my family, and God of course, so this is strange for me. So many people have stepped in to help, but you always seem to know when I need to be talked off the ledge."

"Let's stay away from ledges. I don't want you taking any risks." Kieran smiled but his brow furrowed.

"No ledges. I hear you. Is there anything else about my case we should go over?"

"Ready to get rid of me?"

"No, but I wanted to share my latest findings from my grandmother's letters."

"By all means, proceed. I want to know more of the tale of Nancy Wilson and the elusive Robert."

Her phone buzzed. "I can check it later."

"It's okay. With all that's going on, it might be important."

Megan nodded and looked down to see Reece's name. She'd almost forgotten he wanted to go out.

"You don't look happy. Who is it?"

"Reece."

Kieran pressed his lips together and shook his head. "He's persistent. I'll give him that. You should answer it."

She slowly slid her phone open. "Hello."

Kieran mouthed, "Speaker."

Megan nodded and switched it over.

"Hello, beautiful. How's your day been?"

Kieran raised a brow and tilted his head.

"Fine. Thanks."

"I would have phoned earlier in the week, but I didn't know for sure what day I'd be in London. I worked it out to come Friday and I promised you a date. Will six work Friday night?"

"Oh, I..."

Kieran nodded emphatically. "Yes," he mouthed.

"Yes. Um, Friday at six. I can do that."

"Great. What have you been up to this week?"

"Meetings and that sort of thing today. I did do some shopping yesterday with Kate." She struggled to focus with Kieran looking at her, and she wondered if she made any sense. "What about you?"

"I had a couple of lectures and a tutorial today. Did some research and that sort of thing too." Reece continued chatting about his week as Kieran tapped his fingers.

Megan searched for a way to end the conversation, and before she came up with something, Kieran backed away to the door. Disappointment rose in her chest.

"Megan, I have some things we need to go over," Kieran called out then pointed to the phone.

She nodded. "Reece, my apologies, but I've got to run. Why don't you message me with the details for Friday?"

"Sure. I'm looking forward to it. Goodnight, Megan."

"Goodnight." She hung up, then turned to Kieran. "Thank you for rescuing me."

"Are you sure you wanted rescuing? You were quick to accept the date in the first place."

"I didn't mean to. I was distracted with everything we were discussing." When he raised his brow, she placed a hand on her hip. "I mean it."

"If you say so," Kieran chuckled. "So what were you about to tell me before we were so rudely interrupted?" He rolled back next to her chair.

"Oh, yeah. I read three more letters. Besides Robert waxing poetic about my grandmother's beauty, he mentioned something about taking over his family business. Then he assured her he would work things out."

"Intriguing. No mention of what the family business was?"

"Unfortunately not. Maybe one of the later letters will tell."

"You haven't had the urge to stay up one night and read them all?"

Megan smiled and shook her head. "I've never been one to hurry surprises. At Christmas, I always knew where the presents were hidden, but was never tempted to peek. I like to take my time with important things. I did glance at the signature on all the letters just in case he ever mentioned his last name, but they are all just signed by Robert."

"Another quality of yours that amazes me. I don't think I have that kind of patience. I would have read them all by now."

"Thanks, but I don't feel very patient when it comes to getting to the bottom of what's going on with my necklace and whoever is following me."

"That's different. But we're not going to go down that road again tonight." He looked at his watch. "Declan's mom invited me to stay for dinner. I think it's time." He held out his arm to escort her like a gentleman, and she reached down to lay her hand on it as he turned his wheelchair towards the hall.

Once again she felt that pleasant flutter in her heart...and she liked it.

Chapter Fourteen

Stepping through the front door, Megan reached out from the porch to feel the rain. It was more than a passing drizzle, and she was thankful the security team was sending a "taxi" driven by one of her guards. Normally she preferred to ride a bike, but as anxious as she was today, she appreciated not being so exposed. All week she was aware that someone might be following her, but now *knowing* they were made it much more real. She hoped she would be able to do what was necessary at the right time without freezing up.

The security team thought having her act like she was checking for rain would be a good way to alert the men following her that she was leaving. They wanted their plan of bluebugging the men's phones to have the best chance of success. She smiled at the silly name for the very serious hack. In the wrong hands, it could be used for a lot of bad things. She kept an eye on her watch until five minutes passed before going back out to wait on the "taxi."

Staring at the passing buildings on the way to the museum, Megan wondered if she was currently being followed. She had studied both men's pictures long enough to recognize them easily and would attempt not to react if she saw them. Nervously, she tapped her messenger bag as the driver pointed out random sites along the way.

"Thanks for trying to distract me," she called out to Ben. He had made her feel safe and comfortable from the very first day they'd been introduced.

"I know this can be unsettling, but you are well-protected. That boyfriend of yours is making sure we don't miss anything."

Megan looked up at him in the rearview mirror. "Do you mean Kieran?"

"I do. Sorry, is it not official yet?"

Heat rose to Megan's face. "He's a great guy, but we're just friends." She recalled the beautiful women in photographs with Kieran. "I don't think I'm his type."

"Don't mean to overstep, but a bloke like him doesn't get emotional over something like this unless the girl he fancies is involved. You just wait. It won't be long before he asks you out."

She raised her brow and pondered this new information. "I think you might be misinterpreting his behavior." But something inside her wanted him to be right.

Ben shrugged and began humming a happy tune. She appreciated the time to collect her thoughts as she recounted her recent interactions with Kieran. His hand on hers and the hug the day before made her heart flutter. Could it be possible?

"Megan. What brings you here today? Questions for your book?"

She analyzed Peter's mannerisms as he spoke. He wasn't acting suspicious. Surely he didn't have anything to do with people following her or the attempted robbery. "I just thought I'd say 'hi' before I went to evaluate some of the Egyptian sculptures. We haven't spoken lately, and I was wondering how you were doing." Before the benefit, they typically spoke or texted several times a week, but they hadn't communicated much by text and hadn't spoken in almost two weeks.

"Thanks. I'm fine. The usual for me—keeping things together here at the museum. What about you? Any decision about your necklace?"

"We put it in storage at De Clare's but I haven't decided if that will be long-term."

"Let me know if I can do anything. Has, um..." He rubbed the back of his neck. "Has Reece had any news for you to help figure out how it ended up in your family? He mentioned the two of you had gone out and he was going to follow up on the chevron symbol."

"He has. Ironically, he thinks it's from the de Clare family." Peter's brow shot up at Megan's statement. "But there haven't been any de Clares in existence since 1360, and the family has endless branches and last names now. Unfortunately, none of them ring a bell to my uncle, who is the only relative left on my mom's side, or to me, so I'm no closer to finding out how it came to my family. There is no tie to De Clare's jewelry store, so that's a dead end too."

"That's disappointing. So, you're going to go out with him again?" Peter shifted and looked down at his feet.

"Reece? I am tomorrow." She wanted to add "just as friends," but she needed to be the one to tell Reece that. She had a feeling his interest in her was more about the necklace.

"Oh. He didn't mention that." He looked back up and frowned.

She wasn't sure how to respond. "I should get some work done. It was good to see you, Peter."

"It was good to see you too. Goodbye, Megan."

Peter had a sad puppy dog face as Megan left, and once again, she felt bad and wished he would stop hoping for something that wasn't meant to be. Right now she didn't have time to dwell on Peter's emotional turmoil. It was time to get in place for Operation Bluebug. That's what she called it in her head at least.

P24,601: Isaiah 41:10 "Fear not, for I am with you; be not dismayed, for I am your God; I will strengthen you, I will help you, I will uphold you with my righteous right hand."

Megan smiled to herself as she messaged him back and then texted her security guards.

Ducking behind one of the Egyptian statues in the two story high Egyptian sculpture gallery, Megan calmed her breathing. She'd just seen Stuart, one of the men who was following her. Her guard sent a text confirming it was Stuart and that he was beginning the bluebugging process. She slowly moved away from the statue and towards the wall-mounted limestone stela of Penbuy to take notes. After snapping a picture, she wrote furiously in her notebook. It was a combination of scribbles and jumbled words—not likely to be usable for the book, much less legible.

Out of the corner of her eye, she saw her stalker moving around as if he were studying the art. Maybe he wasn't technically a stalker, but he was close enough. He followed her for no good reason. She wondered if the other man was somewhere nearby. A crowd filled her section of the gallery and it was difficult to see around the imposing statues.

Time seemed to come to a standstill as she waited and continued to "take notes" before moving on to another artifact. She wondered how long the process of hacking his phone would take. In the meantime, her mind played tricks on her and she'd never felt such a strong desire to run. Silently, she prayed for strength to make it through this. She tried not to look at her guard, but every now and then it was helpful to see he was nearby.

At last, she received a text saying that the security team successfully hacked his phone, and some of the stress evaporated. Casually, she worked her way through the next section of the statues then moved towards the museum exit.

"Hey, do you want to get something to eat?"

Megan nearly jumped out of her skin. "Peter. It's you."

"Who else would it be?"

"Sorry. I guess I've been so focused on what I was doing that I didn't see you approach."

"Did you get what you came for?"

"I did, thanks." She could honestly say that.

"We could do afternoon tea at the restaurant here."

"I don't have that much time, but I could get something quick in the café."

They sat in the Court Café and chatted over tea and biscuits for a few minutes until Megan couldn't sit still any longer. She was ready to get home and find out what the team discovered after accessing Stuart's phone.

"Peter, I've got to run."

"You seem anxious. Is there a book emergency?"

Megan realized she'd been tapping her fingers on the table and forced a chuckle. "Something like that. It was great seeing you. I'll talk to you later. Okay?"

Peter tilted his head and analyzed her with a furrowed brow. "Okay then. I'll see you later, Megan." He helped her gather her things.

"Thanks, bye." As she walked away, she could almost feel Peter's gaze burning into her back. Or maybe it was Stuart.

She sent a text to the driver and hurried towards the exit. Only steps from where she sat, she bumped into someone.

"Pardon." The man hurried by with his head down and Megan's heart raced when she realized it was Stuart.

Somehow she forced herself to continue walking out. When she finally made it into her fake taxi, she slumped back into the seat.

"You okay?"

This time Elliot from the security company was driving.

"I don't think I'm cut out for this sort of undercover work. I'm a nervous wreck. As I was leaving, I actually bumped into the man who was following me. It's a miracle that I didn't pass out."

"I'm glad you didn't. To me and the others, you're doing great. Don't give up."

"Thanks. I've never been the type to pass out before. I know God will get me through, but this is pushing me to my limit. Anything I am doing right is completely him."

Gradually, her tension eased and she thanked God for getting her through the afternoon and for the success of hacking into the man's phone. By the time Megan walked into the house, she felt like a new person.

"You're safe," Kieran said as he rolled towards her in the entry hall. He reached for her hand and squeezed it. "Ben mentioned you were nervous when he drove you to the museum this morning. I've been praying all day and following your progress."

Megan's face warmed when she recalled Ben's comments about Kieran's feelings for her. She stared at their connected hands and wondered if he felt the same electricity she did from their connection.

"Come sit in the living room. Agent Gareth, the team leader for your case at Interpol, is here and wants to go over some things." He tugged her towards the living room where she saw a blond-haired man rising from a chair. He was dressed in a collared shirt and dress pants.

"Miss Taylor, it's good to finally meet you in person. As you've noticed, all of those working on this case will be dressed in plain clothes so as not to stand out. Now that we have a working gate between the gardens behind these two homes," he pointed in the direction of the house where the security team and Interpol were set up, "our team can come over as needed instead of always communicating by mobile or computer. Your hosts, Tracey and Richard, have been quite accommodating."

"The path and back entrance to the other home aren't wheelchair friendly, so they have to come here when I'm involved," Kieran commented.

"Without you, we would still be floundering to find a way forward with this case. It's a small accommodation to have your help," Gareth said to Kieran.

"Thanks." Kieran turned back to Megan. "We hacked Stuart's mobile, but we didn't see Billy, the other man following you today. Stuart's mobile is sending GPS locations to another number, but that number has been untraceable. I'm still looking for a way to access that information.

"In the meantime, I discovered that your friend Reece has ties to the De Clare family through the Fairfax name. I've had a strange feeling about him all along, so I am doing a deep dive into his information. Because of this, you will have extra coverage when you go out with him tomorrow night. I want you to be on your guard around him. Have you told Reece where your necklace is now?"

"I haven't, but I told Peter today, and it's possible they will talk before then. It's hard to imagine Reece is behind all of this. He seems like a normal guy." Megan wondered again if she was a poor judge of character.

Gareth spoke up, "When dealing with these types of criminal activities, the criminals can be hard to detect from outward appearances. You would be surprised at what even the most innocent looking people are capable of."

"I'm already surprised that anyone would go to this extent for a necklace. My necklace."

"1 Timothy 6:10 says, 'For the love of money is a root of all kinds of evils.' I read that one the other day, and it made me think of this situation." Kieran turned to Gareth. "I'd like to be at the restaurant when she meets with Reece."

"I don't like it. What purpose will it serve?" Gareth shook his head.

"Being there in person will give me a better chance than working remotely to trace the messages from whoever is following her. Her guard will still be there and can work on bluebugging Reece's mobile to see if he has anything to do with this."

Gareth rubbed his beard. "I'll have to think over the logistics of this. You're somewhat of a celebrity after dating that model, and it might create a sensation that backfires on us. If you draw attention, you won't be able to accomplish anything."

"Disguise me."

"What?" Megan wondered what he had in mind.

"I can dye my hair or wear a wig and a fake beard. Maybe something longer than yours to give me a very different look."

Gareth raised his brow. "Could work. The guards have a selection of things they've been using."

"You'd color your hair? What if it doesn't come out?" The thought saddened Megan. She loved Kieran's dark red hair.

"With your short hair, one of the wigs will work." Gareth threw in.

As they continued to plan, Kate peeked in to tell them dinner was ready. Megan was thankful her friend had been spending more time at her in-laws home. Without her and Kieran, this situation would be so much more difficult.

As they ate, Megan couldn't help but watch Kieran. For a computer guy, he had a magnetic personality. He drew in everyone at the table with his stories and charisma. Seeing him enjoy life brought joy to her heart. Through their past messaging on Pulse and even his attitude when she had delivered food to his Kingsdown home, it was clear he had been in a dark place. She knew God could change someone like that, but it was amazing to see in person.

When Richard pulled out the Articulate game after dinner, everyone joined him in the adjacent reception room and paired off into teams. Kieran partnered with Megan for the word game. It reminded her of Taboo, but this one had lots of British celebrities. They occasionally skipped over some of those cards for her sake. The game moved along quickly, catching everyone up in the excitement. Even Kate's girls shouted out words, though Margaret just copied her sister. The faces Kieran made were entertainment in themselves and she enjoyed seeing that side of him. In the end, Kate and Corbyn won.

"On that note, we're off," Corbyn announced. "I've got to get all my girls to bed."

"I won't keep you up either," Kieran said to Megan. "I want to make sure you are well rested for tomorrow."

They said goodbye to Kate, Corbyn, and the girls.

When Richard turned to get his keys to drive Kieran home, Kieran reached for Megan's hand. "We'll get you through this. Don't worry."

Megan smiled as tingles raced up her arm. "Thank you."

He and Richard took the elevator down, and Tracey wrapped an arm around her. "He really cares about you."

"He's a good friend."

Tracey tilted her head. "I think he may be interested in more. I know he has a reputation, but from what I've seen of him over these last couple of weeks, and the fact that he became a Christian, he may be ready for different things in life. He can't seem to take his eyes off of you."

"We were friends online for a while before meeting in person. I helped lead him to the Lord. It may just be appreciation."

"Maybe, but don't be surprised if he suggests more."

Megan pondered that. Two people in one day had mentioned his feelings towards her, and she liked the idea. She couldn't deny that something was blossoming within her too, but knew she needed to keep her mind from running away with the idea. What she said to Tracey was very possibly the truth.

Her phone dinged.

Kieran: See you tomorrow. (Sunglasses emoji*)

Megan's heart leapt when she saw Kieran's name, and that little spark of hope sprang forth. Maybe he did feel the same.

She said goodnight to Tracey and chuckled on her way to bed as she thought about the sunglasses emoji. What would Kieran look like disguised? Would he change his hair color...or his eyes? She could get lost in those green eyes. She couldn't imagine him not looking attractive regardless of what he did. Her face heated at the thought.

Chapter Fifteen

Megan sat on her bed and stared at the photo of Kieran. Gareth had given approval for him to go to the restaurant while Megan was there with Reece, and Kieran was next door working on his disguise. She chuckled at his black wig pulled into a man bun and the thick beard he sported. She'd never liked man buns, but he pulled it off.

Megan: Your eyes look brown.

Kieran: They have non-prescription colored contacts. Maybe I should start wearing these all the time.

His beautiful green eyes had always been one of the things most striking to her.

Megan: No! I love your eyes.

She immediately regretted sending that text, but before she could hit undo he looked at it. She held her breath, wondering how he'd respond.

Kieran: Well then. Green it is when I'm not undercover.

Megan: Thanks

At least he didn't call her out for flirting with him. She checked her watch and it was 5:40. He was distracting her from getting ready for her date.

Megan: I need to finish getting ready myself.

Kieran: You would look beautiful in a paper sack. If he doesn't realize that, he doesn't deserve to go out with you.

Her heart did a little jump.

Reece: On my way.

Megan: GTG he's on his way!

Reece: Who?

Megan squealed when she realized she'd sent Kieran's text to Reece and was thankful she didn't say all that she wanted to. She texted Reece again.

Megan: Oops. Wrong text thread. You.

This time she made sure it was Kieran.

Megan: Reece is on his way so I really have to go. I accidentally texted that to him and am thankful that's all I said!

Kieran: What else would you say?

She wondered if she should tell him then carefully pulled up the text thread with Kieran.

Megan: That I only view him as a friend.

Kieran: Good to know. I'll stop distracting you now.

Her heart picked up speed. This sure seemed like flirting.

Sitting with Reece at the restaurant, Megan smiled and tried to focus on what he said, though she was distracted by the man in a wheelchair two tables away. Reece had brought lists of the de Clare family lineage. When she pointed out that his last name was part of that lineage, he insisted his family had no connection to the pendant. He did, however, admit to discovering that his family had descended from the de Clares.

She watched him with an analyzing eye but didn't see any tells that he had bad intentions. He wasn't fidgeting. He held her gaze, and he looked relaxed and happy. Then again, Gareth had said that some of the most innocent-looking people were up to no good.

He tried to flirt with her, but it fell flat. Her initial attraction had long been replaced with a simple desire for friendship, regardless of whether he was planning to rob her.

Megan tried to avoid looking at Kieran, but it was hard to ignore when he shifted and huffed each time Reece leaned towards her. She noticed Kieran frantically typing away on his phone. At least he sat in the corner so no one could see what he was typing.

"Would you like that?"

"I'm sorry. My mind wandered." She motioned to the family lineage lists and tried to act engaged in the conversation, though she felt guilty for misrepresenting herself. Was that okay in a situation like this when she had things she couldn't reveal? She was glad they were almost done eating because acting like someone she wasn't made her uncomfortable.

"Would you like to come out to Oxford for a few days? I'd love to show you around. If you come on a Friday, I only have one tutorial early in the day. After that I'm free and you could see what the campus is like with students going to classes and such, then stay through Saturday or Sunday to experience the town's weekend vibe. Next weekend would be good for me."

"Wow. That sounds interesting." The truth was she would love to go, but there was no way she would if he considered it a prolonged date.

"That doesn't sound like a yes."

"I...think we would be best as friends, and I don't want to lead you on." There. She'd said it.

Reece's brow furrowed. "I thought...What's changed? Is there someone else?"

Megan fought the temptation to glance at Kieran and instead looked down at her plate with only bits left of her risotto and lamb. "It's complicated."

"I get it. No worries," he said flatly. "If you'd like to visit Oxford sometime, the offer is still open for me to show you around. But I'd prefer it if you didn't bring the other guy around." He tilted his head. "Unless it's Peter. Is it Peter?"

Megan shook her head, and this time she couldn't keep from glancing at Kieran. When she remembered she was wired and he was listening, she quickly averted her eyes as heat rose to her face.

"Okay, I won't ask. I can't say I'm completely surprised. You seemed off when we spoke last."

"It's all of this with the necklace that has me distracted." That was the truth, at least part of it. "I apologize if I mislead you."

"I'll be fine. I'm glad I could help with the de Clare history. Let me know if you find anything out. Peter mentioned you put it in De Clare's vault. That's smart. If you decide to go the museum route, let me know. I have connections."

"Thanks." She hoped her guard was able to see if there was anything suspicious on Reece's phone. If it were up to her, she would call him innocent and move on.

As he drove her home, Reece made small talk about life at Oxford. It sounded interesting, but once more she had trouble focusing. She wondered if they had found any new information and considered if it were possible that Reece was behind all of the problems with the pendant. Again and again she went through their conversations, trying to recall if he'd said anything that might indicate he was behind it. She still came up blank.

Even though she had rejected him, Reece was a gentleman and walked her to the door.

When she stopped to say goodnight, he gave her a smoldering look and said, "I'm fine with friends, but if things don't work out with the other guy, maybe you'll give me another chance."

Before she could respond, he leaned down and kissed her on the cheek.

"Goodnight," she said shakily as he pulled back. He'd caught her off guard, and she internally panicked, thinking he was leaning down to harm her. Apparently deep down she thought he was capable of bad things.

"Goodnight, Megan. Let's keep in touch."

Inside, Megan plopped down on a sofa in the reception room, replaying the night in her head. She checked in with Tracey to let her know she was okay before going upstairs to her room.

Her phone rang and pulled her out of her thoughts. It was Kieran.

"I'm sitting here watching the video feed from the front door camera and he's kissing you! I thought you said he was a friend. You even told *him* that at the restaurant. It's dangerous territory to be fraternizing with the enemy."

"Hello to you too," Megan rushed out when he was in between breaths.

"What? This is serious, Megan. Your life is in danger."

"You're the one who has been telling me that everything is going to be okay. Anyway, you are jumping to a lot of conclusions. Maybe you need to stop and listen again to the audio they recorded through my wire. I never led him on."

"Maybe I will, though I'm not looking forward to listening to a repeat of him trying to distract you by coming on to you. I saw it with my own eyes at the restaurant, and that's definitely what he was doing."

"I promise it wasn't that bad, and for the record, he kissed me on the cheek."

"Oh, it was bad. Even after you told him you should be friends, he still looked like he was trying to get you to fall for him." Kieran breathed heavily into the phone. "Wait. Did you say cheek?"

"I did, but I don't think this is the conversation we should be having. Why are we talking about this and not about what you found out through your mad hacking skills?"

"Hmph."

Megan covered the phone and silently laughed. He was reminding her of the Kieran she knew from delivering food to his beach cottage. "Well?"

"I wasn't able to get through again. This time it was Billy following you, and it was basically the same story. I found messages that he sent to the same number as Stuart's mobile has been. The messages were updates of your status and GPS location. The number is too well-hidden and I couldn't trace it. The best I can do is keep tabs on their messages and hope for some kind of meet up or drop off that brings the person at the other end to us."

"Okay." She'd hoped he was able to trace the number so they would be further along with things. "What about Reece's phone? Did you guys find anything there?"

"No. Nothing, and it was easy to get into. If he has anything to do with this, he's using a different mobile."

"Or maybe he really doesn't have anything to do with this."

"Are you sure you don't have feelings for him?"

Megan chuckled into the phone. "I don't. I'll admit that in the beginning, I thought he was very good-looking, but even that has diminished since I've gotten to know him. He's not my type."

"Well...It seems you're very lenient when it comes to him."

Megan smiled to herself. "If I see him again, I'll be careful, but I have a feeling I won't be seeing him. Anyway...If there's no new information about the case, I wanted to tell you about my grandmother's letters I've read." She was ready to change the subject to one that didn't put Kieran so on edge. Could it be he was jealous?

"There's no other information. Tell me what you've found."

"It's still not much. Robert continues to extoll my grandmother's virtues, but he also tells her that he's expected to marry for the sake of his family business. He called it a merger of families and said both families would benefit. He insisted that he would make sure it didn't happen and said he plans to meet with his father and discuss other options that would help the family business. Unfortunately, there's still no mention of what the family business is or any other thing that would give a clue about himself. I only have a few letters left to look through."

"I'm sorry. I know you were hoping for more from those letters. It's getting late, but I can come over tomorrow and we can read the last few together."

Her heart raced at the thought, and finishing the last of the letters without finding anything out no longer sounded so bad. "I'd like that."

Chapter Sixteen

Megan gingerly carried her grandmother's jewelry box downstairs to the reception room where Kieran was waiting. After the break-in, Corbyn told her of a place that restored antique furniture, and they had the wooden box looking better than before.

"That's your grandmother's jewelry box you told me about?" Kieran rolled her way as she entered.

"It is." She sat in the chair beside his wheelchair, lifted the lid, and showed him where the letters had been hidden.

"Mysterious."

"It is. I'm surprised she saved them since they weren't from my grandfather. These are the ones I've already read." She set the box on the table in front of them then held up the small pile. "You're welcome to look them over after we read the others. Maybe there's something I've missed." She laid them next to the jewelry box.

Kieran shook his head and smiled. "Doubtful."

"These are the ones we're reading today." She opened the first one.

28 August 1970
My Dearest Nancy,

I earnestly beg you to be patient with me while I come up with a plan to get out of this marriage. Even though my father did not respond well during my first meeting with him to discuss it, I have hope that I will be able to get him to come around. My mother has always been against the idea of the marriage to merge the families, though that is how she and my father ended up married.

According to Mum, their first few years were difficult, but they did eventually find love between them. Indeed, now they are very much in love. But I do believe she wants me to be able to marry for love. With me being the only child, and a son at that, my father's plans are different.

Regardless of how much he pushes the marriage, I can never love her. I love you. The connection I have felt with you is like nothing I have ever felt, nor will I ever again.

My darling, you have promised your love to me as well, so again I urge you to be patient with me while I figure out another way to approach this. Let's meet at our secret spot tomorrow at dawn.

Love forever and always, Robert

"You're right, his letters are evasive and give no concrete facts that can be traced back to him. No last name, not even the name of the location where they are to meet. Almost as if he is worried his letter might get into the wrong hands." He held up the envelope. "Even the envelope has no return address."

"I forgot to mention, last night it hit me that my mother would have been conceived soon after these letters." She pointed to the date on the letter Kieran had just read. August 28, 1970. "My mother was born only ten and a half months later—June 24, 1971. I messaged my uncle and asked if he could find out my grandparent's wedding date. I fell asleep last night before he replied."

She pulled out her phone and checked her messages. When she saw her uncle had replied, she tensed, wondering what she'd find. "It says they married December 4, 1970. He also found her return ticket to the U.S. and it was dated October 2, 1970." She held up the last two letters and flipped them open. "Here is the last letter. It is still addressed to my grandmother in London and it is dated September

30." She looked between her phone and the letter, trying to process it. "My grandmother was in love with this man and married another just over two months later. And what's crazier? Mom was born *less* than nine months after Grandmother left England." Megan's chest tightened.

Her eyes met Kieran's piercing green ones, and she knew he saw her pain and confusion as he reached out and squeezed her hands.

"My grandmother got pregnant out of wedlock." There seemed to be no way around it. "It doesn't coincide with the things Grandaddy used to say about her. He talked about what a wonderful Christian woman she was and how much she loved the Lord. And he told the sweetest stories about how in love he and my grandmother were. I hung onto every word and as a child hoped that if I ever married, my husband would feel the same way about me. I wanted to be like this stalwart woman he described. She died before I was born. Did he lie?" She rubbed her forehead with her free hand until she was distracted by Kieran's thumb rubbing circles on her other hand.

Kieran reached up and wiped tears from her cheek. "People change. I'm a perfect example of that. I never want to be the man I was before you introduced me to Christ. Maybe that's her story too."

She gave a sad smile. "Maybe." Conflicting thoughts swirled in her mind. "That's true. God can do anything."

"We are checking into these three men who were present at the benefit you attended. In our background checks of the attendees, these are the ones who have had run-ins with the law," Gareth said. "And since our guys haven't hacked into Peter's mobile yet, we haven't ruled him out. I want to keep you abreast of our plans and what we're finding so we don't work against each other. We'll have you followed this next week.

You're still planning a surprise visit to De Clare's on Monday?" Gareth's voice came through the speaker on Megan's phone.

"Yes. That's my plan," Megan replied.

"Excellent. We'll get to the bottom of this. These people will slip up at some point. Let me know if you have any change of plans over the next few days. The security company will have you covered tomorrow for church, but our file doesn't currently show you have plans for today. Correct?"

"Yes, today I'm taking a break from the stress of going out and worrying about being followed." Megan locked eyes with Kieran. Unfortunately, it didn't mean her Saturday was without stress.

"Got it. Enjoy your day, you two. We'll speak later."

"Bye." After Gareth hung up, Megan turned to Kieran. "Thanks for helping me sort through these things today. With what I've learned about my mom's conception, I needed someone to talk it through with."

"I've got a shoulder you can cry on too, should you need it."

"Thank you," Megan's voice caught in her throat.

"Should we tackle those last two letters?"

Megan nodded. "I think subconsciously I worried I would find something I didn't like in these letters and that's why I haven't been in a rush to get through them."

"I get it. Sometimes it's easier to stay in our ignorance."

Megan laid out the last two letters on the coffee table. The letter they looked at first was dated September 17, 1970, and had disappointing news that Robert's father was still against ending their family agreement to have him marry the other woman. Robert denounced his family business and said he would use his skills to work for the competition. He mentioned filing for Nancy's spousal visa and said he was finalizing the plans for them to marry.

They both reached for the final letter, and his hand brushed hers sending tingles up her arm. She glanced at Kieran and together they slid it closer.

30 September 1970

My Beloved Nancy,

I rejoice that I can soon call you wife now that your visa paperwork and our marriage application are ready. I have a date set with my new employer to begin working after our brief honeymoon. Meet me tomorrow at our designated spot and we will check into the hotel for the last time under separate names!

Thank you for making me the happiest man alive. I do hope my family will eventually forgive me and understand. I imagine when little ones are running around they will have a change of heart.

I love you with all of my heart, my darling. See you soon!

Love forever and always, Robert

Megan pressed a hand against her chest. "It hurts here. They loved each other, but obviously something happened and it didn't work out. I have a grandfather out there that I never knew. I loved my grandaddy, but it's strange thinking there's someone I missed out on."

Kieran rolled his chair closer to Megan and pulled her into a hug. "I'm sorry. You've had so much hit you lately."

Megan relaxed in his arms and breathed a sigh of relief as a weight lifted off of her shoulders. When she pulled back, she saw her sadness reflected in his face. His eyes dropped to her lips and she felt that pull towards him that had been building.

Kieran moved back but still held her, and his voice was shaky as he spoke. "I'm here for you as you work through it all."

"Thanks. I don't know what I would have done without you." Megan was glad when he finally released her. She had never had such a strong urge to kiss a man and had no plans to until she was in a serious relationship. It was hard to think when she was staring into his eyes while he held her. Something was still lurking in the recesses of her mind. "Do you know...this means my mom never knew her biological father. She always thought Grandaddy was her father. That's so strange to think of. I wonder if Grandaddy even knew. Did my grandmother act like my mom was his daughter?" She shook her head and rubbed her forehead. "I can't believe she would leave us with such a big lie."

"Don't do that to yourself. You said your grandfather told you stories about her being a strong Christian. You don't know the background. What we're missing here is her story and the end of her story with Robert. Maybe he refused to marry her when he found out she was pregnant. Only God knows. Or maybe she did do those things you are thinking but couldn't ever bring herself to tell those around her. God can still forgive that, and you can too."

"You're right." But it still pained her to think such things about the grandmother she previously held so high in her mind. It would be a challenge to give it over to God.

"In the short time I've been a Christian, I've not always done everything I should. We've talked about how Paul said that he does the thing he doesn't want to. I imagine there are a lot of Christians out there who have baggage in their past and don't go around advertising it—even to people close to them. Sometimes we make judgments about sharing things because we worry not only about what people will think of us but about how it will change their view on lots of things. There are things in my past that I might not ever share with my mum or sister. If they flat-out asked me about something, I would tell them the truth, though."

"I didn't think of it that way." He was right. Everyone is still plagued with sin even after they become Christians.

"And think of how this discovery has you feeling like you missed out on a grandfather you never knew. What if you found out your dad was not your biological dad? You might be tempted to go on a mission looking for some other man and doubt your whole existence and worth. What if you did find that other man and he had a wife and children and the new information destroyed their family? There are so many what-ifs. Maybe things like that caused your grandmother to keep it hidden." He shrugged. "I would grapple with those questions if I were her."

"Those are all good points. I suppose I should trust the fact that I know my mom and Grandaddy were both strong Christians, and they thought she was. My mom claimed that her mom had a huge impact on her faith and the way she lived it out."

"God has allowed you to find out these things that others in your family never knew. Hold it up to the light of what you know. God is trusting you with this. God wants to bear our burdens and give us peace. His peace is not like the world's peace. It's a fruit of the spirit that comes from having his spirit in us. I learned that from an amazing Christian woman." He smiled with a gleam in his eye.

Megan chuckled, recalling her conversation with him through Pulse before she knew who he was.

"Now that's a sound I love to hear."

Her heart skipped a beat when she saw the smile he gave her. "Sorry, I've been making this conversation all about me. I'm excited that you're coming to church with us tomorrow."

"I'm looking forward to church with you too, but I'm apprehensive about it being my first time in public in a wheelchair—not counting the other day when I was disguised."

"I didn't realize it would be your first time out. Are you worried your notoriety will cause a stir?"

"Something like that. I suppose I shouldn't complain. You've been going around every day worrying about being followed." He shifted in his chair. "Being watched didn't bother me before the accident. Though I've come to terms with my condition, I imagine everyone will be focusing on it at first."

"We have lots to pray about in the coming days."

"That we do." Kieran took her hand and prayed about her discovery with her grandparents, the situation with people following her and protection from whatever they had planned, and his first time publicly in a wheelchair. He prayed that they would both glorify God in their actions. Megan felt an overwhelming peace.

"Thank you, Kieran, for being here for me."

"Megan, I'm beyond thankful for you. I can't imagine being anywhere else."

Chapter Seventeen

P 24,601: Matthew 11:28-30 "Come to me, all who labor and are heavy laden, and I will give you rest. 29 Take my yoke upon you, and learn from me, for I am gentle and lowly in heart, and you will find rest for your souls. 30 For my yoke is easy, and my burden is light."

Megan immediately dialed Kieran. "It's probably a good thing I never met my biological grandfather. I had such a good relationship with Grandaddy. I don't need another grandfather."

"Good morning to you too, Megan. This seems to be a habit for us —skipping over the pleasantries."

She chuckled. "Sorry. I couldn't stop thinking about things through the night. So...are you ready for church?"

"As ready as I can be. And good news, I convinced Toby to come."

"That is great news. Why don't we meet at your van and we can all walk in together."

"Fabulous. We should be there twenty minutes early. I'll be rolling in with the most beautiful woman there."

"You'll see that's not true, but thank you."

As they walked into the church, Megan and Kieran both glanced around. By now she knew he was checking their surroundings for the same things she was—the men following her and the security cameras. Interpol had come out the day before and placed cameras around the entrances and also facing the parking.

She didn't see Stuart or Billy, but she'd seen her two guards and also noticed two of the cameras so far. She wondered how likely it was that anything would happen at the church. What kind of person committed crimes on church property? It was hard to imagine that someone would thumb their nose at God so blatantly, yet history had proven time and again what mankind is capable of.

Megan imagined the best scenario would be for Stuart and Billy to follow her into the church and sit through the service. They would hear about things of God. Would it change their hearts? The image of the man on the cross next to Jesus came to mind. Jesus told him he would be with him in paradise.

Just as Kieran imagined, his arrival had heads turning. It was mostly the younger set looking his way.

Megan leaned down to whisper to Kieran. "You can tell the ones who pay attention to celebrity gossip."

"I'm thankful you don't. It wasn't until I wanted to get out of the limelight that I realized how destructive it is."

Kieran caught Megan's eye when Megan's friends, Yasmin and Chelsea, arrived at church and both of them recognized Kieran. At first, they oohed and aahed but they soon settled down and joined the group in finding a seat. Megan also wondered if some of the oohing and aahing had to do with Toby. He was quite a presence on his own with his body-builder physique.

During the service, Megan saw a message in her security group texts that said both Stuart and Billy were outside in the parking lot in separate vehicles. Megan still couldn't figure out why someone was going through so much trouble having her followed for days without attempting anything. Not that she wanted anything to happen, but what were they waiting for?

As the days ticked by, her circumstance became more and more unsettling. Repeatedly she laid down her worries before God, but she also kept picking them up. "God, help me trust you more," she begged.

"Kieran, I'm having such a hard time trusting God the longer this goes on." Megan didn't expect a solution, but she couldn't hold it in anymore. "This situation is wearing on me. I know I can trust him, and I think I'm trusting him until something pushes me and I realize somewhere along the way I've stopped trusting."

Kieran nodded. "I can see how that would happen. All I know to say is keep studying your Bible and talking to God, and at some point I imagine your heart will catch up with your head. I go through the same thing with my paralysis. When I first became a Christian, I knew God had taken away the strong need I felt about being healed, but even in this short amount of time, I find I keep struggling with it. We keep praying and keep waiting until he gives us a breakthrough." He reached for her hand and clasped it tightly in his.

That simple gesture was beginning to mean so much.

"Did Toby say anything about the service before he left?"

Kieran smiled. "No, but he didn't say anything negative so that's good. What's more, he and Yasmin seemed to have hit it off, so I think that will be a draw for him. I'll keep praying that his heart will be stirred by the things I talk to him about and the things he hears at church about what God has done through Jesus."

145

"I've been praying for him too. From the changes he's seen in you, he has to be affected."

"I don't know about that, but I've learned God can do miracles. My mum and sister have been praying for me for years. Ever since my dad died I turned away from the idea of God. I didn't think a God who would let my Dad suffer and die so young, and leave my mum, my sister, and me without him, was a God who deserved for anyone to worship him. I didn't understand. From the time my dad died, I took things into my own hands. I believed it was up to me to make sure my family was provided for because God surely wasn't going to."

"You were only eleven. That's so young to carry such a burden."

"It is, and it was a messed-up understanding in my young mind."

"You must have loved your father so much."

Kieran sucked in a breath. "You have no idea. It was me and Dad against the world. I struggled to make friends when I was young. I know, it's hard to believe."

Megan chuckled and raised her hands. "I said nothing."

"It's true, and my dad was my defender and closest friend. When I was little, I preferred to read and solve math problems. My dad taught me to have fun and helped me learn to be a friend and be friendly. Otherwise, I would have been stuck in my own world. When he died...it felt like I lost part of me. In a way, I guess I did. I lost the part that wanted to follow God. I knew my dad was a Christian, but it was the one thing he taught me that I could no longer get behind. In other areas I emulated him—always being friendly and the life of the party, but also working hard and providing for my family."

The usual spark in his eyes had disappeared and the tremble of his bottom lip nearly broke Megan. "I'm sorry. I didn't mean to bring up something so sensitive."

"No, it's good. I've not spoken about my dad since...I can't remember. I shoved all my feelings down, worried that talking about them would make me seem weak. But honestly, it feels good to think about those times and share them with someone. For years my mum and sister tried to share their memories with me but I stopped them. I need to change that."

"I'm sure they would like that. It's obvious that they care for you and are overjoyed by the recent changes—you becoming a Christian especially."

"I think you're right. I have been making an effort to talk to them more than I had since the accident. I'll keep working on that. Tell me about your relationship with your mum. From the things you've said it seems you were close."

Megan took a deep breath as she thought about her relationship with her mom through the years. "Yeah, we were very close. I was an only child, and since she lost her mom not long before I was born, we were the only women in the family. When my mom was sick with her first round of breast cancer, I was little, so I remember laying on the bed with her when she didn't feel good. We entertained each other and took naps together. Even when she went into remission that first time, she made sure we spent a lot of quality time together as a family.

"The realization that we don't know how long we have on earth made a difference in our home life. Both my parents were very intentional when raising me. We came full-circle when the cancer came back. I would hang out on her bed or at her bedside in the hospital and this time we were working on her book—the one I'm finishing."

"I'm glad you had that extra time with her—especially that you had her for so long."

"I treasure that time. I know it hurts that you didn't have that much time with your dad, but one day you'll see him again and never have to say goodbye."

"I'm counting on it." He reached out and patted her shoulder. "We're a sad pair. Two people who lost parents to cancer."

"Yeah, but we also have a lot to be happy about."

"We do." He smiled. "So tell me, Megan Taylor, did you always want to write?"

"What I really always wanted to do was go to China as a missionary."

Kieran grinned. "I could see you doing that. Do you still think you'll go?"

"Maybe, but I've learned that I need to be listening carefully to God and what he calls me to do each day and in the near future. I know he called me to be a missionary, and I'm learning I can do that anywhere."

"You're doing a bang-up job with that here in England."

"Thanks. That's the thing, if I'm too focused on China, I might miss opportunities where God has placed me in the present."

"Like with me, or Yasmin and Chelsea."

"Exactly. It may be that God was just getting my attention to draw me into missions and not China specifically, or maybe he was calling me to China for the future. After I got past my initial sadness when Mom became sick the second time, I also dealt with disappointment that I wouldn't be going to China on the schedule I had given myself. Once I got past that, I realized I still had the opportunity to do ministry, just in a different country. And not only that, I could be effective more quickly here since I wouldn't have to go to language school first. In China, even after language school, it would have taken me a while to truly learn the language."

"I love your positive attitude. It makes sense now that I've studied the scriptures, but so many still struggle to get there. Your positive attitude and encouragement have helped pull me out of my own depression."

"Thanks, but more than anything, I'd say it's the Holy Spirit in you."

"That is true. The Holy Spirit lit the fire, but you brought the first spark. The Holy Spirit in you spoke to me,"

Joy welled up inside of Megan as Kieran described his transformation. "It was a gift to be part of that."

Kieran's eyes lit up. "We should celebrate."

"You becoming a Christian?"

"Celebrate you being part of me becoming a Christian and also you almost completing your co-authored book with your mom."

"It's not finished yet. I should be sending in the draft tomorrow for its final edit. They've edited most of it except for the last few chapters. I may still have some changes to make, but my part should be done next week."

"Then we should begin planning the celebration now. What do you want to do?"

"What do I want to do?"

Kieran chuckled and looked around. "Is there an echo? Yes, what kinds of things do you like to do? Is there something we could do for a day—a place you've been wanting to visit?"

"There *are* lots of places I'd like to visit around here." She clasped her hands together and twisted them. "But I think what I'd like right now, is to go back to Kingsdown for the weekend before it gets too cold."

Kieran's wide smile said he approved. "We could make some new memories that help you forget me being so grumpy there and help me forget how depressed I was there.

"If you want to stay the weekend, we should talk with Tracey to see if you can stay at their beach cottage. I'm still new at being a Christian, but I don't think it would be appropriate for us to be alone in the same cottage even if we are in separate rooms."

Megan nodded and her heart raced. Did that mean he thought of the weekend as a date?

He added, "We could even ask if Kate and Declan wanted to go with us. That might make it feel more like a celebration."

Maybe she was getting ahead of herself and he didn't mean it as a date after all. She hid her disappointment and pasted on a smile. "I love the idea. I'll talk with Kate."

Chapter Eighteen

The half-mile walk to De Clare's felt like ten knowing someone was following her. At every intersection, before crossing, Megan casually scanned the pedestrians and wondered if she'd see Stuart or Billy. The crowded sidewalks made pinpointing them difficult, and it eased her mind knowing her security team had people and cars set up at several locations along her route.

It was a path she'd taken numerous times while in London. Part of her longed to slow down and look more closely at everything—the homes, the shops, the offices. She felt the contradiction within. If she got there quickly, she could check this off her list, but at the same time, she dreaded the possibility that it might be a dead end too.

After she passed her last posted guard, she saw the door for De Clare's up ahead. They had taken every precaution and there was already a guard inside posing as a customer.

Feeling the urge to pray, she lifted up a prayer asking God to get her through this and help them find answers. With only a few steps more to her destination, she heard someone approaching quickly and shifted to the side. As she turned to make sure they could pass, the sound of a man hitting the ground startled her.

There on the ground, Kieran wrestled with Billy. Megan moved to help Kieran, who had fallen out of his wheelchair, but she was quickly swept away by one of her guards. He guided her into the waiting security van. As the van zoomed down the road, she looked back at the scene. She saw another man from the security team place Billy into a van while someone helped Kieran into his wheelchair.

"What just happened?" She spoke to no one in particular. One of the Interpol officers drove, and her guard, Elliot, sat in the back with her.

"Right now we just want to get you to safety, Miss Taylor."

"Elliot, I've told you to call me Megan. Please."

He nodded and a partial smile broke through his serious demeanor.

Megan looked outside at the passing buildings. "Why are we turning away from the house?"

"We're taking you to Scotland Yard until things are under control. Gareth will explain once we're there."

She checked her phone to see if Kieran had messaged and found three missed messages from him about five minutes before everything happened. They all said the same thing, "Don't go into De Clare's."

She messaged back.

Megan: Are you okay?

No answer.

"Does one of your guys have Kieran? Is he hurt? He's not responding to my text."

"I'm sure he's okay," the Interpol driver answered. "We had lots of men there to help."

"Lots of men? More than I knew about?"

"Gareth will explain."

How could she sit there when Kieran might be injured? She could still see Billy sprawled out on the ground and struggling with Kieran. Kieran might not be able to use his legs, but it was obvious he kept his upper body in top shape. He was holding his own with Billy. He'd worn the black wig and beard disguise, but she'd recognize him anywhere. *God, be with Kieran. Protect him.*

With only a table and four chairs, the sterile room looked like a place where police questioned suspects. They left Megan there alone, saying it was for her protection. At least they didn't take her phone.

She opened it and found her contacts before dialing her friend. "Kate, I'm so glad you answered."

"What's going on? Your voice sounds shaky. Are you okay? Did they find out something when you went to De Clare's?"

"I never got in. I'm at Scotland Yard right now. I don't know what's going on."

"What do you mean you don't know what's going on?"

Megan recounted all that happened over the last half hour, and Kate promised to get Corbyn and come there as soon as she could. Within minutes, Kate called back and said they were sending over a solicitor to make sure her legal rights were protected.

"But they're not accusing me of anything."

"I understand, but Corbyn said the police might try to make decisions that are not in your best interest. You have too much at stake. We'll be meeting you there, too, as soon as I can get the girls dropped off with Tracey. Corbyn is on his way to pick me up, so we can keep talking. I imagine that it's scary sitting there all by yourself with no answers."

"It is. Even though they said I'm here for my safety, it doesn't feel like it. At this point, the only reason I believe them is because they didn't take my phone."

"Let's talk about something fun to distract you."

"Fun..." Megan tried to shift her thoughts from what had just happened. "I'm struggling to think of anything." She rubbed her temple. "I take that back, Kieran and I were making plans—he wanted me to pick out a way to celebrate finishing my book. I told her I'd love to go back to Kingsdown before it gets too cold to enjoy. We were wondering if you and Corbyn wanted to come too for a weekend getaway without the girls. Kieran suggested I stay with you guys since he and I are both single and he wants to be respectful. He said he's trying to do the right thing as a Christian."

"Wow...that's...is there something going on officially with the two of you?"

That familiar flutter filled Megan's chest. "He's not said anything. I'm not sure he was meaning for it to seem like a date. Also, I still think he may feel like he owes me something since I led him to Christ."

"Hmm."

"What are you thinking?"

"I'm thinking that you two have been spending a lot of time together and he wants to spend more time with you. Do you feel the same about him?"

"I do, but I don't want to get my hopes up. He's a great guy. Since he became a Christian, he has pursued God with everything he has and he's no longer the depressed, angry man that yelled when we delivered food." She recalled his attitude about Reece but decided not to mention how he acted about that.

Kate chuckled. "And clearly he doesn't want to treat women the way he has in the past. I'd say he's worth giving a chance."

"He is and I want to, but I'm also worried that I won't compare to the women he's been with in the past. He's dated a supermodel and the other women pictured with him on the internet are beautiful enough to be."

"So you've been stalking him online? Seems like you want there to be something more between you."

"The cyberstalking was before I met him. After he yelled at us for delivering the food, I wanted to put a face to the voice."

"Okay. I'll let it go, but I think you underestimate yourself. You are naturally beautiful both inside and out. Those pictures you saw were women who spend so much time adorning themselves outwardly that we probably wouldn't recognize them on the street. I also doubt that any of those women have the living hope in them like you do. It lights you up in a way that sets you apart. From the way he looks at you, I think he appreciates that you are the whole package."

Tears ran down Megan's face, and she blinked them back.

"Are you okay, Megan?"

"I think all of the stress from the day has caught up with me and with your kind words...I'm feeling overwhelmed. He may not feel that way, but I appreciate you saying it."

"I'm going to hang up for a few minutes while we drop the girls off and head your way. Call me though if you need to."

"Thank you, Kate."

Her phone went silent and she stared at it, alone again. She tapped her feet and her eyes shot to the door. "I'm not alone," she whispered when she realized how wrong her thinking was. "I'm not alone," she said more loudly. "Thank you, God. You are my treasure and my protector. I don't know what is going on, but you do and I can trust you."

She opened her Bible app to Ephesians and read.

Ephesians 6:10-20 Finally, be strong in the Lord and in the strength of his might. 11 Put on the whole armor of God, that you may be able to stand against the schemes of the devil. 12 For we do not wrestle against flesh and blood, but against the rulers, against the authorities, against the cosmic powers over this present darkness, against the spiritual forces of evil in the heavenly places. 13 Therefore take up the whole armor of God, that you may be able to withstand in the evil day, and having done all, to stand firm. 14 Stand therefore, having fastened on the belt of truth, and having put on the breastplate of righteousness, 15 and, as shoes for your feet, having put on the readiness given by the gospel of peace. 16 In all circumstances take up the shield of faith, with which you can extinguish all the flaming darts of the evil one; 17 and take the helmet of salvation, and the sword of the Spirit, which is the word of God, 18 praying at all times in the Spirit, with all prayer and supplication. To that end, keep alert with all perseverance, making supplication for all the saints, 19 and also for me, that words may be given to me in opening my mouth boldly to proclaim the mystery of the gospel, 20 for which I am an ambassador in chains, that I may declare it boldly, as I ought to speak.

"Yes, Lord, help me to remember these things and to boldly proclaim the mystery of the gospel. Thank you for trusting me with it."

Her phone buzzed twice with texts from Kate and an unknown number. Kate's text informed her that a woman named Stacey Marshall was her solicitor and was about to text. It also included Stacey's number.

She glanced at the other text, and it was from Stacey's number. It informed her that she wasn't to speak to anyone or make any comments until she arrived. Stacey was currently parking.

Just as she finished reading the text, Agent Gareth came through the door.

"It seems you're at the center of quite a stir today."

Megan almost responded but remembered Stacey's text. "I have an attorney...I mean a solicitor named Stacey Marshall who is on her way in. We can talk then." She wanted so badly to ask about Kieran but decided to wait on Stacey before asking that either.

Gareth's jaw tensed, but he nodded and walked out.

Twenty minutes later, a middle-aged woman entered the room. "Megan, so nice to meet you, though I'm sorry it's under these circumstances. Corbyn speaks highly of you. I've been working with his family for years." She reached out to shake Megan's hand before joining her at the table.

"Thank you, Mrs. Marshall. I appreciate you coming so quickly. I have no idea what I should be doing. I didn't even think to get an attorney...I mean solicitor. Pardon, I'm not used to saying that."

"No problem. I knew what you meant. You have good friends to look out for you like this." Mrs. Marshall reached down into her leather messenger bag and pulled out a notepad. "I can use technology, but I also have an old-fashioned streak and like to write things down."

Grinning, Megan spoke up. "I get it. I tend to carry around notepads or journals to write in too."

"There's something about pen and paper, isn't there? Let's discuss your situation, shall we? Corbyn and Kate gave me as many details as they could think of while I drove over, but I'd like to go over them and make sure I have all of the information."

Megan nodded. "This may take a while."

Mrs. Marshall's firm but kind eyes focused on Megan. "Don't worry. We'll get this sorted out and get you out of here as quickly as possible."

Megan went through everything related to the case, beginning with the day she found out that her necklace was so valuable through the incident outside of De Clare's. Mrs. Marshall's pen scribbled away in her notepad. Now and then she would stop and ask for clarification, then resume writing furiously.

"Anything else you can think of?"

Thinking through all that she had just shared, Megan slowly shook her head. "No, wait. I do have one thing, and it's that I don't know where Kieran is. He hasn't responded to my text and that's not like him. On the way over, the driver said that Gareth, the Interpol agent, would answer my questions. By the time Gareth came to speak with me, you were in the parking lot and had just requested that I not say anything. So I still know nothing about Kieran. He's been working with Interpol, my security team, and Scotland Yard to help find the people behind all of this. Oh, and also Kieran texted me this three times while I was walking to De Clare's." Megan opened her phone and showed the text thread. "See? He said, 'Don't go into De Clare's'."

"Okay, let's get Gareth back in so we can find some answers."

Chapter Nineteen

"Kieran is fine. A couple of scrapes and bruises that our nurse took care of, but that's it. He's meeting with some of the guys here at Scotland Yard to review things," Gareth said as he entered the room.

Megan breathed a sigh of relief at the news. "Okay, that's good. Now please tell me what happened today."

"We're still trying to make sense of it all. Scotland Yard brought in Billy, Stuart, and all the staff from De Clare's for questioning. We'd not intended to go to such extremes until we had more information, but Kieran forced our hand. We do know someone in De Clare's was communicating with Billy and Stuart. I am not at liberty to say more yet. It looks like this jewelry-theft ring goes further than the person at De Clare's. We're working to find how far it goes. At this point, we have to decide if our operation is salvageable and can still help get us that information."

"That makes sense." Inside she was cheering for Kieran when Gareth said that he had forced their hand. She knew whatever he had done was for her benefit. She wanted to ask Gareth more but had the feeling she wouldn't get many details from him. "I need to speak with Kieran. Can I go to where he is?"

Gareth shifted on his feet and looked down. "I'll bring him to you."

Mrs. Marshall spoke up. "Why can't she go to him? Are you holding her here? She hasn't been charged with anything."

"Hold on, Mrs. Marshall." Gareth held up a hand. "This is for her own good. We are taking the De Clare's men in and out of interrogation rooms. We don't know which of them is working with Billy and Stuart, and we don't want them to accidentally see her. Also, if she leaves and there is someone else behind all of this, she will be exposed. I know she has a security team, but all of the Scotland Yard guys who have been working the case are here doing interrogations and making plans to lure this other person in. This is not a good time for her to go out. We need more time."

"Well, you can't keep her here indefinitely."

"We'll make it possible to get her to a safe place tonight."

Mrs. Marshall looked at Megan and back at Gareth. "Why is she at risk? Did I miss something? If the people behind this know the necklace is in the store's vault, why would they still be after her."

"That we don't know."

Megan's heart raced. "How do you know they're after me? I thought we hired security because we weren't sure if the thief knew that my pendant was in De Clare's vault."

"Kieran can explain that to you."

"Okay. And can you let my friends Kate and Corbyn come back?" They'd messaged her a while back saying they had arrived.

He checked his watch. "Yes. This place is getting to be as busy as King's Cross St. Pancras station."

When Kate and Corbyn came in, Megan rushed to hug her friend. "Thank you for getting me in contact with Mrs. Marshall. She has been such a comfort and support."

"I'm glad." Kate pulled back. "And you're okay?" When Megan nodded, she continued. "It's a madhouse out there. I thought they'd never let us back. Will you be able to go soon? They wouldn't tell us anything."

"That's partially because they don't know very much themselves. They've got all the workers from De Clare's and are trying to find out which one is working with the guys who've been following me. Gareth never said what made them realize it was someone working there. I'm guessing it's something they found on Billy or Stuart's phones."

"Billy or Stuart?" Kate questioned.

"The guys who've been following me. Kieran created an app to hack into their phones. Did I already tell you that? I can't keep up with who knows what anymore."

"It's okay. It sounds like there is still a lot that needs to happen."

"What does Kieran say?" Corbyn asked.

"I haven't spoken with him. Gareth said he's been meeting with Scotland Yard and Interpol people to go over things. He's supposed to send him in soon."

"We'll leave you then so you and he can discuss things while Stacey is here. Do you have any idea what time you'll be heading home? We can let Mum know when we pick up the girls."

"Gareth made it sound like I'll need to stay somewhere else tonight. I don't know where."

"Stay somewhere? They're still worried you're in danger?"

"They are but haven't said why."

"Oh, Megan, this has been a nightmare for you." Kate put an arm around her friend.

"Can I pray over you?" Corbyn asked.

"Yes, thank you."

Corbyn's prayer renewed Megan's courage and reminded her that God had given her a gift with these friends who would intercede for her when she needed it.

"Why don't you text me when you find out where they are taking you tonight and also when you leave here and arrive there," Kate said. "I know Scotland Yard is supposed to be keeping you safe, but I would feel better if people who care about you know where you are."

"Thanks." She gave Kate another hug. "I can give you access to my location. Half of London already has it." Megan forced a smile. "That reminds me, I haven't spoken with my dad. He has no idea what's going on."

Mrs. Marshall spoke up. "My suggestion is to speak to Kieran first so you have some answers before you contact your father. If you leave him with more questions than answers, he's going to be worried."

"You're right. I'm sure he'll still worry, but I don't need to make it worse. I've already given him enough cause to worry with all that has happened and him being an ocean away."

After saying their goodbyes, Megan asked the guard at the door to send Kieran in.

"Megan!" Kieran rolled up to her with his arms out. "Forgive me for not getting to you before now. We had to act fast on some things to try and salvage the operation." He reached for her arm and examined her from head to toe. "You're okay?"

Megan nodded but did her own inspection and noticed a bruise just beneath his left eye and one on his arm. His shirt was wrinkled and torn at the collar and his pants had dirt stains.

"I should be asking you that question. I wanted to go to you when you fell out of the chair but they grabbed me and pulled me into the van."

"I'm fine. These scrapes and bruises are nothing compared to my last accident." He smirked and pointed to his legs.

"That's not funny. It had to have hurt."

"I don't want you to worry about me. It was *your* safety that mattered at the time, and they did just what I would have done if someone else had taken Billy down and I was in their position." He tugged her towards himself, almost causing her to fall on his lap as he hugged her.

She relaxed into the hug, satisfied to know he wasn't hurt worse. A wave of peace rolled through her as he stroked her hair.

"I don't know what I would have done if he had stuck that needle into you," He whispered.

Megan pulled back and looked him in the eyes. "Needle?!"

Kieran's brow furrowed and he nodded. "I..." He looked to the side as if seeing Mrs. Marshall for the first time. "Is this your solicitor?"

"Oh." Megan stood and cleared her throat. She too had forgotten Mrs. Marshall was there. "Mrs. Marshall, this is Kieran. Kieran, Mrs. Stacey Marshall, my...solicitor." Mrs. Marshall smiled at Megan as she stopped herself from saying "lawyer."

Kieran and Mrs. Marshall shook hands before they all joined around the table.

Mrs. Marshall spoke up. "What is this about a needle?"

Megan had momentarily forgotten about that. It was good she was sitting. She'd seen so many needles with her mom's illness that just the mention of them made her woozy.

"The needle is why I knocked Billy down." He laid both hands on the table. "Sorry, I thought they would have talked to you about it by now. I need to start at the beginning. Did you see my last three messages?"

"I did. Why didn't you respond when I messaged back?"

"If you mean after the incident, it's because my mobile flew into the road and was run over when I went after Billy. They were supposed to tell you I was okay." He motioned to the door.

"Gareth did eventually, but I needed to hear it from you." When he frowned she added, "Now that I see you, I feel better. Please, go on with the story."

"All I can say is that God intervened from start to finish. I had a bad feeling about your visit today, so I had extra security guys watching you. This morning I spoke with Gareth, and he said those names from the benefit looked like a dead end. We still had our eye on Peter, but I didn't think that would amount to anything.

"After speaking with Gareth, we brought in Scotland Yard and decided to have even more boots on the ground today. We had vans parked in locations on your path and an undercover officer in the store in addition to your security guys already stationed there and on the road. While we were waiting, I searched that jewelry sale site on the dark web, and this time it showed your necklace."

"What? How?"

"Exactly. However it got there, it had to have something to do with De Clare's. I messaged the team. Theoretically, we had plenty of men in place while you walked to De Clare's, but I couldn't sit by and take a chance, so I got out of the van and followed you and Billy." His eyes went to the door and his head shook. "Gareth was angry, saying I was going to blow our cover, but honestly, my only concern was you. I did have my disguise on so I wouldn't attract extra attention.

"Gareth's priority is to find whoever is the head of this stolen jewelry ring, but mine is to make sure *you're* safe. It's a good thing I followed God's nudging because Billy came at you with what we've now discovered is a tranquilizer syringe. Who knows what his plan was after that? Stuart was in a getaway car. It didn't look good."

Megan's hand went to her chest and Mrs. Marshall gasped.

"It doesn't make sense that they'd be after me. I told Gareth the same thing. If Billy and Stuart were working with someone from De Clare's, then they know I don't have the necklace. Why me?"

"That's what we're trying to discover. For now, we have to keep you safe. I'm glad you've had the security with you all this time or there is no telling what might have happened. Let's get Gareth back in here and see where they plan to take you for your protection. I'd like to get you there sooner rather than later, and I want to make sure it's somewhere comfortable." He scanned the room. "This is about the least hospitable place you could be after such a traumatic experience." Kieran turned back to the table. "What about you, Mrs. Marshall? Do you have other things you need to find out while you're here?"

"I'd like to know what they've done with her necklace. Is it still at De Clare's, and if so, can they trust that it's secure? Obviously, their security has been compromised by one of the employees. I'd also like an update on what they've discovered about De Clare's employee involvement. But most importantly, I want to know how they plan to keep her safe."

Kieran nodded. "That's my top priority too. They've had people at De Clare's all afternoon, and they've brought in jewelry experts to go through the vaults and check for authenticity of the items."

"Authenticity? Did they not check the items' authenticity when they were deposited like they did with mine?" As soon as Megan said that, her stomach tightened and queasiness overtook her. "You think someone might be replacing the originals with forgeries?"

Kieran pressed his lips together. "It's a possibility. Several artisans work for the company."

Megan rubbed her chest and softly spoke. "I hope mine hasn't been replaced. It's not the financial value that matters to me."

"I know." Kieran reached for her hand and squeezed. "If it's not there, we have high hopes of getting it back since it was just now posted online. I'll be assisting them every way I can. Earlier I helped Interpol scour the mobiles of the employees. In the meantime, we've got to get you out of London. Is there a place you would prefer to go if they give you a choice? Somewhere at least an hour from London and not a place that you've been before."

Megan swallowed down her anxiety and tried to focus on his question. "This could be a chance to see something new. Give me a few minutes to think." Megan opened her phone map to England, zoomed in, and scanned the names of the surrounding areas. An epiphany hit her. "What about just north of Exeter in Devon?"

"What's north of Exeter that you want to see?" said Keiran.

"That's where the Dashwoods moved when their brother requested they leave Norland Park in *Sense and Sensibility*."

Kieran blinked and looked from Megan to Mrs. Marshall then back. "Did you just speak in another language?"

"Funny. Surely you know of Jane Austen."

He nodded.

"The Dashwood sisters are the heroines of Jane's book, *Sense and Sensibility*. It's my favorite book, and I started reading it again just before my life went sideways with all of this pendant drama. I've been so distracted that I've laid it aside. If I'm going to have to stay somewhere for a few days, I think I'd like to go there and finish reading my book. It looks like a peaceful area with a variety of places for day trips and activities. There's a river nearby, the coast is only about an hour away, and the town of Exeter seems like it would have anything I could need."

"Sounds perfect. I'm going with you," Kieran said.

"You are?"

"Yes. Gareth already suggested that you have two guards with you at a safe house, and that's fine, but I'm not leaving you alone with the two guards. I'm going. That's also about three and a half hours from here which is too far to get to you quickly if you need me. I'll speak with Gareth and make sure we find a place that is handicapped accessible."

"Kieran, I can't expect you to give up your life while I'm there." Though she would love to spend more time with him.

"You're not asking and I'm not giving anything up. I work with computers. I can do that from anywhere. And you should remember, if it weren't for you, I'd have no life."

Megan frowned. "So you feel like you owe me? I don't keep a tally. You owe me nothing. And you've already put so much effort into all of this."

Kieran looked across the table at Mrs. Marshall. "Could we have a few minutes alone?"

Mrs. Marshall smiled and gave a knowing look. "Sure. I'll go see if they've found Megan's pendant. Good to meet you, Kieran. Megan, I'll come back before leaving and let you know if I have any news."

"Thank you." When the door closed, Kieran turned back to Megan and grabbed her hand. "Megan, you mean a lot to me. I don't feel like I owe you. I'm being selfish. I need to know you are okay and that everything possible is done to keep you safe. Doing this is not a burden. Staying here when I'm worried about you would feel like a burden."

Megan searched his eyes. "Do you really think I'm in danger?"

"I don't know and I'm not taking any chances. If you don't want me there, I'll make sure it's a big house and try to stay out of your way."

She shook her head. "It's not that. If you feel so strongly, of course you can come. I'd love to have you there. How can you think otherwise?" A mix of emotions tore through her. His desire to protect her and be with her made her happy, but it was tempered by the concern on his face which had her worried she was in grave danger.

"We agree then. Let's look at places in that area of Devon and see what we can find." He pulled out his computer and within minutes had several rental websites open.

Chapter Twenty

Dreams of being chased by a faceless man with a needle gave Megan a restless night of sleep, and when she woke, she couldn't go back to sleep. After studying her Bible and praying, Megan sifted through her suitcase to see what Kate had packed for her the day before. Considering how rushed Kate had been when Megan explained the plan to leave for Devon after dinner, Megan wasn't sure what she would find, but she was pleased with what Kate selected. They didn't let Megan go back to the house herself for security reasons.

With the village of Cowley three and a half hours from London, they'd been anxious to get on the road the previous day and settled in at the cottage before it was late. It was dark when they arrived, but from what she could tell, the home was idyllic. It had two stories and stone covering the lower level of the exterior with stucco above. With its hipped roof, it looked just like the cottages she'd always imagined herself visiting in the English countryside. The inside was modernized with all the necessary amenities. Best of all, it was set apart from other homes on several acres and looked quite peaceful...and safe.

Before leaving Scotland Yard the day before, the jewelry appraiser confirmed that the necklace in De Clare's vault was the original she had given them. All of the jewels from the De Clare vault, including Megan's, were taken offsite to a high-security safe deposit vault while the investigation continued. That news removed much of her stress. She would have to trust her guards and Kieran to keep her safe until they knew why she had been targeted.

Leaving town was best for her, as well as the safety of her friends, but it was still stressful. Determined to make the best of the hard situation, Megan scoured the internet for things to do and the top restaurants in the area. Once dressed for the day, she went downstairs to figure out a plan for breakfast. She was pleasantly surprised by the smell of bacon and eggs.

"Good morning," she called out to Shaw, one of her guards who was busy at the stove.

He turned his head. "Morning. I went out for groceries and am finishing up fried eggs. Care for some brekkie?"

"How nice. Thanks." She peered into the sitting room. "Have you seen Kieran?"

"Workout room. Want to tell him breakfast is ready?" Shaw removed the pan from the hot eye and pulled another pan out of the oven. It was filled with bacon, tomatoes, and toast.

"Yes, I'll get him." She eyed the food, suddenly hungrier than she was when she came down. "That looks delicious. Which way is it?"

"Just at the end of the hall. The door facing you." He pointed to a long hall with a door at the end, and Megan headed that way.

During her brief tour the night before, she'd somehow missed the workout room. She had seen the two bedrooms off of the hall. One had twin beds that Kieran and Shaw claimed. The second had a queen bed, and Phoebe, the other guard, slept there. The guards strongly suggested Megan take the upstairs room for her protection. She'd seen them setting up portable perimeter cameras soon after they arrived. Between their care and Kieran's skills, she felt well taken care of.

Megan opened the door and found Kieran sitting on one of the machines, working his upper body. His eyes were closed and his arm muscles rippled as he strained to push the handles of the machine up. She'd seen signs of his strength before and wasn't surprised. Blushing, she cleared her throat then looked around the room at the exposed whitewashed brick contrasted with a shiny new-looking wood floor.

"Megan."

She glanced Kieran's way and blushed more as he wiped his face with the hem of his shirt. "Breakfast is ready," she called out before turning on her heels.

Before she closed the door, she heard him chuckle then call out, "I'll just be a few minutes in the shower first."

After a hearty English breakfast, Megan invited her new roommates to join her in the sitting room so she could show them the places she wanted to visit. There were several sites in Exeter, and the nearby coast had some lovely towns.

"Can we all go?" she questioned.

Shaw and Phoebe looked at each other, and Phoebe nodded before saying, "Since the security cameras seem to be working, I think that's fine. Kieran, I would suggest you take your computer in case something comes up and we need more than our mobiles."

"That was my plan." He shifted in his wheelchair. "I checked in with Gareth before my workout, and he said it looks like Bernard Blake is the only one from De Clare's who was involved. He's been creating forgeries of the jewelry and selling the originals. He left the forgeries in the vaults. We're lucky yours wasn't gone yet. I don't know how many of the other original pieces have already been sold."

"Mr. Blake?" A mixture of hurt and anger welled up inside of Megan as she thought about the man's deceit. "I trusted him. How could he? He's the face of the store right now since the owner is old and unable to be there. I wonder how long this has been going on? Does the owner not have anything to do with it?" Her mind fired in so many different directions.

"Gareth said the owner had no idea and is devastated, especially since Bernard is married to his cousin's daughter."

"I remember Mr. Blake mentioned he was related to the owner. This makes me so mad." She clenched her fists, then an idea popped into her head. "Does this mean we can go home now that they know who did it?" Tension dissipated from her body at the thought.

"Afraid not. Bernard Blake said he didn't have anything to do with hiring Stuart and Billy, and he was just the middleman. The men have never seen the person who hired them, so they can't corroborate or deny his story and don't have any more information. Bernard offered to help

Interpol in their search for the ring leader if they cut a deal with him. Gareth will let me know if they make any progress. The bottom line is that we still need to be on high alert protecting you."

"Oh. I had hoped it was over." She fiddled with the edge of her sleeve as the tension returned. "I feel so violated."

"I'd like to pray for you and this situation." Kieran looked at Phoebe and Shaw. "I want to pray for the two of you too if that's okay."

Phoebe and Shaw nodded and Kieran prayed that God would protect them and give Megan peace. He also prayed for a breakthrough in the case.

The vaulted ceiling in Exeter Cathedral took Megan's breath away. She craned her neck up to scan its details and imagined what it was like to worship in such a majestic place.

"I don't need to be somewhere so grand to worship God," Megan whispered to Kieran, "but it would be amazing. It makes me think of being before the throne of God in heaven."

Kieran smiled at her like she was the best thing he had ever seen, and her heart took flight. The more these moments occurred between them, the more she found herself hoping he had similar feelings. He was the bright spot in this bad situation.

As they toured the cathedral she studied the facts on the plaques.The elaborate Gothic details like the ribbed vaults and pointed arches were added about the time her necklace was made around the late twelve hundreds. Her hand automatically went to her neck and she deflated. Would she ever have the chance to wear it again? Kieran caught her gaze and, judging from his look, guessed her thoughts.

Except when driving, Phoebe and Shaw stayed separate from Keiran and Megan so they could keep an eye on the surroundings and protect

Megan if necessary. Megan appreciated that the two took their job seriously. She prayed that she would have opportunities to talk with them about God.

Museum visits, driving around town, shopping on quaint narrow cobbled streets, and eating filled their day. After their early dinner, Megan was ready to return to the cottage and explore.

"Do you feel like one of Austen's characters?" Kieran questioned as he and Megan sat surrounded by a lush garden to the side of the cottage.

Megan grinned and scanned their surroundings. "I do. This house is probably just like the place the Dashwood sisters lived." Sipping her Earl Grey tea, this was the most relaxed she'd felt since nearly being attacked the day before. "The grounds here are beautiful. It feels so peaceful and secluded."

"Those were the two things I wanted for you, so I'm glad you're pleased." He nodded towards the book on the table. "Go ahead and read more about the adventures of those Dashwood sisters."

He had coaxed Megan into reading *Sense and Sensibility* to him while they were at the cottage. She picked it up and continued from where she left off moments before. "Oh, you'll like this part about Colonel Brandon." She chuckled.

"I will? Something about that smirk on your face says I might feel otherwise. Go on then."

"'He was silent and grave. His appearance, however, was not unpleasing, in spite of his being in the opinion of Marianne and Margaret, an absolute old bachelor, for he was on the wrong side of five-and-thirty; but though his face was not handsome, his countenance was sensible and his address was—'"

"The wrong side of five-and-thirty? An absolute old bachelor? I know I was doing life all wrong before becoming a Christian, but this makes it sound like my life is over. Too late I suppose to marry." His eyes lit up and he tried to hide his smile.

"Yes, too bad for you since that is your age exactly. I suppose you are destined to a solitary existence unless those around you feel compassionate." Why did he mention marriage?

He quirked a brow and his face became serious. "Maybe *you* might feel compassionate towards me."

The flutters inside became a herd of elephants rampaging over her heart. "Kieran... what are you saying?"

"I'm saying I think something special is happening between us, and though my thirty-five is much older than your twenty-six, I wonder if you would be willing to date me?"

She took a deep breath and tried to calm herself enough to answer, but before she could, he added, "And just so you know, I've been speaking with Declan about how to approach dating as a Christian. I'm sure you've heard that I don't have a good track record dating women. I haven't treated them with the honor and respect I should have. I want to do things better for you."

His words were more than she had hoped for as she'd recently begun to acknowledge her feelings for him. "You do?"

He nodded. "You're worth my very best."

Swoon. "Yes, I think my twenty-six would be more than happy with your thirty-five." Perhaps she'd found her Colonel Brandon after all.

His face lit up as he reached for her hand and lifted it to his mouth to place a gentle kiss on her palm. "I'm sorry it's taken so long for me to ask. I've wanted to for a while, but so much was happening in your life that I felt I should wait. After talking it over with Declan, I realized we don't know what tomorrow will bring. It seems new things just keep popping up, and hiding my feelings for you was getting hard."

"I'm glad you asked. I've felt the same way. This is a bright spot in all the darkness surrounding my life lately."

"I've also thought about your desire to be a missionary, and I want you to know that I won't hold you back. If you feel like God is nudging you to go to China or elsewhere, I have the flexibility to work from anywhere."

Was he saying what she thought he was? She looked into his eyes and searched for answers.

"Yes, it means what you think." He smiled. "I'm not asking you to marry me now, but I'm entering this relationship with that as the end goal. I hope that doesn't make you uncomfortable. We can go as slow as you want, though I have to admit that after communicating with you for months before we met, I feel like I was a goner from the moment I saw you on our video call. This is new for me, but I want to do things right, and dating serves no purpose if we aren't considering a future together."

Everything within her leapt at his words. Dating anyone, much less Kieran, seemed so far away only weeks ago—she'd not let herself think about it because she didn't want to be deterred from her plans. She never imagined finding a man who loved her and would follow her wherever God led. But now the very man she hadn't been able to get out of her mind or heart was saying everything she needed to hear.

"Does that scare you? I'm not asking you to commit to forever right now but to keep an open mind."

He fidgeted with his napkin and his smile tightened. For the first time since the day they met in person, Kieran seemed nervous.

"Kieran, yes, my answer is still yes."

"And...you don't feel hindered by my paralysis? I have to have help with things occasionally, and I can't go everywhere easily."

Megan chuckled. "Yesterday you proved you can manage more than most men. You were the one who brought my attacker down while I was guarded by several men with four functioning limbs. I trust that you are more than enough for me."

Kieran's face tensed, and it reflected the thoughts she'd had of what could have happened.

"We were having a beautiful moment. I'll not spoil it." Megan shook her head and grabbed the book. "Where was I?" She resumed reading, trying to push all of the worries away. *God, help me.*

The sun began to set and she couldn't suppress her yawn.

Kieran looked at his watch. "It's not yet eight, but you might need extra rest after yesterday's events. Are you ready to head inside?"

"You're right. I didn't sleep well last night." Her dreams of being chased flashed in her mind.

They locked eyes and she saw his concern. She didn't mean to worry him.

Kieran rested his hand on top of hers. "Maybe tonight you'll have sweet dreams of a man in a wheelchair who...cares about you deeply."

Warmth radiated from her hand, and she lost herself in his beautiful green eyes. He knew her so well. "I think I'd like those dreams."

Chapter Twenty-One

Megan woke feeling energized the next morning and realized she'd slept without any fitful dreams. Hopping out of bed, she rushed to get ready so she could spend time with Kieran. Once again breakfast smells greeted her, but it was Phoebe standing over the stove.

"Good morning! I don't seem to be able to beat you and Shaw up in the mornings. I'd love to make breakfast for everyone too."

"Good morning, Megan. It's no trouble. We take turns keeping an eye on things through the night, so one of us is always up. May as well find something to keep busy with."

"Well...thank you. I'm happy to help."

Phoebe turned to her and smiled. "You can set the table."

"Of course." Megan gathered the flatware and napkins to take them to the dining room where she was greeted by a beautiful bouquet filled with red roses and a mixture of other flowers that looked like they were freshly plucked from an idyllic British garden. Lavender, pink, and white flowers complemented the roses. "Where did these come from?" she called to Phoebe.

"Look at the card."

Her heart leapt in anticipation and hope when she saw her name written in Kieran's handwriting on the small envelope. She pulled the card out and read the words.

Megan,

I'm overjoyed that you consider me worthy to date. Our beginning is unusual, but it will be uniquely ours. I look forward to every minute with you.

Yours, Kieran

She pressed the card to her heart and turned towards the hallway to see if he was working out. When she entered, he was there doing leg exercises on the floor with a strap this time. She watched as he extended his leg and pulled it in with a strap looped around his foot, then he slid his leg out to the side and back. He repeated the combination before he realized she was there and his face lit up.

"Megan, good morning. I'm almost finished here, then I'd love to join you for breakfast."

"That would be nice. Thank you for the flowers. They're beautiful."

"My pleasure. It was the least I could do considering that our relationship is starting during such unusual circumstances."

"It's kind of nice, though, since we have so much time together."

"It is nice. There's a positive in this situation after all."

Megan couldn't stop grinning. "God gives good gifts."

"That he does."

"Look at that!" Megan pointed ahead of the kayak as they toured the coast just south of Exeter. "It's beautiful!" They were headed towards an enormous natural arch formation that rose from the ocean. "The beaches I grew up going to are nothing like this. No cliffs or rock formations. Just flat and sandy."

"It is beautiful. I think the southern coast has some of the most unique landscapes."

As they glided underneath the arch, Megan looked up. "I feel so small." Her voice echoed. "Things like this remind me how small I am in comparison to God and all that he is doing. Yet he still cares about the details of my life."

"I'm starting to realize that. It's helped me let go of the anger I held towards him about letting my dad die and about my injuries."

She laid her paddle down and twisted around to see Kieran. She wanted to look into his eyes and see the light that shined in them when he spoke of his newfound hope in God.

He gave her a grin and continued to paddle. "You're welcome to take a break from paddling. I've got this."

"Thanks. Are you sure? I turned around just to see you, but my arms are getting tired."

"Of course. That's why I work out, you know." He chuckled. "So I can shuttle my girlfriend around in a kayak."

"Girlfriend. I like that."

"Good, get used to it." His gaze shifted from her. "Look over to the right on those rocks."

Megan looked, and there lounging on an outcropping of large flat rocks were several seals. "I've never seen them out in the wild before. Only in a zoo." One sat up and looked at them as they passed. "Hey, big guy. How's your day going? Any new fish in the sea?" Kieran chuckled behind her.

As they turned back to follow the guide, she saw Phoebe and Shaw in their kayak and was reminded why they were there—not that she could forget with Kieran wearing his wig.

Kieran had been doing more work with Interpol on her case, but they'd still not found the person behind it all. The rest of the afternoon, she tried to keep those thoughts at bay so she could enjoy the sights. Yet now and then they crept in and she would glance around, wondering if anyone was following them. The day before, the guards said they had not seen anything suspicious since they left London. Along with constant prayer, this news helped calm her fears.

Strolling and rolling along the boardwalk overlooking the coast after kayaking, two small children playing in the sand with their parents caught Megan's eye. They tossed a beach ball around. She smiled as she remembered beach time with her parents. "Did you go to the beach with your parents when you were young?"

"Yeah. We usually went to Kingsdown because it was the closest. That was part of why I bought the cottage out there. So many memories. When I was little, I always thought I'd like to have one of the cottages overlooking the water so I could go to the shore any time."

The beach ball bounced their way. Kieran caught it and threw it back. "Megan." Sadness shone in his eyes.

"What?" She glanced around, wondering if he had seen something.

"I should have brought this up before...The doctors have said it may be difficult for me to have children. Not that it's impossible, but . . ."

"Oh." She'd always loved children and imagined it would be wonderful to be a mom, yet it had seemed like something far in the future.

"Do you want children? I don't want to set you up for disappointment."

"I love children, but I've been so focused on ministry and knew that I might never marry. So I didn't set my heart on having children to be happy."

"Are you sure? If you start to have doubts please let me know. There's always adoption too." He smiled, but his brow was furrowed.

Megan's heart raced as she thought about a future with Kieran. "Yes, adoption seems like such a wonderful thing. I would be on board with that." He seemed so worried that his handicap would keep him from being enough for her, but it was obvious he was more than capable of caring for her and even children. She looked into his beautiful green eyes and imagined having the rest of her life to stare into them. Yes, she could see a life with him.

She reached down and grabbed his hand, interlacing her fingers with his as they continued along the coast. "Kieran, you are more than enough for me."

During an early dinner at a restaurant overlooking an inlet on the River Exe, they feasted on a variety of shellfish.

Kieran moved closer to Megan and placed an arm around the back of her chair. "I like that you have a hearty appetite and we have similar tastes."

"Is that your way of saying I'm a pig?"

"Not at all. You eat a normal amount and a good variety of things like a person should. I've been out with way too many women who practically starve themselves by only eating a small salad or vegetables. I like being able to order appetizers to share or splitting more than one meal like we did so we can try a variety of things. In fact, I'm counting on us ordering two desserts to share because they all look so good. I hope you'll indulge me."

"Well, if that is what will satisfy you, I guess I should take a look at that dessert menu."

He winked at her. "Now we're talking. Have you ever had banoffee pie? Or maybe you're a chocolate ganache tart kind of girl. I also imagine their sticky toffee pudding is good."

Megan bit her lip and tried not to laugh. "Now you're just teasing me. I've had sticky toffee pudding before and it was delicious. Chocolate is always a winner for me too."

"Noted." He gave her another wink.

"And I'm always interested in trying new things like banoffee pie."

"Three desserts it is then."

"That's too much."

He slipped his arm up to her shoulder and pulled her close. "I think not. We can take the leftovers home for later."

"If you say so. You're the one who is usually so conscious about healthy eating."

Kieran's phone vibrated and his face became serious as he read a text.

"Kieran, what is it?"

"They've made contact with the seller by posing as a buyer for your necklace. In about," he looked at his watch, "three and a half hours, I'll need to get online and help them do a trace. Hopefully, we can get to the bottom of things."

Megan wholeheartedly agreed with that sentiment.

Megan wore a path across the floor of the sitting room. Kieran was in his room hacking into the conversation between the person Interpol had posing as a jewelry buyer and the person selling the jewelry. She'd prefer to sit with him and watch, but if their roles were reversed that would keep her from thinking clearly.

Before he went online, he explained that the phones for Mr. Blake, Billy, and Stuart were all still being used to communicate with this person to keep the person from knowing they had been discovered. Through Billy and Stuart's phones, they told the person they lost track of Megan. The hope was that with her out of town, the person wouldn't know where to start looking even if they hired someone else.

Unfortunately, so far the communications between the three men's phones and the person in charge's phone had been untraceable. Kieran hoped with the online interactions, he would have a better chance to locate the person.

"God, please break the case open so we can find out who is behind this. Reveal the things that are hidden. Thwart those who would harm me and others. Hold them accountable for their actions. Give Kieran and everyone working on this wisdom as they search for this person or people. Convict the hearts of the men who have been arrested. In Jesus' name, amen."

Feeling more settled, she sat on a sofa with her journal and decided to write about her day instead of dwelling on what Kieran was doing. Memories of their time together quickly turned her sadness into joy and she thanked God for the gift of Kieran.

Never in her wildest dreams would she have imagined herself dating the handsome man who made her heart race. She thought back to those first pictures of him she saw on the internet. *Dreamy* was how she would describe him, but at the time, she knew him only for his bad qualities and they negated all of his physical beauty.

Then there was Jean whom she had been messaging and starting to find herself attracted to because of his personality and the way he had been drawing nearer to God. She had known he was close to becoming a Christian.

Megan was still stunned by the way God brought everything together and that both men were one and the same. The best qualities of both had risen to the surface and left the man she was falling in love with—or perhaps had already fallen for. She fell back against the sofa.

"I'm already there, aren't I?" she softly spoke to God, the one who had orchestrated it all, and a smile rose to her face.

A loud noise in Kieran's room pulled her from her reverie, and moments later he passed through the door with a storm brewing in his eyes.

"I lost him," he bit out. "This guy is good. He covers his tracks." He began rolling his wheelchair back and forth across the room much like her pacing earlier. "I feel like we're at a dead end. He wants to be paid with Monero and wants it put into an escrow account."

When he looked up and saw her confusion he added, "Monero is a cryptocurrency like Bitcoin, but harder to trace. Once it goes into the escrow, there's no way we will find out who he is. We will have just thrown away millions. He never has to show his face because he assumes Blake is putting the jewelry in a safety deposit box, then he would just send the buyer, us, there to get it. He would be completely hands-off. I don't like this one bit. There has to be a weakness somewhere—some way we can get him to come out of hiding."

Kieran came to a stop and looked at Megan. "I'm sorry. I shouldn't be saying all this in front of you. I'm supposed to be protecting you, not leaving you scared right before bed."

"No, I don't want you to keep things from me. We need to start learning to bear burdens together, don't you think?"

He furrowed his brow and held her gaze.

"You were the one who said we need to be looking towards marriage," she persisted and his face softened, then he rolled to her.

"You're right. I'm not used to this kind of relationship. What we had before we started our relationship was already much deeper than any relationship I've ever had."

"I'm new to this too, remember. We're figuring it out together."

He reached for her hands and began caressing them. "True, but I want so much to make this all go away. I want to know that you're safe. I can't imagine losing another person that I love." His eyes went wide and Megan's heart flipped. "I didn't mean for it to come out like that. You must think I'm crazy." He rubbed a hand over his face and left it there.

"If you're crazy, then I am too."

Kieran slid his hand down and looked at her with sad, hopeful eyes.

Megan nodded and smiled. "I was just having that very conversation with God before you walked in. I love you too, Kieran."

His face relaxed. "You love me? I thought I might have just scared you away with it only being the second day since we started dating." When she shook her head, his face lit up. "You love me. Thank you, God! Megan, I love you so much. I think I started falling in love with you the moment you said 'Goodbye, Mr. Davies' loud enough for me to hear, that day you delivered my food alone.

"I'd already seen how beautiful you were when I watched you from the window playing with Kate's girls. You were so carefree and lovely. I could tell that they were enamored with you. Even if we can't have biological children, I want to adopt so you have the chance to share all of that loveliness with others. You'll be an amazing mum. I love you." He lifted her hand and kissed it, then his eyes found her lips.

Her heart leapt.

Kieran leaned towards her then stopped. "May I kiss you?"

"I..." She didn't want to hold back, but..."I always thought my first kiss would be when I got engaged." She never imagined how hard it would be to wait once she fell in love.

His brows rose. "You've never been kissed?" He leaned his forehead against hers. "Megan, I've never wanted to kiss a woman as badly as I do right now, but I want your first kiss to be exactly the way you imagined." He pulled back and she thought she heard a groan deep in his throat.

"I'm sure it seems silly to you. You've probably kissed so many times that it's no big deal." She stopped herself and scrunched her nose. "Sorry, that sounded bad. I didn't mean to make it sound like you're some kind of awful person."

Kieran chuckled softly. "No, there's nothing to be sorry for. It's the truth. I've kissed too many women. I'm sure Kate told you the story of what I did when she turned down my offer to date. I brought a woman home and kissed her right when I knew Kate was watching. That was the kind of person I was before. I had no physical boundaries with women. Though I'd like to think I treated them well when I was with them, the truth is that I did...much more than kissing, without the least inclination to marry them. Looking back, I see it was more than disrespectful.

"I bought into the world's definition of what relationships should be like and figured that was good enough. At the time, the physical aspect of a relationship was all I had to give because I was so broken.

"So as much as I want to kiss you right now and as much as I will struggle in days to come not to—" He raised his hand when she made a pouty face. "Just being honest. I will wait because you are worth it." He lowered his voice and whispered into her ear, "But just you wait until we're engaged. I'll be kissing you until your lips are raw."

She giggled.

"You think that's funny? I'm giving you fair warning. If that's not what you want, you'd best break things off with me right now." He leaned back and folded his arms.

She bit back a smile before speaking. "Kieran. I love you, and once we're engaged I give you full permission to kiss my lips raw." She burst out laughing, not able to contain herself.

"Good, we agree." He held out a hand for her to shake on it and then pulled it to his lips to kiss.

Chapter Twenty-Two

Megan pushed the bar up on the exercise machine and felt her muscles wobble. She was trying to stay busy while Kieran worked on her case. After seeing him so frustrated the night before, she hoped he had a breakthrough today. A noise drew her eyes up, and there he was—her green-eyed boyfriend.

"Do you have time to talk?"

"Sure. I'm just trying to keep up with my boyfriend."

His furrowed brow softened and he gave her a wink.

"I've done about all I can, which isn't much. I was lifting the bar with no weight added and still got tired." She stood and walked to him. "The sitting room?"

He nodded and followed her while explaining his call with Gareth. "I spoke with Gareth and we came up with some ideas. One was for me to message our suspect from Bernard Blake's number to try to pull more information out of him about you."

"Me?"

"Yeah. When I did it, I told the person I, as in Bernard, had some ideas about how to find you and asked what I should do. I was trying to get a feel for what he was thinking, hoping he would clue me into why he's after you."

"Good idea."

He motioned for her to sit, then rolled beside her. "Wait until you hear his response. He told me that it was up to me and that he wasn't concerned about you."

"Why would he say that? What could that mean?"

"I think it means Bernard is the one who wanted to get to you. I then messaged the person and asked if he would back me up if I came up with a new plan to go after you, and he said that was the agreement for the pendant and he would keep his end of the bargain."

"It doesn't make sense that Mr. Blake would be after me." Megan tried to imagine what Bernard's aim was. "Is he just some sick man who enjoys harming people? Or maybe he was worried that I would keep asking to physically see my necklace and recognize that it was a fake."

Kieran rubbed his hand over his face. "Oh, he's sick all right. I'd prefer not to imagine what he planned if they had caught you, but I do think he was trying to keep you away from that fake necklace once he switched them. Regardless, it makes me wonder what else he's lied about. I think he needs more questioning and I plan to be there for it."

"So can we all go back to London then if it was Mr. Blake?"

"No. You need to stay here." He shook his head and pinched the bridge of his nose. "Sorry. Please. I don't mean to make demands, but I don't want to take a chance until we are sure that's what the conversation meant. Also, there is still a chance that some sort of backup plan was in place. I don't like the idea of leaving you for the day, but I don't see a reason to take any chances."

"Okay. I trust you."

"I've also spoken to Phoebe and she is going to train you in self-defense while I'm gone. Regardless of what happens with this, I want you to be prepared in the future."

"I can do that." Megan wanted to lighten the moment. "If you stay the night in London, we'll have to talk on the phone so I can read more of our book to you."

Kieran rubbed a hand down her arm and smiled. "Yes, I'm anxious to find out how poor *old* Colonel Brandon fares with Marianne. I realize Edward is supposed to be the hero in this story, but I think Brandon is the one who shines through. Edward is just pushed around by all the women in his life."

"Shh." Megan glanced around the room as if sharing a secret. "Don't dare let other women hear you speak ill of *the* Edward Ferrars."

"Is that right?" He smirked. "You think women might decide I'm the worst kind of scoundrel if I speak ill of our dear Edward Ferrars?"

"Yes, I'd say so."

"I think I've figured you out enough to know that Brandon is the one who would capture your heart."

"I have to admit I'm drawn to a more mature man who stands up for those in need." She leaned into him, already dreading him leaving for London.

"Bernard Blake is still lying. I could see it in his eyes. I told him what I texted to the ring leader and Bernard still insisted he had nothing to do with Billy and Stuart coming after you."

Megan heard the tension in Kieran's voice through the phone and knew he was on edge but had no idea what to say. She silently asked God for wisdom. "We'll keep praying that God will show us what's next."

"I think I'll speak with De Clare's owner. Maybe he has some insight about how to get Bernard to talk. I can't speak with Bernard's wife. She thinks he's out of town working with the government on something top secret and has no idea it's because he's been arrested."

"Speaking with the owner is a good idea. Mr. Blake acted like he was dealing with dementia or something, but I'm guessing that was a lie to keep him away from the people he's stealing from." She recalled the time she'd asked Mr. Blake about the owner.

"True. Keeping the items away from his employer's eyes so he didn't know what was supposed to be in the vaults would have given Bernard Blake more control." He sighed. "I'm sorry, that's enough negativity. There's nothing else I can do tonight."

"I've been praying for him."

"Who?"

"Mr. Blake."

"Bernard Blake? The one who started this whole thing with your necklace?"

"Yes. I'm praying God will convict him that what he did was wrong and he'll come forward with more helpful information. I'm also praying that when he realizes how wrong he is, he will turn to Jesus."

"You're a good woman. I don't know if I could do that. I've missed you. Tell me about your day."

"First, I made the final edits to my book. My part is done."

"Congratulations! My girlfriend is an author."

"Thank you."

"You said that was first. What else did you do?"

"This afternoon, we drove around the countryside and had a picnic by the river. It felt very Austenish."

"Austenish. Sounds nice. I hate that I missed it."

"Yes. It would have been perfect if my boyfriend had been there. Oops, I forgot, no more negative talk. Actually, it was just a practice picnic, so I'll have a plan for when my boyfriend can go."

"I like that idea. Have you spoken with your dad? How has he been handling this situation? When I first spoke to him about the plan to bring you here, he was upset with himself for being so far away when you were attacked."

"He's okay. His church family has been rallying around him knowing that he's had a hard year with Mom and now with me. They had a time of prayer for him the other day."

"That's good. And he's still able to work?"

"He keeps pushing through. I know it's hard for him though."

"Yeah, I can't imagine being so far away and knowing my daughter was going through all of this."

"Lots of prayer."

"And maybe even some fasting. In fact, I'm considering a day of fasting this weekend if we still haven't made progress. I've been studying about fasting and how it was used in the Bible. It was always to draw near to God and often to seek his wisdom and help in a situation. If ever there was a need for his wisdom and help, it's now."

"What a good idea. I've never fasted from food but have often thought about it. I should fast tomorrow and petition God about your meeting with the owner of De Clare's. I'll also be praying for you as you try to figure out what to do next."

"Thank you. Be sure to drink plenty of water. You'll just do it until dinner tomorrow, right?"

"Is that your way of telling me that's what you would like me to do?"

"Yeah. It's probably a good idea with it being your first time, and especially with you being away from home. If anything went wrong... Well, I just don't know how I would handle it if you got sick and I wasn't there."

"Aww. That's sweet. I won't give you more cause to worry."

"Thank you. I love you, and I already have so many reasons to worry."

A thrill went through her at his "I love you." It didn't feel like this could be her life. "I love you too. Goodnight."

"Praise the LORD! For it is good to sing praises to our God; for it is pleasant, and a song of praise is fitting. 2 The LORD builds up Jerusalem; he gathers the outcasts of Israel. 3 He heals the broken-hearted and binds up their wounds. 4 He determines the number of the stars; he gives to all of them their names. 5 Great is our Lord, and abundant in power; his understanding is beyond measure. 6 The LORD lifts up the humble; he casts the wicked to the ground. 7 Sing to the LORD with thanksgiving; make melody to our God on the lyre! 8 He covers the heavens with clouds; he prepares rain for the earth; he makes grass grow on the hills. 9 He gives to the beasts their food, and to the young ravens that cry. 10 His delight is not in the strength of the horse, nor his pleasure in the legs of a man, 11 but the LORD takes pleasure in those who fear him, in those who hope in his steadfast love. 12 Praise the LORD, O Jerusalem! Praise your God, O Zion! Psalm 147:1-12."

Walking around the grounds of the cottage, Megan prayed the words of Psalm 147, then continued to call out to God in her own words. "You are God of all knowledge. Please share some of that with us by whatever means you desire. I pray you will make a way with De Clare's owner, and I continue to pray that you will convict Mr. Blake to provide more information. Protect Kieran and all of the officers who may have to get involved..."

As she turned down a path, she noticed Shaw, who nodded at her. He was getting an earful with her prayers and scripture reading today as she fasted and petitioned God for help with her case. That morning when she didn't partake in the bounteous breakfast Phoebe made, she took some time to explain her fast. Shaw and Phoebe looked perplexed that she would go to such an extreme. She'd not been able to share much about her faith with them because they stayed separate from her when they were in public, but she hoped what little she had shared would point them to God. From their response when she had brought up spiritual things, she didn't think either was a Christian. Megan added their salvation to the requests that she brought before the Lord.

The night before, she had texted Kate, Corbyn, and her father to ask them to join her today in praying for forward movement with this situation. Just like Esther, she wanted people in prayer before Kieran spoke with De Clare's owner or tried again with Mr. Blake. God had done greater things than this.

"But if you don't answer the way I hope, God, help me to trust you. You are still God, regardless of how you choose to act."

"There's a text for you from Kieran," Shaw called out as he approached Megan with her phone.

Her whole body tensed wondering what it was.

Kieran: Bernard Blake says he has more he wants to tell us. Keep praying about that. Also, Gareth convinced one of the people with jewels in the De Clare vault to let him take a picture and use them as bait to get the leader talking again. Praise God things are happening!

Megan looked at the time and it was a little after one in the afternoon. "Thank you, God, for movement!"

Just as Megan finished breaking her fast with a late dinner, her phone rang. "Kieran," she answered, anxious to hear his voice.

"Megan, I think we've found him. He's Russian. Bernard gave us a name and a city, and when he responded to the lure with the jewels, we got the location. Gareth is in contact with the head of the Russian arm of Interpol and tomorrow the Russian police are going to scope out the location and come up with a plan. They want to get as many people working with him as possible so it may take a few days."

"Thank you, God! This is wonderful news."

"Yeah. It's good to finally make some progress. Thank you for fasting and praying over this."

"I should be thanking you. You keep spending so much of your time on this. I know you have plenty of other things you could do with your time."

"This is the best way to spend my time. His location in Russia is three hours ahead of London. If they don't have him by five tomorrow night, I'm heading back to the cottage with you."

"I'd like that. Phoebe and Shaw are nice, but they take their job very seriously and don't say much."

"So you just want me around because you're bored?" He chuckled into the phone.

"Hardly. I've grown quite attached to you. At least when we were both in London you could come by every day."

"That was nice. I think we're close to the end of all this, and I'm looking forward to taking you out without having guards or wearing a wig."

Megan grinned as she thought of his disguise. "You look cute with the wig and beard, though I like you best without them."

"Since I won't have the disguise, be prepared for our picture to be posted all over the first time we go out. It was bad enough after I showed up for church last week."

"I don't look forward to that. Maybe since it won't be your first outing, things will have blown over."

"Maybe. I don't want you to be upset if it continues though. Mostly I don't want you to regret going out with me."

"No regrets. If it happens, it happens. My love for you is strong enough to withstand that. I don't pay much attention to social media other than posting on the Pulse app anyway."

"I love you, Megan. Get some rest, beautiful, and keep praying."

"I will. I love you too. Goodnight."

It was hard for Megan to settle her mind that night. They were so close to finding the Russian man and she was ready to get back to London and her life. If they found him, she could even move back into the mews house. But the part she looked forward to the most was her dates with Kieran.

Chapter Twenty-Three

"It's time to come home, baby."

"Did they get the Russian?"

"They got him and a bunch of people working with him. Bernard is in jail, and the Russian, Ivan Morozov, is in jail. You're free!"

"Praise God! Kieran, this is so hard to believe." Megan sank into the sofa in the sitting room. The stress from weeks of worry escaped her body all at once and left her boneless. "This...is a burden lifted." Her voice wavered as she spoke, and she found herself crying uncontrollably.

"It's okay, Megan. Just let it all out. I'm here for it all."

Kieran patiently waited while she let the pent-up stress escape until her tears slowed.

"Thank you," she sniffled as she spoke. "Thank you, Kieran." She took deep breaths and tried to get her breathing under control. "I didn't realize how stressed I still was. I've given it to God over and over, and I do trust him, but somehow I still feel like a huge burden has been lifted."

"It's okay. God doesn't expect you to be perfect. You've done great considering the circumstances."

"Thanks. What's next? Can I go home?" *Please say yes.*

"Yes, please. I spoke with your security team that's here, and they should be speaking with Phoebe and Shaw now. If you pack quickly you can be home by dinner. We can have dinner anywhere you'd like—your place, my place, out, whatever you feel like. If you don't mind me joining you, that is."

"Of course I don't. I'll speak with Kate. It might be nice to have a meal with all of them at the big house. I think I want something low-key tonight, but I also want to see everyone. I've even missed her girls."

"Hmm."

"What?"

"You're going to make such a great mum. I love you."

"I love you too." She loved it when he spoke about their future together. With the two men responsible for her problems in jail, a happily ever after finally seemed possible. Before Kieran's call, she had a hard time imagining her life without the constant worry that someone was after her. Now it was like this new life was opened up and she could start living again.

It hit her that he'd called her *baby* at the beginning of the call, and she liked it. Joy filled Megan's heart as she imagined seeing him again and all of the necklace stress being out of their lives.

"Kieran, I've got to go. I need to pack quickly so I can go see my boyfriend."

"Well don't let me hold you back from him." Kieran chuckled and they said their goodbyes.

Megan raced off to find Phoebe and Shaw and make sure they knew it was time to pack. She didn't want anything to slow her down.

Watching the cottage fade into the distance as they drove away, Megan let out a sigh. Despite the horrible situation that placed her there, it would forever be the location where Kieran asked to date her.

Her dad said he wasn't surprised. She recalled her conversation with him four days before.

"Kieran loves me, and he's asked to date me. I love him too and said yes. Do you think it's too soon?" There'd been no sense in tiptoeing around it.

"It doesn't surprise me in the least, and no, it's not too soon, the fact that you got to know each other before meeting in person seems to have accelerated things in a positive way. From the very first time we spoke with him on the video call, I could tell he was interested in you. At the time, it concerned me because I didn't know that the two of you had been talking, but once that came out, I knew it was a matter of time."

"You thought he was interested in me back then?"

"You may have been distracted with everything happening surrounding your necklace, but the way he reacted when you were speaking with Reece on the phone that day spoke volumes."

Megan smiled as she tried recalling Kieran's face that day, and she remembered him telling her that he started falling in love with her the second time she delivered food to his beach cottage.

"You must have a direct line to God," Shaw said from the front seat, pulling her out of her thoughts.

"A direct line?" She caught his eyes in the rearview mirror.

"Yeah, I saw all that praying you were doing yesterday, then suddenly the guy was caught and we're heading home."

She pressed her lips together. God *had* answered her prayers more quickly than she had imagined and in a way that she had hoped. "As a Christian, I do have a direct line through Jesus, but I also realize the things I want are not always the things he wants me to have. Sometimes he has a different plan and it may even be a hard one.

"My time yesterday was devoted to God and lifting up my worries and desires, but I was also praying for his will to be done and for him to align my heart with his will. Even if he did not answer as I had hoped, I would still trust him and praise him. In fact, there have been times that has happened to me before. The hardest was when my mom died last year from cancer."

"My condolences. I didn't know." He stopped and then added, "That didn't cause you to lose your faith?"

"It drew me closer to God. I was reminded how this earth is just a temporary home. We're all dying, as morbid as that sounds, but for Christians, we know that this isn't the end. We'll be able to reunite with our loved ones who were Christians, and God has promised to give us new bodies and make a new earth where there is no more brokenness, sickness, death, and—most importantly—sin."

"I guess there's more to Christianity than I thought."

Phoebe sat quietly all through the conversation, but now and then Megan saw her look out of the corner of her eye. She even thought she saw Phoebe wipe a tear away. Megan wondered what her story was. What caused Phoebe so much pain?

"It's not just a religion, but a relationship. God who made the heavens and the earth also made mankind to be in a relationship with him, but we battle with our pride. It's easier to think we have control over everything and push God away as if he is irrelevant, but that doesn't make him any less himself—the all-powerful creator, sustainer, and savior of the world. We are still dependent on him for our life and breath whether we admit it or not. We look for satisfaction in accomplishments, money, relationships, and all kinds of temporal things, but he is the only one who will truly satisfy us."

"I know what you mean about not feeling satisfied. Sometimes I think there has to be more to life, but I don't know where to start."

"I'd encourage you to read the Bible. When we get back, I can give you one. The book of John is a great place to start to understand who Jesus is. If you'd like, I'm sure Kieran would be willing to go through it with you. He's a new Christian, but he has already read the whole Bible through and studied it extensively."

Shaw looked at her in the rearview mirror again. "You think Kieran might have a problem if I met with you privately to talk more about the Bible, huh?"

Megan could tell from his voice he was smiling. That was the closest to joking he'd come since she'd known him. "Yeah, I think he might." It had been different communicating with Kieran through messages on an app when she didn't know him in person and also didn't have a boyfriend. As part of a couple, she needed to change the way she interacted with men. She'd never had to consider this before.

As she continued to talk with Shaw, she shared the essentials of becoming a Christian, answered more of his questions, and prayed for him and Phoebe. The longer Phoebe sat in silence, the more Megan felt God prodding her to pray for her. Before they arrived at the London house, she invited them both to church. Shaw readily accepted, but Phoebe politely declined. Megan didn't let that deter her and would continue praying for her.

"Surprise!"

Megan entered the Belgravia house to find Kate's family and Kieran gathered to welcome her. Kate's girls, Madeline and Margaret, wore the cutest party hats and held balloons.

Richard stepped forward. "We have been praying constantly for you. You have been through so much, and God has brought you through."

Tracey agreed and pulled her into a hug. One by one, the others joined in. All the while Megan's gaze kept wandering to Kieran. He smiled and waited patiently. How did she get so lucky to have so many who cared about her? She may have lost her mom months earlier, but God had filled her life with others who felt like family.

"Sorry," Kate said to Kieran as she released Megan. "I'm sure you want to give your girl a hug and we're hogging her."

"His girl? Are you two dating?" Tracey questioned.

"We are," Kieran proudly announced as he rolled towards Megan and reached for her arm to pull her close.

As she leaned into his arms, she felt at home—safe, comfortable, and like she belonged. She never wanted to be away from him again. Was this what it felt like to be in love? Reluctantly, she pulled back and saw her disappointment reflected in his eyes.

"The mews house repairs are complete and it's ready if you want to move back in. It's up to you. No rush," Richard said. "When you decide, let us know what you'd like to do."

"Thank you." Megan forced a smile, but the thought of staying in the mews house alone made her tense.

"Didn't you want to go out to Kingsdown for the weekend?" Kate questioned with a furrowed brow. "Corbyn and I spoke, and if Tracey and Richard are up for it, they could keep the girls this coming weekend and it could be an adults' weekend getaway."

Tracey looked at Richard and he nodded. "We're free. Of course, we'd love to have the girls."

"Yay, Nan and Pop!" Madeline squealed.

"Nan...Pop!" Margaret copied.

Megan looked at Kieran and he nodded. "Sounds like a plan."

As the evening wore on, thoughts of staying in the mews house kept haunting Megan. She tried reasoning with herself that there was no cause for fear. Why did she feel so worried now after everyone had been caught?

When Corbyn was gathering the girls to leave, Kate pulled Megan aside. "Are you okay? Ever since Richard brought up the mews house, you've seemed tense. Are you worried about going back?"

Megan nodded. "I know it seems strange now after the arrests, but I feel unsettled."

"Tracey and Richard aren't in a rush to move you back there. Give it some time. Maybe after our weekend trip you'll feel differently. Corbyn and I will be praying for you."

"Thanks. You guys have been so good to me, and Tracey and Richard too. I don't want to keep imposing on them."

"We all want what's best for you. With God's help, I know you'll be okay, but I imagine it's going to take some time to feel safe. Just know that we're here for you." She hugged Megan. "We'll get out of here. I'm sure you're ready to have a few minutes to speak with Kieran alone."

Megan grinned and marveled at the fact that just the mention of Kieran's name made her worries melt away.

"Having so much time with you at the Devon cottage spoiled me." Kieran squeezed Megan's hand and brought it up for a lingering kiss once everyone left them in the sitting room. "Tell me how you're feeling about things."

"I was relieved when you first told me the Russian man and others working under him were arrested, but now that I'm back in London, worry is creeping in again. I know it doesn't make sense. I've been praying and trying to turn it back over to God. The past few weeks, I have had so many ups and downs related to this that I'm left feeling on edge like it couldn't possibly be over."

"I'm sorry you've had to go through so much. I wish I could take those feelings away and make it instantly better. God and time will help."

"That's pretty much what Kate said."

"She's a good friend. I'd like to pray for you."

"Thank you."

Kieran took both of her hands in his and prayed for Megan to have peace. As he spoke, Megan thanked God for bringing him into her life and for Kate and all of her family. God had blessed her abundantly.

"On a happy note, I'd like to plan for our first real date. Are you available tomorrow afternoon and evening?"

"Hmm, let me check my busy calendar." Megan held up her phone and winked. "Oh, look, tomorrow is free. That will be a wonderful way to end the Lord's day."

"Perfect. If you have anything that you aren't interested in, let me know. I'd like to surprise you...if that's okay."

"I don't think there's anything you would choose that I wouldn't like to do. And you know what I like to eat by now."

"I need to get out of here then. I have to plan a date with my girl."

"Don't stress over it. Just being with you will be special."

"I feel the same way." He lifted her hand to kiss it again before he pulled her into a hug. "But I still want this to be special."

Megan's heart fluttered as she imagined what their first date might be like.

Chapter Twenty-Four

"These Gothic arches are beautiful. I've never seen a home with as much Gothic detailing as Strawberry Hill House. It's almost like being in a cathedral." Megan tilted her head up to better see the gallery ceiling. The gold lacelike designed trim seemed to radiate from the edges of the room and meet in the middle. Next to the walls it met up with similar trim that moved down the walls to form golden Gothic arches. "Look at the ceiling design, Kieran."

When Kieran didn't respond, Megan looked down to find him watching her and grinning. "I've been before. Right now I'm enjoying your reactions to it all."

"Thank you for bringing me. I never would have found this place. It's so fantastical and playful. Not dark or depressing like most Gothic homes"

"It is. Horace Walpole wanted the house to revive Gothic design and was influenced by buildings, tombs, and cathedrals he'd seen during his travels. He also had no qualms doing it in a way that wasn't precisely accurate."

Megan entered the library and giggled. "Can you imagine having such a beautiful library?" She approached the fireplace and looked closely at the golden decorative trim above it and the way it contrasted with the forest green walls. The trim design was repeated above each bookcase. Turning she noted the windows above the bookcases at the end of the room. "Look at these windows. I love their shape with the four circular pieces coming together."

"It's called a quatrefoil. Do you want something like this for our home?"

Megan's heart skipped a beat and she looked at Kieran. "Don't tease me."

He rolled closer. "Megan, this isn't a joke to me. I'd marry you tomorrow if I thought you'd have me."

There went the heart flutters again. "I...tomorrow?" She wanted to jump into his arms and say yes, but that would be crazy. Wouldn't it? Besides, her father couldn't get there that quickly.

"I don't expect you to answer right now, but if you feel so inclined to marry soon... let me know and I'll ask you properly. Our first real date doesn't seem like the right time." He smiled secretively. "But I won't keep you waiting long."

Later when they toured the grounds of the Royal Botanic Gardens at Kew, she couldn't keep her mind off Kieran's discussion of marriage. As they passed through the various gardens and greenhouses, she felt like she was floating through a dream. This man was her match. Though he was a new Christian, he loved the Lord as much as she did and enjoyed talking about the things of God in great depth with her.

When she mentioned he might want to work with Shaw to help him understand scripture, Kieran quickly accepted and started talking through what might work. Kieran had texted Shaw the night before, and when he came to church, Kieran scheduled a time for them to meet and discuss what he was reading in John. Kieran had also been sharing with Toby. He was so excited about his own relationship with God that he shared it with everyone he could. She imagined what it would be like to work alongside him as they ministered to people and shared the gospel.

"You've been quiet." Kieran looked up at Megan.

She laid a hand on his shoulder. "You've given me a lot to think about when you mentioned marrying soon."

One side of his mouth lifted. "Oh? I thought the trees and bushes had you deep in thought."

"They are nice, but I had you on my mind."

"Yeah? Do you want to talk about it?"

She looked away and the Japanese Gateway momentarily caught her eye, but her mind was elsewhere.

"If you don't want to, that's fine too."

"No, I do." She quickly turned back to Kieran. "There's so much going through my mind. I love the idea of marrying you. I love you."

"But you're not sure if you want to be married to an invalid?"

The worry on his face nearly broke her heart. "Don't put words in my mouth. There are no buts. Actually, I was thinking how perfect you are for me."

"Oh." The worry faded and he smiled again.

When he smiled Megan's heart soared. "You're the one who should be worried about me. Both my mom and grandmother died of breast cancer."

Kieran's brow furrowed.

"Don't worry, when my mom's cancer returned this last time, Dad insisted I get the genetic testing. I don't have the gene mutations for it, so my chances aren't any higher than the average person's."

Kieran tilted his head. "We think alike. I was tested too and don't have the markers for colon cancer. Regardless, I try to eat lots of vegetables and unprocessed foods to decrease my chances even more."

"I've noticed you eat really healthy for a guy."

"Oh yeah? You've been watching what a lot of guys eat?"

"I did have some guy friends growing up and they burned through the calories because of sports, so they felt it didn't matter that they ate garbage."

"I did a bit of that myself when I was younger, but once I went to university, I started thinking about how I needed to make changes so I didn't end up like my dad. That's also when I got the genetic testing."

"I'm glad that you started taking better care of yourself." She leaned down and hugged him. "I want you to stick around for a long time."

"That sounds good to me. Or if we go to heaven at the same time, I'd be good with that. I plan on hanging with you in heaven. I hope you don't mind."

"That's a bit morbid for a first date, but honestly, I like that idea."

"See, we were made for each other."

"Yeah." Megan smiled down at the man who held her heart.

Kieran checked his watch. "It's almost time for our dinner booking. We should probably head towards the exit. The restaurant gets great ratings, but keep in mind it doesn't have the Michelin rating like our lunch spot did."

"Got it. Lower my expectations."

"I still think you'll like it. It's Italian, but not the kind with pizza and heavy sauces." He winked. "Since we've been talking about eating healthy."

"I like to eat healthy, but I also like a good dessert now and then, so don't be worried if I get the tiramisu."

"I'm all for tiramisu or maybe the panna cotta."

Megan's eyes swept around the restaurant as they settled in their seats. It was elegant with a contemporary feel—white walls, dark wood floor, black and white pictures of Italy in sleek black frames hanging over dark wood dining tables.

"You made it sound like this place was a hole in the wall. It looks really nice and from the smell of that platter the waiter just carried past us, it will be delicious."

Kieran grinned and tilted his head. "A hole in the wall?"

"Yeah, some sketchy little rundown place most people would walk right past."

He chuckled. "I would never take you to a sketchy little place for our first date. Now, the second... it's debatable."

Megan's breath caught in her throat. How was this her life? Biting back a grin, she dramatically cleared her throat and looked down at her menu. "I think I can make a meal of these appetizers. They all sound so delicious—grilled calamari, artichoke topped with creamy spinach, fresh mussels, king prawns with garlic butter—" Megan stopped and looked up at Kieran who was grinning at her. "Oops. I'm practically reading out the whole appetizer menu."

Kieran chuckled. "It all sounds good to me, and I'm game if you'd prefer to just do appetizers. We could maybe add a pasta to split. That black truffle ravioli sounds good."

"Ooh. I haven't even looked at the rest of the menu." She glanced down and skimmed the rest of the menu. "Yeah, let's do that."

"Hi, I'm Olivia and I'll be your server today. What can I get you to drink?" Olivia looked between Megan and Kieran, then her eyes settled on Kieran. "Wait, I know you." She tapped her chin. "You're Natalia Moreno's ex." Leaning down to touch his shoulder she added, "I'm so sorry about your motorcycle accident. It's great to see you doing so well." She moved even closer to him. "Can I get a picture with you?"

Kieran leaned away from her. "I'm here on a date with my girlfriend."

Olivia looked over at Megan. "Oh, sorry. I...I'll just take your drink order then."

Moments later, she was gone and Kieran let out a breath. "I had hoped that wouldn't happen since we were away from London."

"I guess it really was a good thing that you wore the disguise when we were in Devon."

"I wasn't going to take any chances."

"I imagine it was worse than this when you were with Natalia. How did you handle it?"

Kieran frowned and shrugged. "I was a different person back then. I know it wasn't that long ago, just over half a year, but it seems like a lifetime."

Megan slid her chair closer to his and grabbed his hand. "I'm glad you're different because I'm in love with this Kieran."

"Thanks. I'm much happier with this new me too. Before, I acted happy on the outside, but it just covered up the emptiness. I'm especially glad that God changed me because I know you would have never considered being in a relationship with the man I was before."

"I don't like to think about the what-ifs, but it's true. I always knew that if I didn't find a man who was as in love with God as I was, then I would rather not marry."

"I do love God with everything in me, and I'm trying to be a man who is worthy of you."

"I couldn't ask for more." She looked into the depths of his green eyes and saw the truth of his words. This handsome man was her match in every way.

For the rest of the meal, their waitress was all business, and they wondered if someone had said something to her. They were grateful regardless of the reason.

As they ate, a string quartet strolled around the restaurant and eventually made its way to Megan and Kieran's table. They both smiled at the men, who eventually moved on.

"I assume that was Italian. Did you understand anything they were singing?"

"Just *ti amo* which means I love you," Kieran said.

"That's perfect like this whole day. I can't imagine a better first date, Kieran. Thank you."

"It was fairly simple, but I knew I wanted time for us to talk, be outside, and not have huge crowds."

"Maybe it seems simple after your last girlfriend, but to me, you went all out. This was a lot more than dinner and a movie that I always hear about for the standard date."

"Good, I like to avoid being standard." Kieran chuckled.

"I was glad to see Toby at church today. How has he been?" Megan asked as Kieran drove her back home.

"Good. Now that I am doing most things on my own, he is picking up more hours at a clinic. He'll still be doing therapy with me, but we're more like roommates now than caregiver and patient like before."

"That's good for both of you."

"Yeah, it wasn't cool depending on my best friend to do so much for me. But his training and instruction have given me the confidence that I could take care of myself. Having this MPV I can drive is another breakthrough. It gives me the freedom to go places without depending on others."

"It was such a surprise to see you roll up in this today. I'm happy for you." Megan studied the handicapped accommodations incorporated into the van. "The setup is impressive. Back home we call these vans. I'm not sure what MPV stands for."

"Multi-purpose vehicle," Keiran said as he pulled up to the front of the Belgravia home.

"You don't have to get your chair out to walk me to the door."

Kieran grinned and shook his head. "You're not getting out of this, baby. It's our first date, and according to you, your first real date. There's no way I'm not escorting you to the house—if you don't mind waiting the extra couple of minutes it takes for me to get my chair out."

"I can wait. You've been a perfect gentleman the whole night. I should have known better than to suggest it."

"I'll have to stop here, at the foot of the steps, since we're not at the handicapped accessible back door."

"I think this is more than appropriate for a first date."

Kieran was using his electric wheelchair and raised it to its highest position. "I always knew this adjustable height wheelchair would be handy, but I didn't imagine I would use it for this when I was stuck in my depression," Kieran said. He was almost at her height when he reached over and pulled her into a hug. Into her ear, he whispered, "No kisses on the lips until we're engaged, but can I kiss your cheek?"

"Yes," she whispered back.

When he pressed his lips to her cheek, they lingered there and she wanted to swoon. *This was worth twenty-six years of waiting.*

"Just wait until I kiss you when we get engaged," Kieran said as he pulled back and looked her in the eyes.

Megan giggled. "I didn't realize I said that out loud. Thank you again for the most wonderful first date."

"I'd like to stay here staring at you forever, but it's been a long day, so I'll say goodnight, my love."

"Goodnight. I love you." Megan turned to walk up the steps, then stopped at the door and looked back.

Kieran hadn't moved. He winked at her just before she entered.

Once inside, she leaned back against the door and sighed. The whole day felt like a dream, and those green eyes would surely be the star of her real dreams very shortly.

Chapter Twenty-Five

"Kate, I got my next job from Corbyn Publishing! I'll be working with an author on a textbook about Ancient Greek art and artifacts. I spoke with the author already, and I'll be helping her do research and editing. The most exciting part is that we'll be taking a trip to Greece at some point." Megan shifted her phone so she could lean back on her bed.

"That is exciting. I'm so happy for you. I heard they were impressed with your work on your mom's book. Maybe you've found your niche working with books on historical artifacts."

"I think you're right. I feel like I'm in the perfect location for it with the British Museum nearby, and being so close to the locations of ancient civilizations."

"Your mom would be so proud."

"Thank you." Megan's thoughts drifted to her mom. She never would have discovered how much she enjoyed working on books if her mom hadn't gotten sick again and died. God gave her a gift in the midst of the pain. Her mom would be pleased.

"Are you packed for this weekend?"

"Almost. I have a few more things to throw in my bag." She thought about her weekend getaway with Kieran, Kate, and Corbyn. All of them were blessings who wouldn't be part of her life if her mom had not died. It was a strange paradox to consider.

"I'm glad Kieran agreed to stay with the rest of us at the Corbyn cottage instead of at his place alone. It would have been silly for him to stay next door by himself when we have plenty of room and even a handicapped accessible bathroom."

"He's been trying to be very careful not to put us in situations that will place us in temptation's way. After his past, he's still trying to figure out what's best, and he knows his weaknesses."

"He's made such a turnaround. I'm happy for you. To convince him to stay at the Corbyn house, I reminded him you guys had stayed in the same house when you were in Devon."

"Yeah, I think that's what got him to agree. I'm looking forward to a tour of his cottage, though. It will be different going there now that we're dating."

Kate laughed. "I bet. It's no longer the home of the grumpy stick in the mud."

Megan joined in the laughter. Her feelings towards that stick in the mud had changed drastically. "Are the girls excited about their time with —" Her phone buzzed with another call. "That's strange. There's a call coming in from De Clare's."

"De Clare's? What could they want? You should answer it. I'll message you when we're headed that way tonight."

"Okay, bye." Megan switched to the other line. "Hello?"

"Hi, this is Bailey Woodhouse. I'm calling from De Clare's."

"Yes?"

"Mr. Henry Stafford has me calling all of those who were affected by the vault...situation. He would like to meet with you personally to extend his apologies."

"Oh, I...When did he want to meet?"

"He's very flexible and happy to meet you as soon as you're available. You can meet at the store or at another location if you prefer."

"I wouldn't be able to meet this weekend." It occurred to her that Interpol or her solicitor might advise her against meeting with him. "Let me check some things and get back to you."

"That's not a problem, Miss Taylor. I'll be looking forward to hearing from you."

After saying goodbye, Megan messaged Gareth to ask his opinion, and her phone rang a minute later.

"Gareth. Did you see my message?"

"I did. I had heard that Mr. Stafford was planning to speak with all of those whose vault holdings were affected by this. It shouldn't be a problem for you to meet with him. We didn't find anything concerning about him in our investigation. If you want, you can always have someone join you. I realize your situation is a little different than the others in that you were personally targeted, not just your jewelry."

"Okay, that's a good idea. I do think I would feel better with someone. I'll speak with Kieran and see if he wants to go or what he suggests."

"He's a good man, Megan. I'm glad you two ended up together. It's nice when something good comes out of situations like this."

"Thank you. It is a blessing and was a wonderful surprise." She wasn't going to explain to him that they had met through Pulse first. It was a long story. "Well, thank you. I'm going to call De Clare's back and set that up. The sooner I get all of it behind me, the better I'll feel."

"Don't feel like you have to meet with Mr. Stafford if you don't want to, Megan."

"No, I do. I think it will give me a sense of closure."

"Good. Let me know if you need anything else."

"That's it for now. Thank you, Gareth. You have been a great help."

"You're welcome, but we couldn't have done it without that boyfriend of yours. I hope you don't mind, but we plan on contracting him to work for us a lot more. He's got a knack for this type of thing and he's a genius with computers."

"I agree with you on both counts. Actually, I think he's a genius in a lot of areas. I guess I'll be speaking with you in the future even once my case is closed. Goodbye, Gareth."

"Goodbye, Megan, and good luck with that genius of yours."

Megan chuckled as she hung up and pulled up De Clare's number.

"Yes, may I speak with..." She tried to recall the woman's name. "I think she said her name was Ba-"

"Yes, that would be Bailey Woodhouse. Just one moment."

A few minutes later, Megan had a meeting set up with Mr. Stafford for Monday at 10 a.m. She wasn't sure how she felt about it, and she was absolutely taking a man with her. If Kieran couldn't come, she was sure one of the men she knew would come; if not, she would hire one of her security guards for the day. She scrolled to Kieran's number on her phone.

"Hey, baby." Kieran sounded out of breath.

"Are you okay?"

"Yeah, just getting in a workout before we leave. What's up?"

"Someone from De Clare's called. Mr. Stafford wants to meet personally with everyone affected by their vault situation. I spoke with Gareth and he says it's fine, so I'm going Monday at 10 a.m. Can you go with me? I don't feel comfortable going alone after everything."

"I'll be there. Are you sure you want to go?"

"Part of me doesn't, but another part knows if I don't, I'll feel like I don't have closure."

"Then that's what you should do."

"Thank you. I'll let you get back to your workout. I've got a few loose ends to tie up before we leave."

"I love you."

"I love you, too. See you soon."

"I've missed being out here. It's so relaxing. Thanks, everyone, for agreeing to come to Kingsdown this weekend," Megan said as they enjoyed dinner and the last of the sunlight from Kieran's deck.

"Of course. After all you've been through, I can understand the need to come to a place that feels safe. I get it. The Kingsdown Coast has held a special place in my heart for the last few years." Kate winked at Corbyn.

"That's right, you guys met here didn't you?" Megan tried to recall what Kate had told her.

"Yep, right over there in my gran's garden." Corbyn looked slyly at his wife and they both laughed.

"What are you not saying?" Kieran asked.

"Where to begin?" Corbyn smirked and gave Kate a side-eye. "Firstly, I think she fell in love with me that first day when she saw me working in the garden with my shirt off."

Kate blushed but said nothing.

"Secondly, she thought I was the gardener, and thirdly she didn't know I was Gran's grandson." He looked at Kate pointedly. "She thought Gran just had random employees of Corbyn Publishing who showed up, trimmed bushes, and stayed the night at her home."

At that, everyone broke out in laughter.

"In my defense, you introduced yourself as Declan, but I had only heard you called Corbyn by your grandmother and mom."

"Oh, yes, the Declan-Corbyn conundrum." Kieran shook his head. "You'll always be Declan to me."

Megan looked at Kieran. "You do always call him that, even when others around are calling him Corbyn."

"I answer to both. Declan is my first name and I like it. It helps me remember everything is not always tied to Corbyn Publishing. Mum started the whole thing when I was little. She was determined to keep the Corbyn name in the family, but when my dad refused to have it as my first name it became my middle name. Then just to spite my dad when they were having issues, Mum started calling me Corbyn. It became my name around the family and later when I began working at Corbyn Publishing. I still like to be called Declan, so with non-work friends, that's what I go by."

Kate spoke up. "I called him Declan until the day we got engaged. It was hard to transition, but all his family calls him Corbyn so it seemed appropriate. I should also admit I was jealous that his ex-fiancé called him Corbyn, and I wasn't about to be left out on that when I had the opportunity."

Corbyn's brow furrowed. "You never mentioned that."

Kate shrugged. "You know how things were with her. It was playing games with my head. I had been through so much the year and a half before we got engaged."

Corbyn pulled Kate into a hug and whispered something into her ear, making her sigh.

Megan looked over to Kieran and thought about their short relationship and all that they had been through together. They'd have their own stories to tell one day.

As if sensing her thoughts, Kieran grabbed her hand, tugged her closer to his wheelchair, and wrapped an arm around her. Megan relaxed into him. More and more she knew he was her future.

"Do you think the owner of De Clare's will try and convince you to put your pendant back in their vault?" Kate asked before taking a bite of salad.

"I have no idea, but that is not something I would consider."

"Good. There have got to be decent options, but surely he doesn't think you would trust them." Kieran squeezed her shoulder.

"It has got me thinking about what to do again. Once this case with Interpol is completely closed, I'll have to figure something out. I don't want to sell it, but it can be expensive to both insure and keep safe. That was why I put it in De Clare's in the first place. It was such a good deal."

"And now we know why." Corbyn shook his head.

Megan agreed. "I'm starting to think more about the museum option that Reece mentioned."

"How is Reece? Has he tried to contact you lately?" There was tension in Kieran's voice.

"No. Not since that time we went out and I told him we were better as friends."

"Good," Kieran huffed out. "He made me uncomfortable with the way he looked at you."

"Jealous much?" Corbyn chuckled at his friend.

Kieran shrugged. "He may not have been involved with trying to steal Megan's necklace, but something about him didn't sit right with me."

"Mmhm." Corbyn continued grinning at Kieran.

"Corbyn, stop giving Kieran a hard time. Have you forgotten the looks and comments you made towards Aidan when you thought he was still after me?"

"All right, fair enough, dear."

Megan thought that name sounded familiar. "Is that Hayley's Aidan?"

"Yep." Kate grinned. "The very same."

Kieran sat up straighter in his chair. "Do tell."

Kate recounted several instances of Corbyn's jealous antics. The most interesting was when Corbyn's ex, whom Kate thought he had only recently broken his engagement with, along with Corbyn and Kate, joined Hayley and Aidan at the Rose and Crown and were line dancing to Celtic music. "The faces he made at poor Aiden." Kate smirked. "On the way home, I even mentioned that Aiden was dating Hayley, but he was still moody."

"Thanks, man, for taking the pressure off of me." Kieran chuckled.

"What's the plan for tomorrow?" Kate questioned.

"I'd like to go biking," announced Kieran, causing everyone to look at him curiously. "I just bought a recumbent trike that I'd like to try out. It's here at my cottage."

"How does that work?" Corbyn asked.

"It's low to the ground and has two wheels in the front, one in the back, and hand controls. It's electric but moves my legs so they can get exercise."

"What a great invention. We should bike then." Megan looked at the others who agreed. "How about we get dinner cleaned up here so we can head over to the other cottage and get settled in for the evening."

"Sounds like a plan." Kate stood up and started gathering plates.

When Megan joined her in the kitchen, she giggled. "Last time I was in here, I could hear grumpy Kieran in the other room and never dreamed we would end up dating."

"You and I both. God does amazing things when we least expect it."

"You're living proof."

"Amen."

"One day, I hope to have a story as radical as yours, Kate."

"I wouldn't wish a story like mine on anyone. Your story will grow into just what it needs to be. It's already a beautiful one, and you have glorified God in your own difficulties. Not many would start a Pulse account to encourage others when they are grieving the loss of their mom."

"Thanks." Megan shrugged. "It was all through God's power, that's for sure."

Turning to watch as the guys came in with the remainder of their dinner, she sent praise up to God for so many beautiful blessings that had blossomed from her pain.

Chapter Twenty-Six

As Kieran moved from his wheelchair to his recumbent trike, he explained how it worked while Megan, Kate, and Corbyn oohed and aahed before hopping on their bikes. They rode the less-than-two-mile trek to Walmer Castle along the shore.

Once on the castle grounds, they unloaded the picnic items they brought, paid the entrance fee, and found a picnic table overlooking the sea.

"This is one of those rare sunny days." Kate tilted her head up towards the sun from her spot at the picnic table.

"It is perfect for our picnic," Megan agreed as they spread out the tablecloth and covered the table with an assortment of lunch items. "It's so clear, I think I even spotted the French coast across the Channel during our bike ride here."

"Yes, I saw it too." Corbyn nodded at Megan before placing a hand on Kate's.

"This garden is lovely." Megan glanced around. "I look forward to seeing the inside and the rest of the grounds. It's laid out so differently than Dover Castle with its position high up on the hill." She tension in her shoulders eased with the warmth of the sun and the breeze coming off the channel. More than that, she finally felt like she could let her

215

guard down after the worry of the past month. Yet one thing still tugged at her mind.

"Indeed," Corbyn agreed before turning to Kieran. "What has you so quiet?"

"Hmm?" He turned from staring at the water to Corbyn.

"What has you so quiet?"

"Oh, nothing." He shook his head before glancing at Megan.

She smiled at him, unsure of the look he was giving her. Usually, she felt so connected to him that she could guess where his thoughts were. Megan shook it off as they packed up their lunch things and began their tour of the Castle grounds.

"Grandaddy, shall we go look at the Queen Mother's Garden?" A young woman asked an old man walking with a cane as they passed.

Their voices trailed off but left Megan's mind reeling, and she decided it was time to share what had been troubling her. "Now that the necklace and I are safe, my mind has been wandering back to the letters to my grandmother."

Corbyn raised a brow, and Megan summarized what they'd found.

"I'm guessing the necklace is from the man named Robert who sent my grandmother those letters. If that's the case, he's likely my mom's father and that's why my grandmother always told her it was her heritage. I can't explain why, but I feel drawn to find out who Robert is, yet I have no idea where to start.

"My grandmother would be seventy-nine if she were still alive, so I'm guessing he's close to that age. I looked back over the letters this week to see if there was some clue about him that I'd missed. There was nothing. He mentioned a family business but never said what it was. He mentioned a woman his family insisted he marry to help their business financially, but the woman is never named. The letters don't have a return address or his last name. I studied the de Clare family tree since Reece thinks that is what the mark on the back of the pendant represents, but so far I've found hundreds of last names for their descendants. There's no way forward that I can see to find who gave it to my grandmother."

Corbyn nudged Kieran. "Seems like you should develop an app for that."

"Don't think I haven't wracked my brain over that." He wrapped an arm around Megan's waist. "I'm sorry that's been bothering you. I truly have been trying to come up with something, but like you, I don't know where to start."

"It seems silly to worry about when there are so many more important things going on in the world. But it has me feeling like there's a loose end in my life that I need to tie up. I'm glad I read the letters, but I feel like I've unleashed Pandora's box."

"Can I pray for you about it?" Kieran asked, and when Megan nodded, they all moved to the side of the garden path and bowed their heads. "Heavenly Father, again we come to you because you are Lord over all and have all knowledge. I pray that you would either take this desire for answers away from Megan or point her in the direction where she can find answers. In Jesus name, amen."

"Thank you." Megan leaned into him and felt some of the frustration release. It was nice having someone to help her bear the burdens of the things that troubled her heart. Whether big or small, Kieran was consistently there for her. *Thank you, God.*

"Look at the birds." Kate pointed at two jays perched on a low branch on the woodland walk as they entered. "If Margaret were here, she would be toddling over there trying to play with them." Kate looked around at the group. "I know I'm not supposed to be talking about my kids when it's an adult weekend, but they're so much a part of me. It's hard not to."

"Of course you should talk about them. You've not offended us at all." Megan imagined a little boy with Kieran's beautiful green eyes doing those very things. Pushing that thought away, she reminded herself she would be happy with whatever God decided to do in that area of their lives. She looked at Kieran who smiled back with a hint of worry crossing his face. She hoped she was able to convince him that he was enough.

"You look beautiful, Kate." Megan moved away from the armoire in Kate and Corbyn's bedroom at the cottage to admire her friend.

"Thanks, Megan. Sometimes I feel I've become so homely since having Margaret. I've gained a few pounds, and I don't always have the time to put myself together."

"I've only known you since you had her and I've never thought you didn't look put together. Regardless, I'm sure Corbyn will be impressed tonight."

"Speaking of impressing someone, how are things going with you and Kieran?"

Megan smiled as she thought through their time since she agreed to date him and her heart raced. "It's been like a dream. He just swooped in and is everything I never knew I was looking for."

"I'm glad things are working out. You both seem so happy. I know Corbyn has been speaking with Kieran and has been encouraged by the changes in him. I never would have imagined him initiating a prayer like he did earlier."

"Yeah." Megan thought back to his prayer and sighed.

Kate giggled. "You've got that dreamy look again. You've had it a lot lately. With all that's been going on, I'm glad to see you happy."

"What I've been through has been so much better with Kieran by my side through it all. He has been an encourager, and he's great at thinking outside of the box and coming up with solutions. I don't know that Interpol would have figured things out without him. Knowing Kieran was working on my case and praying me through difficult days gave me confidence and peace. It was like God placed him in my life at just the right time."

"And you were in his life at just the right time. It makes all the difference in the world when you have a man who looks to the Lord for his strength and guides your relationship under the headship of God.

Corbyn is night and day different from my first husband. When Mark died, I never wanted to marry again, but through Corbyn, God has shown me how wonderful marriage can be."

"What a wonderful surprise."

"It was."

"I never seriously thought about marriage until Kieran entered my life. Part of me worried marriage would keep me from accomplishing all that God called me to. But Keiran has the same goals as I do—to love God, glorify him, and tell others about Jesus. I can see myself married to him and still serving God in all that God has for me. Already Keiran is mentoring two different guys, and he encourages me in my ministry."

"That's rare for such a new Christian. We have both been blessed." Kate turned Megan to face the dressing mirror. "I think we're ready for a night on the town with our guys. Hayley and Aiden have a babysitter, so they'll be at the Rose and Crown too."

"Rose and Crown is Aiden's place, right?"

"It is. He used to be there all the time, but after Chloe was born, he's tried to be home more."

"It will be interesting to see this Aiden guy that had Corbyn so worried."

"He's a good man, but with Corbyn around no one else had a chance—even when I mistakenly thought Corbyn was torn between me and Alexandra I couldn't get him out of my heart or mind."

"It's a good thing my relationship with Kieran hasn't had that kind of drama or I would have decided he wasn't worth it. I've had enough going on without guy drama."

Kate fully agreed.

"Aiden, it's so good to finally meet you," Megan said as she shook the hand of the muscled, tattooed man before her. His appearance fit perfectly with his pub and all of its dark wood, exposed beams and dark, rich colors. "I've enjoyed getting to know your wife and Chloe. Your daughter is adorable by the way."

"Thanks. She's changed our world. I can't imagine how we lived without her." He turned to Kieran and placed a hand on his shoulder. "How have you been, chap, and what's that silly grin on your face?"

"I'd like to say it's because of this one here," he motioned towards Megan, "but it's because I know Megan was interested in seeing the guy that had Corbyn so jealous way back before you started dating Hayley."

"Ha. You're one to talk. You left Kate a mess from what I understand."

"It's true." Kieran reached for Megan's hand. "And I've changed for the better. This little lady here straightened me out before I even knew her name."

Aiden raised a brow. "Good for her."

"Yeah. She pointed me to Jesus, and for that, I'll always be thankful. Then when God pulled us together in real life, I knew God was doing something more than just guiding me to himself through her."

"Sounds interesting. I'd love to hear more." He turned to the rest of their group and waved them to the back. "Everyone, I've reserved the private dining room so we can actually hear one another. Sometimes it gets noisy even without the band. We can move out to the main dining area once the band starts. I have a table reserved there as well."

"Thanks, Aiden." Corbyn patted him on the back as he walked past into the private room.

Aiden sat across from Kieran. "It sounds like Megan has had a big impact on your life. Tell me more."

Kieran told him about the Pulse app with her witnessing to him and how they met in real life. He skirted around her specific issue with the pendant. That was her story to tell, but he did mention that Declan had him helping with something and he met Megan through Declan.

"Hayley got interested in God through Kate. When she saw Kate's consistent faith through all her ups and downs, she wanted to know the

God that got her through too. I became a Christian through Hayley. God has his ways doesn't he?"

"He does." Kieran caught Megan's eye and winked.

Megan's heart raced and was full as she watched the man she loved, before noticing Aiden shifting in his seat.

Aiden leaned down and whispered something in Hayley's ear and she nodded. He placed a kiss on her lips then stepped away from the table.

When Megan looked back at Kieran, he glanced down at her lips and she knew exactly what he was thinking. She found herself wanting to break her promise to herself so she could kiss him sooner. When she first made her no-kissing-until-engagement rule, she had no idea how hard it would be once she was actually in love. Kieran seemed to share the same feelings as he sighed and moved his hand behind her back to rub circles.

The six of them got along famously and Megan especially enjoyed dancing to the Celtic music. Before Kate, Corbyn, Megan, and Kieran left, they agreed to go to lunch after church.

Upon arriving back at the cottage, Kate and Corbyn disappeared into their room, leaving Megan and Kieran some time alone in the living room. They recounted the day's highlights and he mentioned that Gareth asked him to help Interpol solve crimes using his computer expertise.

"Will you accept the job?"

"I'd like to help them when I can. Now that I'm working again with my company, I won't have the free time I had while working on your case, but I like the idea of helping people. Interpol does a lot with human trafficking, and that has been something weighing on me for a while. This might be a way I can help."

Megan smiled. "That would be amazing. If you want to work with them, I'm behind you."

"Thanks. We can discuss it more later. We should get some sleep so we won't be tired at church in the morning." He glanced at her lips and shook his head before leaning in for a hug. "Just you wait, Megan Taylor."

Chapter Twenty-Seven

P **24,601:** Psalm 100:1-5 A Psalm for giving thanks. Make a joyful noise to the LORD, all the earth! 2 Serve the LORD with gladness! Come into his presence with singing! 3 Know that the LORD, he is God! It is he who made us, and we are his; we are his people, and the sheep of his pasture. 4 Enter his gates with thanksgiving, and his courts with praise! Give thanks to him; bless his name! 5 For the LORD is good; his steadfast love endures forever, and his faithfulness to all generations.

Megan smiled at her message from Kieran. She needed something positive to focus on before meeting with Mr. Stafford. *I am thankful for you, Lord. I praise you.* She meditated on the words of the Psalm as she dressed and ate. A glance at her watch showed that there were still thirty minutes until Kieran would arrive to take her to the meeting. She opened her phone to text and ask him to come early but decided against it. He had already spent so much of his free time helping her. Even if she was his girlfriend, he might have things he needed to do.

Just as she laid her phone down, a text came through. A glance showed it was Kieran.

Kieran: I can come over now if you're ready. I thought we could chat a few minutes before leaving, or we could stroll around. That would be roll around for me ;).

Megan: Yes, please come! You read my mind. I need a distraction.

Kieran: OMW

Within minutes, Kieran arrived and they decided to take a scenic route to De Clare's.

"This is the first time in ages I've walked around London without being watched." Megan scanned the area. "It's so different to not look around and see people following me—both guards and bad guys. It makes me feel lighter. That was an ever-present burden."

Kieran tugged her hand to his lips for a kiss. "I'm glad you're free of that too."

"The strange thing is that for the past month, I walked these streets hardly noticing what was around me other than my final destination and those following me. They could have demolished whole buildings and I would have had no idea. I was that distracted with what was going on. I enjoy the scenery and I've missed it."

"You had a taste of that when we were in Devon didn't you?"

"I did. It was a nice break. I felt safe there, and it was fun visiting a part of England I hadn't explored before. I especially enjoyed roaming around the countryside described in *Sense and Sensibility*."

Kieran looked at her and grinned knowingly. "Looks like we're here."

"Oh." Megan looked up and saw De Clare's across the street. "You brought us around from the opposite direction and kept me distracted. Sly. Let's go get this over with and be done with this place."

"Hang on." He tugged her back. "We need to pray first."

Megan nodded. "Thanks."

"God, you know all of Megan's burdens. Please use this to bring some closure to one of those burdens. Give her peace, wisdom, and the graciousness to represent you well even though this place has caused her so much turmoil. In Jesus' name, amen."

When she opened her eyes, he was staring at her with a look of love and protectiveness.

"I'm ready." She thought she was, but as she approached the entrance, her eyes fell to the place where Kieran had wrestled Billy to the ground. She imagined Billy reaching towards her with the tranquilizer-filled syringe. Her step faltered. *God, you've got me.*

Kieran's brows pulled together, but she shook her head and steeled herself. "I'm okay."

When they entered, they were greeted by a petite blonde woman and quickly whisked to a small room. Several cushioned antique chairs surrounded a coffee table.

"By the way, I'm Bailey Woodhouse. The one you spoke with on the phone. Mr. Stafford will be right in. Can I get you something to drink?"

Megan's throat suddenly felt dry. "Yes, hi, Miss Woodhouse. I'll take water, please." Kieran reached for her hand and she squeezed it. "I feel so anxious all of a sudden," she said softly to him. After what Mr. Blake put her through, paranoia filled her. She wondered if she was being watched and glanced around looking for security cameras.

"You have a good reason."

Megan chose a seat and Kieran rolled his wheelchair next to her just as the door opened. They both turned to see an older, distinguished white-haired man with blue eyes. He looked familiar. Megan recalled seeing his picture on the website. Kieran caught her eyes, boosting her resolve, just before the man approached them and spoke.

"Megan Taylor and Kieran Davies, I presume?" They nodded and he thrust out his hand. "Henry Stafford." He shook Kieran's hand first. "Thank you for all of your work to bring this to light. I am grieved by what has occurred within these walls. I understand that you worked closely with Scotland Yard and Interpol."

"I did. You're welcome."

Mr. Stafford turned to Megan. "And you..." His eyes looked weary and he glanced away before looking at her again. "I feel terrible for the distress and worry that my company has caused you. I misplaced my trust in Bernard, and I feel personally responsible...I—" He turned away and Megan thought she saw tears welling up in his eyes. "Excuse me. I'll be right back." He darted out of the room.

"What was that about?" Kieran moved closer to her.

"I've no idea. It looked like he was about to cry. He's taking this very seriously."

"I'll say. Seems quite emotional."

Megan began to wonder if they should leave when the door opened and the woman from before joined them. "Sorry for the delay with the water. Mr. Stafford will be right back." She set out two water goblets filled with water. "I brought an extra just in case."

The woman quietly slipped back out of the room, and they were startled when Mr. Stafford stood before them. His eyes were rimmed with red. "I apologize." He glanced at Kieran before his eyes landed on Megan and he held out a jewelry box. "For you. Open it." After she took it, he took a seat opposite her.

She pulled open the top and there sat her pendant. "It's..." But as she looked more closely she saw slight differences.

"It's the replica Bernard made. It's yours if you'd like it. The fake jewels are hardly of any value, but the gold in the necklace and the quality of the scrollwork makes it a decent piece of costume jewelry."

"Thanks." Megan forced a smile, feeling happy to have something similar to her precious necklace yet sad at the reminder of all she had been through with it including not being able to wear it. A touch of anger towards Bernard and his associates was mixed in too as she analyzed it.

"Can I...May I ask how you came in possession of the necklace? The original," Mr. Stafford questioned.

Megan ran her fingers over the fake necklace and pictured her mother wearing the original. Tears filled her eyes and she reached up to wipe them away. "It was my grandmother's necklace but I never knew her. She died before I was born, and my mom inherited it.

"Mom wore it almost every day, though she usually kept it tucked beneath whatever she was wearing." A smile broke through as she recalled it. "The necklace is a bit much for most outfits, and red doesn't match everything. My mom died eleven months ago, and since I was an only child, she promised it to me. We had no idea it was of any value." She wanted him to understand how little prepared she was to get caught up in such a scandal.

Mr. Stafford frowned. "I am so sorry about the loss of your mother and never knowing your grandmother." He shook his head and looked pained. "Miss Taylor, what was your grandmother's name before she married?"

It was fresh in her mind after reading the letters. "Nancy Wilson. Why?"

He looked down at his withered hands and then back at her. Moisture once again filled his eyes. "I've done some research. Your mother was born in June of 1971?"

Megan's heart froze and she slowly nodded.

"It wasn't...I didn't know." He shook his head, then rubbed his temple as tears slipped down his face. "I think I'm your grandfather."

Megan gasped. It felt as if she were freefalling down a rabbit hole. Kieran wrapped an arm around her shoulder. Was it really possible her grandfather had been so close all this time? Doubt rose inside and she stopped that train of thought. "What makes you say that?" The letters to her grandmother were from a man named Robert. Was he part of Mr. Blake's scheme after all?

Mr. Stafford glanced at Kieran then back at Megan. "I loved your grandmother and she loved me. We planned to get married but she left suddenly. I gave her the necklace to wear at our wedding." He wiped another tear from his eye. "I never saw her again. We met while she worked with the U.S. Embassy here in London. I was drawn to her the moment I first saw her in a café reading a book. It was Jane Austen's *Emma*." He smiled sadly and stared into the distance. "She loved that book."

"What proof do you have?" Megan felt like she might explode. His answer could change everything she knew about her family.

With a shaky hand, Mr. Stafford pulled a packet of letters from the inside pocket of his suit and retrieved the top one. "This was the last letter she wrote me. You are welcome to read it and any or all of the others. Please be careful with them. They are precious to me."

Megan took the letter and wondered if it could possibly be true. She examined the envelope. It was postmarked 2 October 1970 and addressed to Henry Stafford. She took a deep breath. She didn't know what her grandmother's handwriting looked like, so she couldn't verify his claim that she wrote it, but she *was* curious about the words inside. When she unfolded the paper, it looked aged just like her grandmother's letters from the jewelry box.

Scanning the greeting she discovered it began with *Dear Robert*. Her heart sank. Even if he had researched her grandmother, how could he have known about that? She had those letters in her possession. Was it possible he had something to do with the break-in and the burglar found the letters but left them for her to find? Or was one missing? The jewelry box *had* been tampered with. She turned it over and it was signed *Nancy*. Her heart pounded and she shot a look of worry to Kieran before looking at Mr. Stafford.

"Why is it written to Robert if your name is Henry?"

He got a distant look, then with trembling lips spoke, "Like I mentioned, at that first meeting, she was reading a book. I noticed her and couldn't take my eyes off of her. She glanced up at me while taking a sip of tea and tried to place the cup back on the saucer without taking her eyes off of me." A small smile rose on his face before quickly disappearing. "The teacup missed the saucer and tea spilt onto the table and her book.I was at her side instantly with my handkerchief, wiping off her book. She invited me to sit and join her. When I tried to introduce myself, she stopped me and said she wanted to guess." He paused and his chest rose and fell. "My apologies. This is difficult for me. I can't believe I had a daughter, much less a granddaughter." A tear trickled down his cheek and he wiped it. "I can only imagine what you're thinking. Anyway, she called me Robert. When I asked why, she said I reminded her of Robert Redford. Back then, I had blond hair. From that point on, Robert was her pet name for me."

He stopped and ran his finger over the stack of letters still in his hand. "I loved her. I don't think I ever stopped. Megan..." He shook his head and a deep furrow etched across his brow. His shoulders fell and he no longer looked like the put together British gentleman she saw when he first introduced himself. "I shouldn't presume to call you by your first name. Miss Taylor, I'm so sorry I missed out on all of your lives—

your grandmother's, your mum's, and yours. I'd...I'd like the chance to get to know you and learn more about my...daughter."

More tears streamed down his face after he choked out the last word. If Mr. Stafford was lying, he was a very good actor. The things he said left her heart aching. Part of her longed to believe it all. She wanted to believe she had some link to the grandmother she never knew and she wanted to believe the mystery of the necklace was solved, but she was still smarting from Mr. Blake's deception and torment. She looked at Kieran who placed a hand on her knee and squeezed. It gave her a surge of confidence. "Mr. Stafford, this is quite a shocking revelation... I need some time to think it through."

Kieran cleared his throat. "We should also have a paternity test done. Megan can get back to you with the details about that."

"Yes, of course. I would expect nothing less. I will happily pay for it," offered Mr. Stafford.

Kieran looked at Megan, and from the look in his eyes she could tell he wanted to speak, so she remained silent.

"We'll get back to you with the details." Kieran rolled towards the door and waited for Megan to follow.

She stood, unsure of what to say. What is the correct protocol for someone who claims to be your grandfather? "It was nice to meet you, Mr. Stafford. Like Kieran said, we will get back to you."

Mr. Stafford closed the box containing the copy of her necklace. "Regardless of whether you want to have anything to do with me after this, the fake necklace is yours."

Megan forced a smile as she took the box. As Kieran led her out of the store, the world around her began to spin.

"Are you okay?" Kieran looked at Megan with concern. She shook her head and leaned against his wheelchair. He held out his hand to hail a taxi.

They were silent while Kieran got situated and she stowed his wheelchair.

"Thank you," Megan said shakily as they settled into the car. Her eyes drifted to the window, but the scene beyond was out of focus. She leaned back against the seat and took deep breaths. As she recovered, her mind raced from one thought to another. Was it possible Mr. Stafford was telling the truth?

When they approached the Belgravia home, she found her voice again. "Kieran, will you come in with me?"

"Of course." Kieran had the driver drop them off at the mews street entrance so he could use the handicapped ramp. He paid the driver, moved to his wheelchair, and escorted Megan inside. "Do you want to talk about it?"

"Yes and no." She led him inside to the sitting room. "My mind is filled with conflicting thoughts." She chose a seat with room next to it for his wheelchair.

Kieran moved close to her and wrapped an arm around her shoulder. "I'm here when you're ready to talk, or we can sit here quietly."

Megan sighed. "It's hard to imagine the grandfather I've always known is not my biological grandfather, though I know that wouldn't change the special bond we had." She pressed her hands to her eyes and took a deep breath. "I don't want this to be real. That would confirm that my grandmother lied all of those years and leave me feeling like I missed out on something."

The thoughts continued to work their way out. "Have I really found a grandfather I never knew? I don't want to naively believe, and honestly, I'm still feeling paranoid after everything that has happened so far. What if he's involved with Mr. Blake's scheme but managed to hide the proof?"

"My worry, exactly. That's why the paternity test is important."

"Thanks for stepping in on that. I was so stunned I didn't think of it."

"You're welcome. I didn't like speaking for you, but I could tell you weren't going to get much out, and I didn't want to take a chance that he would coerce you into using his people for the test. I would never trust the results if he had something to do with it. There's too much at risk here. If—" Kieran shook his head.

"If what?"

Kieran frowned. "If there is someone else involved that we missed... That's not a chance I'm willing to take. Do you mind if we call Gareth and let him in on what's going on? I'd also like to get him involved with the paternity test."

"Not at all. That seems like the best plan."

During the call, Gareth agreed they should be on alert until they had the paternity results. He had a lab he trusted and promised to set things in motion for the test. He also suggested it would be helpful if they had something like hair from a hairbrush with Megan's mother's DNA.

Knowing her father, her mother's hairbrush was tucked safely inside the bathroom drawer where her mom left it.

"Considering our recent findings, I don't want to risk anything falling through the cracks," Gareth said.

"What recent findings?" Megan couldn't recall any new information concerning her case since she'd returned. She turned to Kieran and he grimaced.

"I've not mentioned it to Megan." He placed a hand over hers and said to her. "I planned to, but with you being stressed about the visit to De Clare's, the timing didn't seem right."

"I'll leave you to it then, Kieran. Bye, Megan." Gareth hung up and they looked at each other in silence.

Kieran finally broke the silence. "I'm sorry."

"You're scaring me. What is it?"

Kieran's jaw clenched. "The Russian's jewelry forgery ring is part of a larger network that also trafficks drugs and...women."

"Kieran, no." She knew about human trafficking and prayed regularly for those affected by it, but she never had any personal connections to people who had been trafficked, nor had she met anyone who worked with an organization fighting against it. A darkness surrounded human trafficking, and she could feel the weight of it every time she heard a story of someone who had been trafficked or when a trafficking ring was discovered. "Will they be able to get to the traffickers and drug ring through those they arrested for the jewelry theft?"

"That's the goal. Ivan Morozov seems willing to talk. One of the things they have me working on is locating the other parts of the network." His face tensed and his eyes became distant.

"There's more?"

He stared at her but said nothing.

"I can see it in your eyes. Something's bothering you. Please don't keep things from me."

His expression dulled. "I...knowing that this group is involved in trafficking and the fact that they were about to take you..." He shook his head. "It was so close, Megan. Too close." His voice strained and became a whisper. "God saved you."

Stunned, Megan fell back into her chair. "I'm glad I didn't know this when we were in Devon. I would have been paranoid. How long have you known of the ties to human trafficking?"

"About a week. At first, the timing wasn't right. We had our first date, and I didn't want to bring it up during your first few days home. Then the meeting with Henry Stafford arose. I wasn't trying to keep it from you. You're safe now. I feel sure you were of interest because of the necklace. They will have moved on by now."

It bothered her that he didn't tell her right away, but more than that, she understood the reality of what could have happened to her if he hadn't been following God's lead that day. "Thank you for listening to God. You really don't think they are after me anymore?"

"We're covering our tracks with the De Clare's and Russian takedowns. If the organization realizes what happened with the takedown, they also realize that getting near you places them squarely in our trap. If they don't realize they've been discovered, then based on the false information we've sent them from the mobiles of those who have been arrested, they have to believe you are no longer a problem. Regardless, we are making inroads into the larger organization. We have eyes and ears all over."

"You make it sound like you're a detective now instead of a computer programmer."

"I feel like a detective. If you had not been the one in danger, I doubt I would have started down this path, but now that I have, my eyes have been opened to the darkness hiding in the very place I'm most comfortable. I'm compelled to help. Maybe it will change the kinds of programs I develop too."

Megan smiled, once again amazed at the change in Kieran.

Chapter Twenty-Eight

"Psalms 100:1-5 A Psalm for giving thanks. Make a joyful noise to the LORD, all the earth! 2 Serve the LORD with gladness! Come into his presence with singing! 3 Know that the LORD, he is God! It is he who made us, and we are his; we are his people, and the sheep of his pasture. 4 Enter his gates with thanksgiving, and his courts with praise! Give thanks to him; bless his name! 5 For the LORD is good; his steadfast love endures forever, and his faithfulness to all generations." Kieran closed the Bible and looked over at Megan. "Whatever the outcome, we can rejoice in the Lord."

Megan's heart raced. Anxiety over waiting for the paternity test results mixed with the happiness of being loved by a man who was consistently pointing her towards God. "Thank you for coming over. If the results took more than one day, I don't think I could handle the wait. My heart feels so restless."

"Can I pray?" When Megan nodded, Kieran reached for her hand. "God, we trust you no matter the outcome. We love you and praise you. Please protect Megan's heart whatever the result and help her to know what steps to take next. In Jesus' name, amen."

"I'm not sure how I'll feel if I'm related to Mr. Stafford or what I'll want to do about it. I'm glad Gareth will take care of things if the results are negative. I'll be happy to put De Clare's behind me." In the back of her mind, she couldn't help but think De Clare's was about to become a permanent part of her life.

"We'll take it one day at a time and figure it out."

"We?" Megan raised a brow.

Sadness clouded Kieran's features. "I only meant that I'm here for you every step of the way. God willing, I will be for the rest of your life. I'm sure your dad has good advice too. You don't need to feel like you're on your own."

Megan's heart clenched in her chest. "I was just giving you a hard time, Kieran. I'm thankful I have you and want your help in this. I do want to work together for the rest of our lives. We're a team now. Right?"

Kieran blew out a breath. "Yes. You had me concerned. I'm still trying to figure out this dating towards marriage thing and I worry I'm not doing it right sometimes. Megan, you're precious to me and I want to protect you from outward and inward dangers, but I don't want to be overbearing. Please let me know if I am. It might hurt my ego, but I'll get past it."

"You're doing great." Megan couldn't hold back her smile and leaned over to hug him. She found that she didn't want to let go. She breathed in his woodsy scent. It was a smell she had come to associate with happiness, contentment, and safety.

"Why don't we go out for a bit? We'll go bonkers if we sit here stressing over things and checking your emails."

Megan nodded in agreement at his offer.

"Are you ready to go now or do you need a few minutes?"

"I'm ready. Let me go grab my purse."

When she returned, Kieran said, "You look beautiful."

Megan's heart raced at his words. She'd never been overly concerned with her looks, but knowing that the man she loved found her beautiful filled her heart with joy. "Thank you. I didn't change anything from when I was with you a few minutes ago."

"I know. You always look beautiful to me and I don't say it enough." He took her hand and led her towards the back door. "I had a driver on standby. I have somewhere I'd like to take you, but it's a bit of a drive if that's okay and your schedule is open for the day."

"I'm happy as long as I'm with you, and I have nothing on my schedule today except checking emails." She winked at him. "I'll happily put that off."

"Perfect."

"I do have one stop I'd like to make before we head out of town," Kieran said after his driver pulled away from the curb.

"Out of town?"

"Yep. Trust me, you'll love this."

"I do trust you. It just caught me off guard."

The driver parallel parked next to a row of shops and Megan scanned the buildings trying to guess which one they were going to. "The Screaming Peach?! I'd heard one was opening in London. How did I miss their grand opening?" Megan grinned from ear to ear at the familiar café. Back home, the Screaming Peach Café was her go-to place for smoothies, lunch, and dessert. She pulled Kieran into a hug. "Thank you."

"It opened while we were in Devon. Kate mentioned you might appreciate a reminder of home. I thought we could grab something to take along with us."

Megan's mouth watered thinking of her favorites on the menu.

When they entered the café, Megan took in the retro decor and felt right at home. It had the peach leather booths, black and white tile floors, and chrome accents like her favorite Screaming Peach in Chapel Hill. "I may have to get Yasmin and Chelsea to start meeting me here for our Bible studies. Time to introduce them to an American icon."

Kieran chuckled. "I'm glad you're happy."

Megan squeezed his hand and bounced on her toes while they waited in line. She scanned the menu and sighed. "Just like home. They have all my favorites. The problem is it's been so long that I can't decide."

"You know how I feel about it. If you can't decide, order several different things. At the very least, order for you and me and we'll share everything."

"I'm glad you like sharing. You're going to love everything here. We can split a couple of sandwiches, and get two different soups...and salads. The desserts are to die for. I'm thinking Peach of Art Cobbler and Just One Peach of Cake. Does that work for you?"

"Absolutely." Kieran grinned back at her. "Order away."

"And I'll get us a smoothie to share because you have to try one. How about Let it Mango? Oh, and Pretty as a Peach Lemonade." She clapped her hands together.

"It all sounds scrummy."

"Thank you again." Megan leaned down and kissed Kieran on his cheek. "This is the best day ever."

Kieran bit his lip and tried to hold back a grin as they returned to the car with bags of food.

"How long of a drive to the place we're going?"

"Two hours."

"Two hours?! I'm glad I got us this smoothie then." She took another sip from her straw before handing it back to Kieran.

Kieran chuckled. "It's only ten a.m."

"I know, but there is no way I would have been able to sit in this car for two hours knowing there were desserts from The Screaming Peach inside. This smoothie takes that urge away...a little bit."

"Megan, wake up." Kieran's voice sounded far away. A soft kiss warmed her temple. "Wake up, my love."

Happiness filled her heart as she gradually awakened from a sweet dream. "Kieran?" Megan blinked. "Where...Oh." She opened her eyes as everything came back to her. They were on their way somewhere. Heat rose to her cheeks as she realized she'd fallen asleep against Kieran and there was moisture in the corner of her mouth. She swiped at it before lifting her head. "Sorry." Her hand ran over her hair to smooth it down.

"I rather liked it." From the tender smile on his face, she knew he was being truthful. "We're here."

Megan looked outside to find they were traveling down a long drive approaching a huge stately home. Enormous trees dotted the landscape. She turned to Kieran. "Where is here?"

His mouth curved into a sly grin. "Charborough Park. It's in Dorsetshire. The location of Delaford, Colonel Brandon's home."

"Kieran!" Her hand flew to her cheek. "It's beautiful. How did you find this place?"

He shrugged. "We're just here to picnic and tour the grounds, not visit the home itself. They do have a building on the property open if we need to use the facilities."

"That's fine. It's perfectly wonderful!"

Their driver pulled alongside a horse-drawn carriage.

Once Kieran was in his wheelchair, he opened Megan's door and held out an arm. "My lady."

After getting situated in the carriage, they were soon riding across the beautiful lawn. In the distance, she spotted what looked like a bench and table covered with a white tablecloth. As they moved closer, she could make out a vase of flowers on the table and her heart took flight. Kieran was more romantic than she ever would have imagined.

Kieran slid an arm around her shoulders and pulled her close. She looked up at his strong silhouette and silently thanked God for this man who filled her life with joy and knew what she needed before she knew herself. He was beautiful inside and out. God had gifted her with a boyfriend so far beyond what she could have dreamed up for herself.

The coachman pulled the bags of food from the cooler attached to the back of the carriage while Kieran situated himself in his wheelchair and they went to the beautifully adorned table. After Megan sat, Kieran reached for a book, and to Megan's delight, it was *Sense and Sensibility*.

She raised a brow. "We just finished it. You want to read it again?"

"Just the ending. I'm particularly fond of it."

"Me too." She crossed her legs and leaned back on the bench, recalling Elinor and Marianne's happily ever afters in the last few pages.

"Let's see." Kieran flipped to a spot with a bookmark. "Here it is. 'Marianne Dashwood...'" He looked up with a gleam in his eyes. "'She found herself, at nineteen, submitting to new attachments, entering on new duties, placed in a new home, a wife, the mistress of a family, and the patroness of a village.

"'Colonel Brandon was now as happy as all those who best loved him believed he deserved to be;—in Marianne he was consoled for every past affliction;—her regard and her society restored his mind to animation, and his spirits to cheerfulness: and that Marianne found her own happiness in forming his, was equally the persuasion and delight of each observing friend.'"

Megan's heart beat wildly as she watched Kieran. The expression on his face changed as he looked up from the book and into her eyes. His smile became forced and his expression tight. Was he in pain? Just as she leaned forward to ask if he was okay, he spoke.

"Megan, we have known each other for seven months, though only one month in person. In that time, I have changed in ways I never thought possible." He stopped and seemed to be laboring to breathe. "I never knew I could love someone the way that I love you. I never let myself get that far in relationships. After my father, I've been scared of losing others I love, and no one seemed worth the risk. With you, I can't stop myself. I can't *not* take the chance of forever with you. I love you with everything in me. You led me to the one who has shown me what love is. As a Christian, I am finally the man God intended me to be, and I am ready to be the man who walks through life here with you until God is ready to take us home.

"I love you. Will you marry me? Please?"

The strain and urgency would have tugged on Megan's heart if it hadn't already been his. "Yes! I love you beyond words. You are God's gift I never knew I needed. A hundred times, yes!"

The tension on Kieran's face changed to joy and he looked up at the sky. "Thank you, God!" His eyes found hers. "Megan, I've been so anxious. I thought I would go mad if you said no."

Megan chuckled but he didn't join her.

"I'm serious. I've worried about everything under the sun and prayed constantly. Thank you for putting me out of my misery."

Before she could respond, he pulled her into his lap and the look in his eyes silenced her. She remembered his promise as he leaned in. When he hesitated, she nodded and he wrapped his arms around her, pulled her close, and placed a gentle kiss on her lips. She melted into him and his kisses became urgent. Minutes later, he pulled back and looked into her eyes once more. He was breathing heavily.

"I love you, Megan. Will you sit back down on the bench? There's something else I need to do."

She was confident she knew what it was. She'd been so caught up in the moment she'd not thought of it. Megan reluctantly slid off of Kieran's lap and moved to the bench wondering what type of ring he chose for her. As she watched, he reached into his pocket and pulled out a ring box. She patiently waited for him to open it and offer it to her, but instead, he rolled his chair back, reached around, and pulled out a metal pole. It seemed like an odd addition to his proposal.

With a couple of adjustments, he extended the pole to several feet long and turned the top so it had a handle. It was a cane!

Kieran raised his electric chair to its highest position, leaned on the cane to stand, then put one foot in front of the other.

"Kieran!" Megan threw her hands over her mouth and jumped up when he wobbled.

"I'm fine. Please sit down."

"You...You're walking!"

He grinned and she smiled back.

"Kieran, how is this possible?"

He continued smiling. "Our God is a God of miracles. I'm not completely healed, but I'm improving and may get there." He stood before her. "I apologize that I can't kneel, but considering the circumstances, I thought you might like this better." He moved to open the ring box with his hand that held the cane and struggled.

Megan wanted to reach out and help but held back. She knew he needed this. "Oh, Kieran, I'm so happy for you. This is amazing."

After opening the ring box, he held it out to her. The ring gleamed in the sun. As she drew closer, she could see it was oval and the setting matched the surrounding of her treasured necklace. "Oh, Kieran! It's beautiful."

"If you don't like it, or if you don't want a reminder of your necklace, you can pick out something else. At the time it seemed like a good idea. You were missing your necklace, and I thought you would enjoy having a reminder of it. Now I'm not so sure."

"I wouldn't think about changing it. I love it, and I love that you put so much thought into it." She stood and reached for the box, but he pulled it away.

"I'd like to put it on you. If you'll sit back down, I'll join you so I have my hands free."

Megan smiled, liking the idea that with his new ability, he could sit beside her on the bench. Until this point, the only time they sat truly side by side was in a car with a driver who helped him in. She readily sat down.

Kieran hobbled next to the bench then gingerly sat beside her. He blew out a breath. "Where were we?" He chuckled nervously before removing the ring from the box and sliding it on the ring finger of her outstretched hand. "It looks as beautiful on you as I imagined."

Megan stared at her hand, tears filling her eyes. "Kieran, this is perfect. And it fits just right."

"You can thank Kate for that." He grinned.

"Oh, she'll hear all about this, and I'll be sure to thank her." She touched his leg and looked into his eyes. "What is happening with your legs? I didn't know this was a possibility for you."

"Doctors had thought it was a complete spinal cord injury, since I had no feeling or muscle control for months. A few weeks before I met you in person, I started occasionally feeling sensations in my legs. I never said anything to you because we weren't sure if it was phantom sensations or if it would lead to any functionality in my legs. Toby increased my range of exercises and I worked hard, but it wasn't until a couple of weeks ago that it became clear my spinal cord was only partially injured and I began to have some muscle control. I waited to tell you because I didn't want to get your hopes up.

"In the beginning, I didn't think it would amount to much, and neither did the doctors. This past week when I saw I was getting close to walking, I decided to wait and have it be part of our engagement. I hope you'll forgive me for not saying anything earlier. I wanted to surprise you."

Megan took his hands into hers and smiled at him. "I forgive you. I hope you won't keep anything from me in the future, but I forgive you. I'm overjoyed for you and for us. We'll work together, wherever this leads."

"I don't deserve you." Kieran wrapped his arms around her and pulled her close. "We need to enjoy the fact that we don't have the wheelchair between us." He placed a trail of gentle kisses from her ear, down to her chin, and finally on her lips.

It was hard to think clearly in the arms of the man she loved, but Megan silently said a prayer of thanks to God for his abundant blessings.

Chapter Twenty-Nine

While driving back to London, Megan and Kieran busied themselves calling family. First, it was Megan's father. He congratulated them and told Kieran he couldn't have picked a better man for his daughter. Scott said he thought highly of Kieran from the time they first spoke on the video call. He told Megan how Kieran had nervously called two weeks before to ask for her hand and begged his approval even though they had just officially begun their relationship. They spoke of how Megan's mom would have loved Kieran and been overjoyed to see her daughter with such a godly man.

Kate was the next call and said it came as no surprise and she thought they were perfect for each other.

"Were you surprised?" Kieran questioned as soon as she disconnected from the call with Kate.

"I truly was. I thought it was just you distracting me from an incredibly tense and long wait today. Thank you for that too."

Kieran gave her a sly grin. "I like to multitask. It seemed like the best way to surprise you since you already knew it was coming. I spoke to your dad to get his thoughts on waiting until after today or going ahead, and he was all for today. I, of course, preferred as soon as possible—so today it was."

"I can't imagine anything more perfect."

Belgrave Park came into view and Megan spoke up, "Do you mind coming in? I'm not ready to say goodbye yet or for this day to end. We could maybe make dinner or something."

"I'd love to." Kieran gave her a questioning look.

As the driver deposited them at the mews entrance, Megan's thoughts cleared and she frowned at Kieran. "I momentarily forgot. This whole day started with my wait to find out the test results and you had promised to be with me for that. I wondered why you looked at me funny when I invited you in."

Kieran drew his hand down her arm and clasped her hand as they approached the back entrance of the house. "I would have said something if you had tried to send me away. I'm here for you, my love."

"Being around you keeps me from thinking clearly. I guess considering what it kept me from thinking about, it's a good thing."

"That's what fiancés are for." He rubbed circles on the back of her hand. "Let's go to the sitting room."

She thought about his new circumstance now that he could walk with assistance and imagined him cozied up next to her. "Will you join me on the sofa?" Before he could answer she added, "Will you start using a cane or a walker now?"

"Yes to the sofa, and probably a walker. I'm not quite ready for a cane. That took a lot out of me. I didn't bring a walker today because I wanted to surprise you and a walker would have been hard to hide."

"True."

"I hope to graduate to a cane eventually."

"I imagine the walker will feel freeing after months of a wheelchair."

Kieran stopped and tugged her down so he could whisper in her ear. "It will make it easier to kiss you. I have a promise to keep." He wrapped a hand around her neck and pulled her closer for a kiss.

Megan sighed and grabbed hold of the wheelchair arm to keep from falling. She'd never understood the phrase "weak in the knees" until today. She was quite ready for Kieran to show her what he meant when he had promised to kiss her lips until they were raw.

Before she'd had her fill, Kieran pulled back. "Why don't we go get situated on that sofa? This wheelchair is too much of a barrier."

Megan nodded as he clasped her hand and rolled towards the sitting room.

"Surprise!"

"Congratulations!"

Megan jumped at the sound of so many voices. Her father stood in the center of the group and approached first.

"Dad? I just spoke with you on the phone." She wrapped him in a hug.

Scott chuckled. "Yes, and I had to move to another room for fear that you would hear all of the commotion in the background."

"And here I was imagining you sitting at home in your favorite chair. When did you get here?"

"Last night, but don't worry about me. Go greet your other guests." He kissed her on the cheek. "I love you, my pearl, and couldn't be happier for you. Kieran's a good man, and though you haven't been together long, I have every confidence that he has your best interest in mind."

"Thank you, Dad."

Megan scanned the room and began making the rounds to her friends—Peter, Yasmin, Chelsea, Toby, Kate, Corbyn, Tracey, Richard —even Shaw and Phoebe. Phoebe whispered in her ear that they were telling everyone they met her through Corbyn. Indirectly, that was true. Corbyn was the one who connected her with the security company Corbyn Publishing used. Kieran's mom, Susan, and sister, Paige, were even in attendance.

"What a wonderful surprise!" Megan told the group. "Kieran has been full of surprises today." She looked over at her fiancé and grinned.

Kieran rolled next to Megan and spoke up. "I have another surprise for everyone here." He looked towards the entrance to the room where Corbyn pushed a walker forward. Kieran raised his wheelchair and pulled himself up with the walker, then walked several steps. He stopped in front of his mom who held her hands over her mouth.

"Kieran, this is..." Susan sobbed and shook her head. "Pardon the tears, I never dreamed I'd see this day. I'm so happy for you. A future daughter-in-law and this good news both on the same day." She leaned forward and wrapped an arm around Kieran while reaching out to squeeze Megan's shoulder. "My precious, precious, son." When she pulled back, she placed her hands on Megan's cheeks and said, "And future daughter, I'm so thankful God placed you in Kieran's life."

Megan realized that tears filled her own eyes as she thought about what Kieran's mom must be feeling. Those thoughts mixed with ones of her mom. It was the first of many important events her mom wouldn't be part of. In spite of that reality, the joy that filled her heart was too much to express. "I too am so thankful for the way God brought us together." The dam broke and she could no longer hold back her tears.

"Look at us," Susan said. "I didn't mean to make you cry at your own engagement party."

"It's okay," replied Megan as she swiped at the tears streaming down her face. "They're the best kind—happy tears."

Turning, Megan found Kate approaching. "It was so hard not to spill the beans when you called me. I couldn't be happier for you both."

"Your acting skills are phenomenal. I hadn't the slightest clue anything like this was afoot." Megan glanced around. "Where are the girls?"

"With their Aunt Chloe. I knew there was no way I could keep them quiet when you two entered the house. They'll get their chance soon enough to congratulate you. Now..." Kate stepped away from Megan. "It wouldn't be a party without food and cake!"

"If you don't want to end the day by looking at the email, we can wait until tomorrow," Scott asked Megan after everyone but he and Kieran had left.

The laptop screen illuminated the space in front of them, teasing her with the secrets it held. Once again she felt as if she were playing with Pandora's box. Would she be better off if she never opened it?

Maybe, but the questions she'd be left with would forever eat away at her mind.

Megan looked into her father's eyes, then over to Kieran before shaking her head. "I don't want to put it off anymore. I'd rather not have all night to toss and turn imagining the result. I might as well toss and turn already knowing the result. Kieran, I can't thank you enough for bringing my dad here for this." She squeezed both men's hands as they sat on either side of her on the sitting room sofa.

She took several deep breaths before releasing the men's hands. Opening her emails, she scrolled past all of the junk mail and found what she was looking for. Her finger hovered over the email, but before she clicked, Kieran grabbed her hand.

"God, prepare Megan for whatever she will find and help her dad and I to know how best to support her. Most of all, I pray that you will be glorified in this."

As soon as Kieran released her hand, it flew to the keyboard and clicked on the email. Best to get it over with.

Dear Ms. Megan Taylor,

We have used the results from the DNA of Mr. Henry Stafford, yourself, your late mother, and your father to come to our conclusion and would like to inform you that the test has shown Mr. Henry Stafford has 99.999% chance of being your mother's father and a 98.999% chance of being your grandfather. This leaves little doubt that he is your grandfather.

There were more words and numbers explaining the results, but they became a blur as tears filled Megan's eyes. Her chest tightened and she began to shake as pent-up emotion escaped. Her father and Kieran silently wrapped their arms around her as the news worked its way from her brain to her heart.

Eventually, her crying subsided and she was able to slow her breathing back to normal. She was thankful that Kieran and her dad continued to let her sit there quietly. What was there to say? How did she feel? She couldn't express it and never could have prepared herself.

She wasn't sure how much time had passed before she closed the laptop and sighed. "Can we discuss this tomorrow?" she said softly. "Right now I have no words." Her voice strengthened before she turned to her dad. "Thank you, Dad, for being here."

Next she looked at Kieran. "I love you, and regardless of what happens with this, excluding the day I became a Christian, today is the happiest day of my life."

He kissed her on the cheek and whispered, "PG for your dad." Megan chuckled, and he spoke more loudly. "Very soon I hope to supplant this day with our wedding day."

Megan stared into his eyes which were filled with love and longing. "I'll hold you to that, Mr. Davies."

"On that note, I think I'll head to bed and let you two lovebirds share some time alone. I'm still suffering from jet lag anyway." Scott gave both Megan and Kieran hugs before heading to his room.

Kieran pulled Megan closer, and she sighed. "This day has filled me with a multitude of emotions. Mostly happy, though I'm unsure how I feel about my newfound grandfather."

"That's understandable." He nuzzled her nose and she found his lips. They felt like home even though she had only kissed him a few times. She looked forward to kissing him for the rest of her life. "We can speak about it tomorrow after you've had some rest."

Megan blinked, and it took her a moment to recall what they had been speaking about. His kisses made her senseless. Another cliché that she now understood. She giggled and he placed another kiss on her lips.

"So, future Mrs. Davies, when do you want to make this official?"

"I guess we do need to figure that out."

"I'm not rushing you. Just wondering if you have any thoughts on it. Like I said before, I would marry you tomorrow if you would have me."

She smiled and stared into his eyes while running her fingers down his cheek and along his chin. "Let's talk about that tomorrow too. All of the excitement of the day has caught up with me and my brain is shutting down."

"Are you ready for me to leave, or would you like to sit here silently for a bit?"

"I think I have enough energy to snuggle some more. It may even help me have more restful sleep." She gave him a sly smile.

"I'm all about encouraging restful sleep for my fiancée." He kissed her on her forehead, then pulled her close.

Chapter Thirty

With the sun peeking in her room, Megan lay there thinking. Her newfound grandfather was at the forefront of her mind. She was happy to have found him but disappointed in him and her grandmother. She wanted to know more but didn't want to bring drama into her life—again. Blowing out a breath, her mind turned to Kieran—much more pleasant.

An idea popped into her head, and Megan pulled out her phone and looked at her dad's work calendar. His Christmas break ended Wednesday, January 8. If they had their wedding the Saturday before, he would have plenty of time to get back home for classes. The fourth of January was almost three and a half months away. In some ways, she wanted to marry Kieran sooner, but she could use a few months of calm to get her bearings and get to know her fiancé better. She added "Wedding" to her calendar with several emojis—a ring, a heart, a bride, and a groom. As she laid her phone down it vibrated and she saw a message.

P24,601: Psalm 42:1-5 ESV - 1 To the choirmaster. A Maskil of the Sons of Korah. As a deer pants for flowing streams, so pants my soul for you, O God. 2 My soul thirsts for God, for the living God. When shall I come and appear before God? 3 My tears have been my food day and night, while they say to me all the day long, "Where is your God?" 4 These things I remember, as I pour out my soul: how I would go with the throng and lead them in procession to the house of God with glad shouts and songs of praise, a multitude keeping festival. 5 Why are you cast down, O my soul, and why are you in turmoil within me? Hope in God; for I shall again praise him, my salvation.

P24,601: Good morning my love, my fiancée! I hope you were able to sleep well. My night was filled with sweet dreams of you. Let me know when I can join you and your dad.

She grinned and began her reply but an incoming text stopped her. It was from an unknown number, and the words she could see on her phone said, "This is Henry Stafford. I'm sure you have received the same email that..."

And so it began. Opening the text, she braced herself for the surge of emotions.

Unknown Number: This is Henry Stafford. I'm sure you have received the same email that I did. I apologize for intruding on your privacy, but I retrieved your number from our database. I hope that you will consider meeting with me. It is my greatest desire to share with you what I can and also to learn about my family and the daughter that I never knew. If you would prefer never to speak with me again, that is your choice, though I hope you understand that I did not knowingly abandon your grandmother. I loved her more than I have ever loved another woman. Please let me know if you are willing to meet.

Megan texted Kieran.

Megan: Can you come over in an hour?

She was excited to share her thoughts about their wedding date, but she also wanted to talk to him and her dad about Mr. Stafford.

Kieran: I'll be there. I love you.

Megan: I love you too!!!

Laying aside her phone, Megan pulled out her Bible. It was time to feed her soul. There would be plenty of time later to figure out the other matters of her life.

"We don't have to do this if you don't want to. We can turn around right now," Scott said as they approached De Clare's.

"I want to. I need this. You know how I am. I don't like to leave things unfinished for very long."

Kieran squeezed Megan's hand and gave her a wink. He was back in his wheelchair. It would be a while before he could walk more than a few minutes at a time, even with a walker. Megan momentarily got lost in his eyes and smiled at the memory of their morning conversation. He'd been quick to accept the wedding date in January and promised to open up his schedule for a couple of weeks afterward so they could have a two-week honeymoon.

When he tugged her hand, her face heated as she turned to face him again. Kieran gave her a knowing smirk.

She felt like she was walking on a cloud. "No matter what happens today, I have been truly blessed. I have a man that I love dearly." She turned to her dad. "And a wonderful father. It's more than many have."

"Megan, my pearl, you are a treasure. May God guide this time today." Scott wrapped an arm around his daughter and the three of them entered De Clare's.

"Hi. Miss Taylor, nice to see you again," said the blonde woman she had met before. "You're here for your meeting with Mr. Stafford?"

"Yes, thank you, Miss Woodhouse. And this is my father, Scott Taylor."

"Hello, Mr. Taylor and Mr. Davies. You may call me Bailey." She smiled and guided them to the same room where Megan first met Mr. Stafford. "Waters for everyone? Or we have hot tea."

"Water would be good. Thank you, Bailey." Megan wondered if Bailey had any idea what she was discussing with Mr. Stafford.

Before sitting, Megan's father helped Kieran out of his wheelchair and into the cushioned chair next to Megan.

The door opened and Megan tensed as Mr. Stafford entered. He froze in the doorway, then blinked before joining them in a seat. "Megan." His hand went to his heart. "I never dreamed I'd see this day."

Watching Mr. Stafford, she realized why he looked familiar. His eyes...Looking at them was like looking in the mirror. She had his blue eyes. Megan had not wanted to see it when they first met. It was hard to accept that they might be related and easy to ignore when they had no proof. Now everything had changed. She had a grandfather.

Tears gathered in Mr. Stafford's eyes. "My apologies for being so emotional." He wiped at his face. "Please forgive me for any part I had in your grandmother having to go through so much alone. I never knew and I had no way to reach her. Communication was so much more complicated back then."

"I have wondered how it all came about. My grandfather always spoke so highly of my grandmother and what a godly woman she was. It's hard for me to reconcile that with this woman who became pregnant out of wedlock, and it doesn't leave me thinking very highly of you either."

His brow furrowed and he frowned. "It's a long story, Megan, and I want to tell you all of it. Do you want to hear more? I don't want to say things that may pain you, but I will say that it only happened once and your grandmother and I truly meant to marry the very next day."

Time seemed to slow down as Megan processed this new information. Did she want to know more? How could she leave only hearing part of the story?"

"Please continue. I want to hear it all, even the difficult parts."

Mr. Stafford looked at the others before his eyes found Megan's again and he smiled sadly. A knock on the door broke the trance holding Megan captive and time sped back up to normal. Bailey asked if she could bring in their drinks and left quickly.

"Where to begin? You'll have to be patient with me. I've replayed the events in my mind hundreds of times, but the process may be slow to put them back into order for you.

"Your grandmother, Nancy Wison, came into my life and nothing has ever been the same. I think I told you about the first day I saw her... when she spilt her tea at the café. It seems I fell in love with her that first day, but I didn't attempt to pursue her at that time. My father had been planning to have me marry the daughter of a friend of his, Linda. I didn't love Linda, but I was willing to marry her to help save the family business.

"De Clare's was struggling financially and my father's friend had done quite well with his investments. Linda was young, only twenty years old, and had no idea what she wanted in life, least of all who she would marry. She'd been in awe of me because I was older—twenty-seven, but there was nothing between us other than friendship. Still, when I first met your grandmother, I was hesitant to pursue her because of the verbal agreement.

"It wasn't until we accidentally met again a few days later that I began to question my decision to marry someone I didn't love. That second meeting, the draw to Nancy was so strong. I enjoyed her company immensely and at the end of my lunch break, I could hardly bear leaving her, so I begged her to meet me again the next day.

"It became our thing—meeting during our lunch breaks. We shared so much during those lunch dates. After a few weeks, we started to branch out and took turns bringing lunch for one another. Instead of meeting in the café which was centered between our offices, we met just outside it and used the time to tour London together. It was wonderful to see things from her perspective." He gazed past Megan as if he could see the very scenes he described. "So much of the city had become little more than background noise to me.

"After a month, I was done for. I knew she was the one for me and I was determined to convince her. She knew my situation with Linda—we had shared nearly everything about ourselves—so she was reluctant to consider more than friendship. I convinced her that I would work on my dad and all would be right. With my assurance, she continued meeting me, but we still kept it private.

"I dropped hints with my father, but it was to no avail. At that point, about three months into our relationship, I wasn't giving up. I loved Nancy too much and knew I would never be happy with anyone but her. We decided it would be best for me to leave the family business and take my talents elsewhere. I was in talks with several other jewelers and finally worked out a deal with one who was excited about having the historical de Clare/Stafford family name tied to his start-up company.

"Nancy and I decided to give my father one last chance before I agreed to work at the other company. I took her to my parents' home and introduced her as the woman I loved and the reason I could not marry Linda. My father flew into a rage and dismissed us from his presence.

"The next day, I agreed to begin working at the other company with the guarantee that I could take a week and a half off for our honeymoon. Thankfully I had some money from an inheritance that my grandfather on my mother's side had left me. This allowed us to make a start. I applied for her spousal visa and our marriage paperwork."

Megan nodded, recalling something to that effect in her grandmother's letters.

"I booked us separate rooms for the night before the wedding in a hotel close to the chapel where we were to wed." At this last sentence, his brow furrowed and color rose to his cheeks. "I'm ashamed to say that we gave into temptation that evening. Our rooms happened to be connecting, and it was too much. We had no chaperones, and at the time, it seemed trivial to worry about such a thing with only hours until the marriage was official. Clearly, we were both wrong." He pressed his fingers to his temple and shook his head.

"That evening, I went out to pick up dinner and bring it back for us to eat in my room and when I returned Nancy was nervous and upset. She tried to talk me out of getting married and said she didn't want to come between me and my family. I gathered it was last-minute nerves and reassured her. After a while, she seemed to calm, so I thought she would get past it. Even when she barely ate and said she needed to go to bed immediately after dinner, I told myself things would be fine in the morning. After what we had done, I had hoped she would stay in my room, but she insisted on her own room and locked the door between us. I was too far gone to see what was coming.

"It wasn't until the next morning, when she didn't respond to my knocking or calls, that I discovered she was gone. The front office informed me she had checked out the night before and left me a note. It said that she loved me and would never forget me, but she couldn't be the cause of my family falling apart, so she was returning to South Carolina. It was devastating, and I couldn't understand what changed her mind until I read the letter that was included with her note.

"It was from my father. I had picked it up just before I left my home, but upon opening and seeing it was rubbish, I shoved it in my bag. At the hotel, when Nancy asked to see our marriage papers just before I left for the food, I pointed her to the bag, forgetting about the letter.

"My father's letter said that if I married Nancy I would be shunned. He claimed my mother was distraught, and Linda was devastated as well. According to him, Linda had loved me for years and we had a good relationship until I was led astray by this American. He accused your grandmother of being the family's undoing and some other things I won't repeat. Needless to say, I was furious with my father.

"I couldn't believe she was gone and checked everywhere. She wasn't at the boarding house where she had been lodging, nor was she at work. I even checked our favorite restaurants. I didn't have her U.S. contact information. My world spiraled out of control that day.

"I was angry at God for leaving me in such a predicament and I was angry at Nancy for leaving me without giving me a chance to prove myself. That very day, I had words with my father, and several days after that, he had a heart attack.

"When my mum begged me to step in for him, I threw myself into replacing my father and righting the wrongs I found in the business accounts. Linda and her family's money was not an option I considered.

"Cooler thoughts prevailed a couple of weeks later, and it hit me that rather than accepting Nancy's explanation, I should be showing her we could still make it work.

"I went again to the U.S. Embassy and begged for her contact information in the U.S. and they refused to give it to me. All I knew was that she was from Greenville, South Carolina. Nothing could deter me, so I went back to the boarding house and gave a letter to the woman who ran it. My letter explained how things had changed for the better and that I thought my father would accept her now. I told her that with me running the company and already turning the accounts around, he could not complain.

"I never received an answer. The finances were not at a place where I could travel to South Carolina, nor could I hire an investigator to search for me. It wasn't until over a year later that I felt like I could finally go, but days before I left, my father had another heart attack. This one he did not recover from.

"A couple of months later, I left for Greenville, South Carolina, determined to find Nancy. I discovered she had moved with her husband to Columbia. At that point, I wouldn't believe she could have married so quickly until I saw it with my own eyes.

"When I arrived in Columbia I found the home where she was said to live with her husband and I saw the two of them. The man had his arm around her and was guiding her into the house from their car. I saw the look of love in his eyes. I only saw her profile as she looked up at him. It was just over a year and three months after she left me."

Tears streamed down Henry's face. He sucked in a breath and whispered, "I was again devastated. I didn't see a baby that day, so I had no idea there was anything more for me to question. I felt betrayed. I knew that I loved her too much to marry anyone and at that point, I never thought I would risk my heart again."

Megan pondered what Mr. Stafford told her. It didn't seem possible.

She shook her head. "I can't wrap my head around this. It makes my grandmother sound awful. Why did she never tell you about her pregnancy? Why didn't she give you a chance to decide for yourself how you would be involved?"

"Oh, no." Mr. Stafford held a hand up. "You must forgive her. I left out a very important part that vindicates your grandmother. Upon my return home from South Carolina, my mother admitted that my father had paid my butler to give him any letters from Nancy. She said my father did receive some and burned them without reading them. She also said that he paid Nancy's landlady to collect any communications from me or Nancy and give them to him. And to make sure I had no options, he had a friend working at the U.S. Embassy who agreed not to give me her contact information and to intercept any communications that might come through." Mr. Stafford's face tensed and his hands clenched the arms of his chair. "It was a good thing my father was dead at that point because I would have left him and the business that day and never looked back."

It was difficult for Megan to imagine a father so evil. She looked at her own father and silently thanked God for him. Her dad placed a hand on her shoulder. She could guess the thoughts going through his mind because they were likely similar to hers. Her mom never knew her biological father—a man who seemed to have genuinely wanted all that he missed out on.

Chapter Thirty-One

Megan bit her lip and glanced at Kieran. He reached for her face and wiped off a tear. She'd been affected more than she realized. As she thought about all of the information Mr. Stafford gave her about his relationship with her grandmother, one thing was missing. "What about the necklace?" Questions began to pop into her head faster than she could verbalize them. "How did she get it? Did she know it was so valuable? Grandmother never gave my mom any idea it held such value. Mom said it was a nice piece of costume jewelry that her mother said represented our heritage. Grandmother insisted my mom get it and not my uncle. She put it in her will."

"Your uncle?" Mr. Stafford questioned. "Nancy had other children?"

"Yeah, she and my grandfather had a son. My mom didn't have any other siblings." She tilted her head. "They were only half-siblings. I didn't think of that until now."

Mr. Stafford ran his hand over his face and sighed. "I'm sorry to be the one who has turned your life upside down. This is unsettling for me too. The necklace...I brought it to the hotel as a gift for her to wear to the wedding. For generations, since the de Clare's, it's been worn by the bride of the oldest son in the family on their wedding day." He adjusted a sleeve on his suit jacket and his face colored. "While she was in the bathroom, I tucked it into the dress she planned to wear for our wedding."

"So she didn't know anything about it—its value or history?"

"No. I included a note. If I remember correctly, it just said that it had been worn by the brides in our family for generations. I don't think I said anything about it being valuable and definitely not how old it is. I thought there would be time for that discussion later."

"Oh." Megan furrowed her brow. "So you don't think..."

"That she stole it." Mr. Stafford shook his head. "No. In fact, I would guess that when she first returned to South Carolina and discovered it, she tried to contact me about sending it back. That's the type of woman she was."

He sneered and looked at a photo on the wall. Megan recognized it from their website. It pictured Mr. Stafford and his father. "My father never dreamed that he wasn't just keeping me from marrying Nancy but also ensuring we would never get back our priceless family heirloom."

"I feel bad that you weren't able to give it to your wife when you married. You did marry, didn't you?"

He nodded. "It's okay. The necklace was where it belonged, and I'm glad you have it now. I've been married twice and the first time was a mistake. I'm glad she never wore it. The second time was good, but she wasn't the love of my life." He frowned and looked at the floor.

Megan wondered if the sadness in his eyes was from more than this present situation. It sounded like he lived a very unhappy life.

When his eyes found hers again, they held questions and pain. "I...I know this is a lot and very emotional. It is for me at least. But...is there any chance you will let me be a part of your life? Even if it's in a small way. I would also like to find out about my daughter." He took a shaky breath. "I wish I could find out more about Nancy, but I imagine you don't know much since you never met her. Maybe one day your uncle would be willing to speak to me."

Megan was still unsure about letting another person into her life, but at the same time liked the idea of sharing about her mom. "I'd like to tell you about my mom. I think..." Just as she prepared to tell him they would have to see about him being part of her life, she felt the Holy Spirit nudge her to pray over Mr. Stafford. "I think I would like to pray over you." Her father squeezed her hand, and when she turned his way, his brow was furrowed. She nodded, then released his and Kieran's hands and stood. "Is that okay with you, Mr. Stafford?"

The man who had looked so stately, even when sad and angry, slumped. "I haven't spoken to God in a long time."

"That's not a problem. I will do all the talking."

His mouth opened, but he shut it and nodded slowly.

Megan walked to him and laid a hand on his shoulder. "God, I don't know all that Mr. Stafford has gone through, but I'm sensing so much brokenness and loss. And I can tell that he is angry at you. But please help him see that just like in the book of Joel when you promised your people that you would restore the years that were taken from them, you are even now restoring to us what has been taken. Not just the necklace which is of passing importance, but the lost relationships.

"Help him to see beyond the here and now and know that there is a future and an eternity that awaits if he will lay his burdens down at your feet and repent. Open his eyes to the fact that Jesus died and rose again so that he could be set free from the bondage of anger and pain. Help him to see that you want to replace it with the fruit that comes from accepting Jesus as Lord and Savior—love, joy, peace, patience, kindness, goodness, faithfulness, gentleness, and self-control."

Mr. Stafford began to shake beneath her hand.

"God, you have done something amazing here. After so many years, you have brought us together from two different continents. Guide us as we move past this rough start and lead us into still waters. Give us patience and trust with one another as we both have been deceived by others. I trust you to complete the work you have started. Now to you, God, who is able to do more than we ask or think, to you be the glory forever and ever. In Jesus' name, amen."

Loud sobbing filled the room by the time Megan finished her prayer. It was all from Mr. Stafford. His head fell into his hands and he continued to shake and cry. Megan glanced up, and both Kieran and her father still had their eyes closed. She saw Kieran's mouth move and knew that he was continuing to pray. She stepped away from Mr. Stafford, closed her eyes, and silently prayed for God to complete the work that he had started in him. It wasn't clear to her what his relationship with God was like in the past, but it was obvious he was distanced from God right now.

"I'm a broken man," came Mr. Stafford's shaky voice. "I've been angry at God for so long."

"I've been down that path myself until a month ago." Kieran nodded towards Megan. "For months before I became a Christian, Megan had been telling me about Jesus and guiding me through the Bible. I wanted so badly to blame God for losing my father when I was eleven, but after studying the Bible, I knew I was the one in the wrong.

"My dad was a Christian and is in heaven, and I was pushing away the very one who could eventually reunite us. If you're willing, I'd like to meet with you sometime to begin sharing what I've learned in God's word."

"I..." Mr. Stafford's face tensed then softened. "Yes, I would like that."

When Mr. Stafford stood, Megan couldn't hold back and approached him. "Can I hug you?"

The lines at the corners of Mr. Stafford's eyes creased as he pressed his lips together and nodded. She wrapped her arms around Mr. Stafford who stiffened at first but gradually moved to embrace her.

"Grandfather," she whispered, feeling more at peace about having him in her life.

"What was that?"

"Grandfather," she said more loudly.

"I like the sound of that," Mr. Stafford replied. "I could get used to it."

"Do you have grandchildren?" Megan pulled back and released him.

He shook his head. "I don't have children." He stopped and shook his head again. "Sorry, I guess...other than your mother." The edges of his mouth rose into a smile. "I still can't get used to this. It feels like someone else's life."

Scott stood up. "If Megan wants you in her life, then I am excited to have you as part of our lives."

Mr. Stafford lowered his head. "Thank you, but the honor is all mine. In fact, could I interest you in having dinner at my home?"

"We couldn't expect you to make us dinner with such little notice, but we could go out to eat," offered Megan.

"It wouldn't inconvenience me." Mr. Stafford chuckled. "My house-keeper is the one who cooks for me, and I think she would be overjoyed to know I'm bringing people to the house."

Megan looked at her father and Kieran and they both nodded their agreement. "Okay then, we'd love that." She tapped her chin. "Why don't you let us pick up dessert? There's a brand new Screaming Peach Café here that Kieran took me to yesterday. It's been a favorite of mine for ages. I'd love to pick up some things from there."

"That sounds nice," Mr. Stafford agreed.

"I hope you like peaches...Grandfather, because they have the best peach desserts. Is it okay if I call you that? It seems strange calling you Mr. Stafford after what we've learned."

"I'd like that very much. No food allergies?" When everyone shook their heads, he pulled out his phone and sent off a text. "Jolly good. Can I show all of you around the place before you leave?"

Kieran spoke up first, "Yes, please."

Megan and her father nodded.

While Scott rolled Kieran's wheelchair to him and helped him in, Mr. Stafford turned to Megan and pointed at her left hand. "When did the two of you get engaged?" He glanced between Kieran and Megan as they moved down the hall.

The smile that filled Kieran's face sent Megan's heart into overdrive. "Yesterday," they both answered.

"How did you guess he was my fiancé?"

"I would have to be blind not to see the affection in his eyes when he looks at you." Mr. Stafford tilted his head and his eyes glistened. "I imagine that's how I looked at your grandmother so long ago."

After growing up hearing about her grandfather's love for her grandmother, it was odd to hear her recently discovered grandfather speaking that way about Grandmother.

"I like the design of the ring." He looked at Kieran. "Went to my competition? I see you chose a design similar to the family pendant. I'd like a chance to design the wedding band if you don't already have it commissioned."

"As you can imagine, De Clare's was not an option at the time. When it comes to the wedding band, it's up to Megan."

"I understand." He turned and pointed to a huge metal door. "This is the vault. It has some of the finest built-in security. Unfortunately, I failed in who I trusted with access to it. I'd like to show you my office." He turned to a room and unlocked the door before waving them through.

His office held a large antique wooden desk, a drafting table, and a wall of floor to ceiling built-in bookcases filled with jewelry in shadow boxes, books, and framed pictures.

Megan approached the drafting table and found sketches of several ring designs. They were like nothing she had ever seen, and each was beautiful in its own way.

"I like to hand sketch my jewelry ideas," her grandfather said as he joined her. "Most designers now go straight to the computer. I can do that if necessary, but it doesn't feel as natural."

"These designs are amazing."

Kieran rolled over and raised his brow. "Impressive. Maybe we *can* trust you to design her wedding band."

"I think some of my clients would agree," Mr. Stafford winked and waved towards the bookcase.

When Megan looked more closely at the photos, she saw one of him with Queen Elizabeth, one with Princess Diana, one with Audrey Hepburn, a more recent one with Princess Catherine, and several others of Mr. Stafford with important-looking people she didn't recognize. "These are all clients?"

"They are. I'm a royal jeweler."

"I had no idea there were such things."

"The head of our family has been a royal jeweler since the founding of De Clare's. We're also the oldest family owned jeweler in the UK."

"What an honor." Megan lifted the picture frame with Audrey Hepburn to look more closely at the necklace she wore while posing with her grandfather.

"Has the recent incident with Bernard made you worried about what happens in your office?" Kieran pointed to a tiny black tower that was hidden behind the Audrey Hepburn photo.

"Pardon?"

"This video camera. Do you still have worries about your employees?"

"I am rather paranoid now, but I don't have a video camera in here. Bernard was the only one with a key to access my office, and he is in jail." Mr. Stafford stepped closer. "What is that?"

"It's a video camera. Did you have a security company set things up when you were gone? Maybe they put it in and you didn't know."

"I absolutely did not. Let me see that."

"Wait! Don't touch it. It may have fingerprints which will help you determine who put it there," Kieran shouted. "I'll call Gareth and he can send his guys over to check it out."

Mr. Stafford's Knightsbridge home reminded Megan of Tracey's. It was stately and filled with well-kept antiques. After dinner, they moved from the dining room to the library for dessert. Megan scanned some of the shelves and stopped at a section of leather-bound Jane Austen books. He had all of them. Sitting next to them was a framed photo of a much younger Mr. Stafford with her grandmother. Her chest tightened as she imagined the sudden end of their relationship. It was obvious Mr. Stafford never stopped loving her.

"Your grandmother loved Miss Austen's books," came her grandfather's voice from just behind her. He pulled out *Emma*. "This was her favorite."

Megan touched the book. "You said she was reading it the day you met."

Her grandfather smiled wistfully. "She was."

"I enjoy Jane's books too, but *Sense and Sensibility* is my favorite." She touched the spine of it. "May I?"

"Of course. It's yours if you'd like."

"I'll just look, thank you." She pulled it out and examined the burgundy leather outside before flipping through the book and stopping to view the artwork. "It's a beautiful copy." It pleased her to know that she and her grandmother had similar tastes in reading, but she wasn't going to take a book from a man she barely knew, even if he was her grandfather.

Mr. Stafford invited the group to eat the peach cake from the Screaming Peach. His housekeeper had plated it up on the sideboard. Just as the group sat and began eating, Kieran's phone rang. "Gareth. What did you find?" He switched on his speaker.

"It was as we guessed, Bernard. We questioned him before hacking into the video footage. I figured it would be hard to know what we were looking for. He was quick to squeal when we told him he was going to get more time for illegally surveilling someone on their personal property."

"So what did he say?" Kieran asked.

"He said there was no way he was going to lose De Clare's to a little girl. When I asked if he was referring to Megan, he said yes. But the dates don't line up. He said he placed the camera there back in May."

Mr. Stafford pulled out his phone and began tapping. "May is when I met with my solicitor about the future of the company after I die. I was considering leaving it to Bernard and his wife because she is family —though it's on my mother's side, not the de Clare side."

"That man has no conscience," came Gareth's voice through the phone.

"Don't get me started," Kieran replied with an edge.

"He not only wanted to get rid of your necklace for the money, he wanted to get rid of it before I saw it and...get rid of you before I saw you." Horror filled Megan's grandfather's face at the realization. "He tried to...."

Heaviness from the words left unspoken weighed on them all. Kieran had hinted at his worries right after she was almost attacked and again when the human trafficking connection was discovered. Bernard wanted to get rid of her and make money while doing it...Once again, she stopped her mind from wandering to the what ifs.

"With what we have on him, he will be locked up for the rest of his life. Kieran, I'll check in with you tomorrow about that other project we're working on."

"Thanks, Gareth. Goodnight." Kieran reached for Megan's hand and laced their fingers together.

Megan looked around the room and saw the defeat in everyone's eyes. Another day, another discovery of things Bernard had done. She let out a sigh.

Kieran released Megan's hand and wrapped his arm around her. "Let's look at the positive. He's behind bars. You're safe. You have a grandfather."

"You're right." She looked at Mr. Stafford. He was sitting with his face in his hands shaking. Crossing the room, she sat beside him on the settee. "Grandfather, what's wrong?"

He raised his head and wiped tears from his eyes. "Megan, I've brought nothing but trouble to you. What good has come of you finding me? Only worry and fear have entered your life since you got close to me. I trusted Bernard with too much, and that trust made him into a monster who would do anything for money and power."

God, give me words to say. Megan closed her eyes before lifting them to Mr. Stafford's. "You are not responsible for the choices Bernard has made. I am safe. God protected me. But even if he hadn't, I am his and I have hope. When I chose to be a missionary, I knew that with it would come attacks from the enemy. I never dreamed of these sorts of attacks. Regardless, they are nothing short of attacks from the enemy."

She looked across the room at Kieran and he nodded in affirmation. "And I will not be distracted from what God has for me. I choose to rejoice in God and share his goodness with others, not dwell on the difficult things and turn inward."

When Mr. Stafford's hand touched her arm, she turned back to him and found him looking at her curiously. "Your mother raised a wonderful and strong woman." He shook his head. "I don't feel worthy to have you in my life. For so long, I've had no one. My second wife died over twenty years ago."

"You have me now," Megan assured him. "God has given us both a gift."

Chapter Thirty-Two

Six weeks later, Megan again found herself gathered with a crowd in Tracey and Richard's hot tub room. Today she had the privilege of watching her grandfather get baptized by her fiancé. Kieran had been going through the Bible with her grandfather. The two men grew close over that time, and once again, she thanked God for the gift of a fiancé who loved to tell others about Jesus as much as she did.

A squeeze of her leg drew her eyes down to a smiling Madeline. "Hey, sweetie. Let's watch over there where Mr. Kieran and my grandfather are."

Madeline giggled. "Your grandfather is all wet."

"He is, but it is for a very special reason since he just became a Christian."

"I'll take her so you can focus on what's happening," Kate said as she reached for her daughter and picked her up.

"Thanks." Megan watched as Madeline nuzzled her mother's neck. Even at four, she was still a momma's girl.

Corbyn held Margaret and placed an arm around Kate. It was a sweet, domestic scene, and Megan momentarily felt a pang of sadness. With Kieran's injury, they might never have a family of their own. They were both open to adoption, but there were so few children available to adopt outside of the foster system. With fostering, there was no guarantee of adoption. When Megan said yes to marrying Kieran, she accepted that they might never have children, and she was confident they would have a very fulfilling life ahead regardless of whether God provided them with children. That didn't stop the occasional longing. Kieran's voice broke into her thoughts.

"I have been blessed to have the opportunity to study the Bible with this man, Mr. Henry Stafford, and he has become a good friend and now a brother in Christ. Very soon—" Kieran stopped speaking, and his eyes found Megan's. "I'll also have the privilege of calling him Grandfather. Mr. Stafford...Henry, what would you like to say to everyone on this day as we signify your salvation with baptism?"

Megan's grandfather looked around the crowd and found Megan. His smile grew. "I'd like everyone to know that it's never too late to repent and accept Jesus as your Lord and Savior. From now on, I will be encouraging others not to wait. I wasted so many years giving into sadness and anger when I could have been rejoicing in my blessings. I thank Jesus Christ for covering all my sins. I know I am not worthy, but he is. It is my joy to spend as many days as he gives me showing and telling others about his great love and mercy. And thank you, Kieran, for teaching an old man about God's word." He placed a hand on Kieran's and patted. "I especially want to say thank you—" His voice caught, and he blinked back tears. "Thank you to my beautiful granddaughter for accepting me into her life, reminding me that God loves me, and giving me hope that it wasn't too late for me to turn to God." His tears began flowing and his final words were broken. "She...is just one example...of the good gifts that God has blessed me with."

Tears filled Megan's eyes as she watched Kieran dip her grandfather back and announce that he was baptized in the name of the Father, Son, and Holy Spirit. A picture of introducing her mom to her biological father and Kieran as they reunited in heaven entered Megan's mind. What a joyous day that would be. She greatly missed her mom, but just as her grandfather said, God had blessed her with good gifts.

Several weeks earlier, God had surprised her with another good gift. Peter invited her to attend a special event the British Museum was holding for those of Chinese descent. They had Chinese speakers and displayed several Chinese items that were not in their permanent collection. At the event, Megan made connections and began communicating with a few women who wanted to organize English as a second language classes with her. God brought the people to her and she looked forward to pointing the people to him. Bible passages were perfect for teaching English, and there would no doubt be numerous opportunities to go deeper with her students.

As she watched Kieran help her grandfather out of the hot tub, she rubbed at her pendant. It was good to be able to wear it again. Gareth had referred her grandfather to a security specialist who reviewed his system and protocols. It was a very secure system, but the downfall had been allowing one person to access it without the knowledge of others. Now several people had to approve the opening of the vault. With the new protocol in place, Megan and her father put her pendant back in De Clare's vault, and she was allowed to remove it anytime she wanted. Her grandfather surprised them by insisting there was no charge. He even covered the insurance.

Later that evening, before Megan's grandfather left her and Kieran sitting in one of his reception rooms, he said, "I'm off to bed, but I will remind the two of you that just because you plan to get married, it is not the same as being married." He arched his brow and smiled. "I know all too well how that can turn out, though the Lord brought me my greatest blessing out of it."

"Yes, Grandfather," Kieran responded. "I appreciate your care and protection of Megan." He drew a hand down her arm, shooting tingles through her body. "I promise to honor your granddaughter, and as hard as it will be, we will wait these final two months before we do anything more than kiss. I hope you're okay with kissing because I promised her a lot of kissing." He winked at her grandfather.

"As long as you keep it clean, young man."

Megan bit her lip and fought back a smile.

"I promise," Keiran saluted her grandfather. The minute Mr. Stafford was out of the room, Kieran turned to Megan. "Time to keep my promise to you, beautiful."

"But—" She started to tease him with a smart comment, and he cut her off with a kiss—slow and easy at first, then more urgent and intense. His arms moved from her neck to her shoulders, then he slid them around her waist and pulled her closer. Every time he kissed her, it was as exciting as the first time. The tingles that began when he touched her arm now spread through her body. She longed for the day they didn't have to stop there. When he moved from her lips to her neck, her head spun. Moments later, he kissed her lips again, then pulled away. "What... What is it?" Megan glanced around the room trying to clear her mind.

"I—" Kieran rubbed the back of his neck. "Your grandfather knows what he's talking about."

Heat rose to her cheeks, but she wanted Kieran to clarify. "How's that?"

Kieran cupped her face in his hands. "Stopping with only kisses is getting so much harder than I imagined. Are you sure we can't move this wedding up? Maybe you're getting tired of your new roommate?"

"No, we're not going to move the wedding up, and in this giant house, it would be hard to feel bothered by my grandfather's presence. I'm enjoying having extra time with him."

A couple of weeks after receiving the results of the paternity test, her grandfather invited her to live with him until the wedding, and she was thankful for the opportunity to get to know him better.

"I'm just saying. I don't know if we can keep kissing like this while we wait." He looked slightly pained.

"So you're going back on your promise to me?" Megan smirked.

"I've never dated someone as a Christian. I had no idea how hard this would be. My feelings for you are way more intense than I've had for any other woman."

"It's intense for me too." Her heart raced and she reached up to squeeze one of his hands. "Maybe for now I won't hold you to that promise to kiss my lips raw."

Kieran's face tensed.

"But that doesn't mean I don't want *any* kisses."

"We just won't get too carried away." Kieran agreed with a smile.

"Exactly."

"That will free up more time for talking." He winked. "How is your necklace design coming along?"

When Megan mentioned the idea of incorporating some of the Egyptian designs she'd studied into a line of jewelry, her grandfather invited her to help create a new line. He had been working with her and teaching her his process for designing jewelry. She was surprised at how naturally it came to her. It was a creative side she never knew she had. "I'm happy with my latest drawing and am going to translate it into a trio of bracelets and a pair of earrings."

"Sounds brilliant. I love the way your grandfather brought out your skill in jewelry design." His eyes fell on the coffee table and he picked up a book. "Ah, been reading about the amazing Colonel Brandon again I see."

"You are more perfect for me than Colonel Brandon. Actually, this time I was thinking about how so many of the characters in *Sense and Sensibility*, including the Colonel, are not what they first seem. Colonel Brandon had many layers, and once Marianne got to know him, she no longer thought of him as an old codger. Edward seemed unattached at the beginning but was actually engaged. Lucy seemed to be humble, attached to Edward, and caring towards those around her. But all she cared about was money and working her way up the social ladder. Willoughby appeared to be the perfect hero, showing up when Marianne was hurt and showering her with attention. He turned out to be the worst. Even Mrs. Jennings irritated the girls somewhat when they first met, but later, she was their greatest ally and friend. I could go on with examples in the book.

"Just like in the book, I've realized that my perceptions of many people in my life have changed over the last few months. When I first heard your gruff voice and what you had done to Kate and others, I never imagined you as marriage material, even though I instantly noticed you were devastatingly handsome." Kieran gave her a wide grin. "Peter made me uncomfortable when he wanted to date me, but he has turned out to be a constant friend. I placed my trust in Mr. Bernard Blake, and we see how that went. I didn't trust my grandfather, but he is a wonderful man." She stopped and frowned. "I held my grandmother on a pedestal, but she kept secrets from the family that she took to her grave. I have forgiven her, but she's not exactly how I imagined."

"Those are some deep thoughts. Christ makes a huge difference in how people's lives play out and whether they are what they seem."

"True."

"Are you okay?"

"I am."

"Let's talk about the plans for our wedding that is *much* too far away. What's on the schedule for this week?"

She appreciated the change of subject from her lingering disappointment with her grandmother. "Cake tasting Wednesday. Kate highly recommended this lady, and she has worked our wedding into her schedule."

"Sounds fun."

"You sure, Mr. Health Nut? I'm not ordering veggie cakes with no frosting."

"Ha-ha. You know I can never refuse you desserts, and I'm not opposed to something nicely done. What flavors are on offer?"

Megan opened Instagram to pull up the baker's page and show him the options. "Here. She's got a list through the link in her bio. "

"Nice selection. I look forward to seeing if she lives up to the hype." Kieran closed the list of flavors and scrolled through the cake pictures. "You've got a direct message," he said as he handed the phone back to Megan.

She looked and was shocked to see the name of the sender. "It's from Natalia." She turned to Kieran. "Why is she messaging me?"

"My ex?" Kieran shrugged. "I have no idea. Remember I told you she called me after I posted our engagement picture."

"I do, but it seems strange." Megan opened the message. "It just says congratulations on our engagement."

"You can block her if you want, but she seemed fine with everything after we spoke. She *is* the one who broke up with me."

"True, but from what you told me about the conversation and

about your relationship with her, she really liked you even though you had made it clear you weren't interested in marriage. I imagine it's got to be hard seeing you've changed your mind about marriage. Especially since it's less than a year after your break up."

"I didn't think of it that way. I did apologize to her though. As a Christian, I can see now that I was not treating her, or anyone I dated, with respect. During our conversation, I shared a bit about how I became a Christian and now view things differently."

"I'm glad you apologized to her. I'll be praying about her response to what you said. Maybe it will create an interest in God. I'll also pray that others will come into her life to speak to her more about God."

"That's a smashing idea." Kieran's hand went to Megan's cheek and his eyes became hooded. "I love it when you talk to me about God." He pulled her into a kiss that was all too short then leaned his forehead against hers. "You were made for me. God has blessed me beyond measure."

CHAPTER 33
Epilogue

"Stafford Henry Davies," Kieran said proudly as he lifted their son from Megan's arms and carried him to the hospital recliner where Mr. Stafford sat.

"Megan," Mr. Stafford's voice was thick with emotion. "He's so beautiful." Baby Stafford's little hand wrapped around one of Grandfather's fingers and he sucked in a breath. "Thank you for letting me into your life so I can share this moment. I missed out on your mother's birth and yours. Did you notice?" His voice rose. "I think he's going to have our eyes."

Megan didn't want to mention that sometimes babies' eyes change after birth. She hoped her son's eyes always matched hers and her grandfather's. It had been two years since she met him, and he was a good man. When he became a Christian, he turned his life around and made good on his commitment to make Christ known in any way he could.

In honor of her grandmother, he started a foundation to work with Christian Crisis Pregnancy Centers and provide monetary help for women struggling financially so they could keep their children. The foundation also helped equip them to find jobs and the only requirement was that they join a weekly Bible study. In the year since it began, almost one hundred women had gone through the program. Nearly seventy of them stayed with the program until they had their child and went back to work, and thirty-seven women had become Christians.

"He does have beautiful eyes," she conceded.

"God willing, I am going to teach you to design jewelry too, Stafford," her grandfather cooed to the little one.

"Your mobile is blowing up, darling. I sent that group text and photo to your Chinese language class and they're buzzing."

Megan was overjoyed. The Chinese class was part of another work that God had done. Over the past two years, her language classes had grown into a full-blown program with multiple volunteers teaching classes five days a week at their church. The classes were mostly taught from the Bible and always included prayer time and a verse of the week. Most importantly, the gospel was shared regularly. Their church now had over two dozen Chinese members who had become Christians through the program.

She'd quit her job at Corbyn Publishing so she could spend more time with that and helping her grandfather with De Clare's. Kieran even helped out the business by monitoring their security protocols. She ran her thumb along the back of her wedding band, recalling how her grandfather had let Kieran help make it. They were close, and her grandfather filled a gap in Kieran's life. His father's grandparents had become distant after his father's death, and his mother's father had passed away some years earlier, so Megan's grandfather was the only male family he had nearby.

That was about to change. Her eyes found her father's. He had just moved to London after ending the fall semester at Chapel Hill. Grandfather invited her dad to live with him, and Scott was scheduled to start teaching at King's College London after their Christmas holiday. He would be working in Classical Studies with English. Because of the different teaching style in England, he was working under an older Professor until he felt comfortable with the way the program ran.

Kieran came back to Megan's side and gently rubbed her shoulders. He winced.

"Is your leg bothering you?" She scooted over on the mattress. "Here, there's room for you to sit on the edge."

He was now walking without a walker or cane, but sometimes he had shooting pain in his left leg, especially when he was on his feet a lot. Eighteen hours in labor to deliver Stafford had pushed him to his limit. Kieran never complained. He was happy with his progress after being confined to a wheelchair for seven months.

"Henry, did Megan tell you about the diary?" Scott asked Mr. Stafford.

Her grandfather shook his head. "What diary?"

Scott looked at Megan. "Why don't you tell him?"

"Grandmother's diary," Megan spoke softly. She imagined her grandfather was as curious about it as she was.

"Nancy had a diary?"

Megan nodded. "Dad brought it with him. My uncle found it when he was going through some of her old things. Its first entry is the day of her flight from London to South Carolina...when she left you."

Her grandfather's hand covered his mouth and he looked at the ground. When he looked back up he asked, "Do you think...would you..."

"Yes, of course. Maybe I should read it first though. In case I need to prepare you for anything."

"Thanks. I've always wondered...It will be good to know what was going through her mind."

"I'd like to know too. Maybe it will help me understand her better."

"Regardless of what it says, you have a great life and are surrounded by people who love you. Both of you." Scott looked between Megan and Mr. Stafford.

"Yes we do," Mr. Stafford agreed.

All the men in Megan's life were right here, including little Stafford, the gift that she'd settled on never receiving. As much as she'd read and imagined having him over the past months, nothing could prepare her for the way he captured her heart. Her heart was full. The things she'd given God in order to follow his will for her life, he had multiplied in greater measure than she ever imagined. Everything wasn't always perfect, but with God, it was always good.

The End

Hebrews 10:23-24 ESV Let us hold fast the confession of our hope without wavering, for he who promised is faithful. 24 And let us consider how to stir up one another to love and good works.

Read on for a preview of Nancy's story (Book 3 of the Not Quite Series) to find out what happened when Megan's grandmother left Henry.

Megan stared at the journal lying before her on the coffee table. What would she learn about her long-revered grandmother? She hesitated before pulling it to her chest and praying. *God, help me accept whatever I find inside and help Grandfather find peace instead of pain within its pages.* She took a deep breath, then turned to the first page.

Journal of Nancy Wilson

October 2, 1970

Help me, God. I feel like I'm drowning. It's been eleven hours since I saw Henry. In a few minutes, I'll board the plane that will take me an ocean away from the man I love. Have I made the right decision? Should I turn back before it's too late? This burden is too much to bear. I love him...

Isn't love supposed to be selfless? I'm trying. Just yesterday I was sure I would spend forever with Henry, but after reading that letter from his dad I couldn't follow through with it. I can't be the one to rip a family apart and destroy a family business that has existed for hundreds of years. There's also the fact that my parents don't know my plans. They would be brokenhearted upon finding out I married without them present.

My parents didn't believe me when I told them I was trying to work out a way to marry Henry and that it might be soon. They asked me to hold off so I could be sure, but I ignored them and here I am. Mourning a marriage that almost was.

We're boarding now. Can I do this? Part of me hopes Henry will come after me. I left my contact information with my landlord, Beatrice, and of course, the Embassy has it. Maybe he will...They're calling for passengers on my flight to board. This is for the best...Right?

Standing and gathering her things, Nancy looked around for the first time since checking in at the gate. An older woman met her gaze with concern. Nancy touched her cheek and imagined how swollen and red her eyes were.

Minutes later, the same woman sat next to Nancy on the plane. "Now, now, dear. God will be with you every step of the way. I don't know what you are going through, but he does."

Nancy smiled at the woman. She had followed God for years, but where was God right now? Had he abandoned her in her time of need? Rubbing her temple, she leaned against the window and scanned the night sky. It would soon envelop her and carry her far from all she had imagined would be her future.

"I have some paracetamol for your head." The older woman reached into her bag and produced a small bottle.

Nancy looked at the bottle and recalled it was a common pain reliever. She nodded. "Thanks." After swallowing the medication, she closed her eyes. The plane began its trek across the runway and as it accelerated, she sank deeper into the seat cushion, letting the gravitational force pull her into a fitful sleep.

Tugging her carry-on over her shoulder, Nancy exited the jet bridge and said goodbye to the woman she'd sat beside on the plane.

She fought back the tension in her chest as she imagined the look on her parents' faces. They sounded so worried when she'd made the collect call to tell them she was flying home, but they asked no questions. Her mom said they could talk once she was home. They would have an hour and a half to grill her while driving from Charlotte, North Carolina to their home in Greenville, South Carolina.

She had no idea how best to explain that she'd quit her internship early because she'd foolishly chased after someone she never should have gotten involved with.

Doubts lingered. Should she have stayed? What had she done? She would be a married woman by now if she hadn't fled. She looked back at the jet bridge, wishing she could reverse time. Shaking her head and turning once more to the terminal she trudged forward, wondering if a good night's sleep in her own bed would bring more clarity.

"Nancy. Welcome home."

She followed the sound of the familiar voice. "Walt? What are you doing here?"

Acknowledgments

Thank you for joining me in the Not Quite Series! When I wrote *Not Quite Mr. Darcy*, I had no idea it would be the start of a series. This book was so different, and, though it touches on serious topics, I hope it was fun to sort through the intertwined mysteries.

It has been my prayer that NQCB would touch each reader where encouragement is needed. Hopefully, it has also spurred you to find ways God has gifted you to point others to Him.

As a stay-at-home mom/homeschool mom who has also led the local Woman's Missionary Union for years, I often felt bad that I couldn't "go" on mission trips. What I learned over time, is that the work I was doing at home and in my community was mission work as well. As a Christian, I am a missionary. If you are a Christian, you are a missionary too. Everywhere we go we represent Christ—even at home. Don't discount that important work.

I give my greatest thanks to the Lord, who has given me blessings beyond what I could fathom and has called me to share Him in my writing. It's not that my life hasn't had difficulties, but He has walked alongside me in every circumstance. He is constant. He is my strength and my shield.

To my husband who has made it possible for me to write and has been my best friend and the love of my life for almost 36 years—thank you! You are my HEA (happily ever after).

In writing this book I have worked with some great ladies as Beta readers. I appreciate their encouragement and constructive insight to help this book be the best it can be. Thank you, Elizabeth, Judith, Storm, Marla, Myra, and Nora.

My ARC reader team is an important ingredient in the making of this book. Thank you all for helping me and promoting my book.

Thank you Christian Mommy Writers! You ladies are amazing and have been so encouraging!

A big thank you also to my editor L. Taylor.

And to my dear friends Kim and Caroline—thank you for your encouragement, help, and the fun we have in between.

Blessings, Kim Griffin

If you enjoyed this book you can help me by reviewing it on Goodreads and Amazon! You can find both links on my website here: https://www.kimgriffin.org/home/books/not-quite-colonel-brandon

For more *Not Quite Colonel Brandon* fun check out the special reader-only extras page on my website! Pull up the page with the QR code below. If you have trouble, please email me at kim@kimgriffin.org.

About the Author

Kim Griffin is a former interior designer and homeschool mom who has been leading Bible studies for over 35 years and working in Women's Ministry for over 25. Several years ago, God led her to begin writing words of hope. She writes Christian women's fiction with clean romance and devotionals/Bible studies. Her desire is that her books will draw readers closer to the God who sees all of their imperfections and loves them still.

You can learn more about Kim and her books and sign up for her newsletter at her website:

kimgriffin.org

Made in the USA
Columbia, SC
30 July 2024

39661948R00174